**W9-BTK-593**

### Praise for

*The Belles of Solace Glen*

"Hitting all the right notes of good storytelling, [*The Belles of Solace Glen*] is both touching and revealing, with sparkling moments of gentle humor and honest emotion."
—Earlene Fowler, author of *Delectable Mountains*

"Susan James has written a winner!"
—*Roundtable Reviews*

"*The Belles of Solace Glen* is a delightful, feel-good book. The story is filled with an odd, clever collection of townsfolk, all of them adding a twist to small-town life. Ms. James blends history, humor, and honest emotion to create the first in a new mystery series I look forward to reading."
—*The Best Reviews*

"A promising new series."
—*Romantic Times*

"A charming New England mystery with enough danger, gentle humor, and just a touch of romance to keep any mystery lover's attention."
—*Rendezvous*

"Flip is a wonderful character. She's practical, sensible, and someone you'd like to have as a friend."
—*The Romance Reader's Connection*

# SOLACE GLEN
### ❈
# HONEYMOON

## Susan S. James

BERKLEY PRIME CRIME, NEW YORK

**THE BERKLEY PUBLISHING GROUP**
**Published by the Penguin Group**
**Penguin Group (USA) Inc.**
**375 Hudson Street, New York, New York 10014, USA**
Penguin Group (Canada), 90 Eglinton Avenue East, Suite 700, Toronto, Ontario M4P 2Y3, Canada
(a division of Pearson Penguin Canada Inc.)
Penguin Books Ltd., 80 Strand, London WC2R 0RL, England
Penguin Group Ireland, 25 St. Stephen's Green, Dublin 2, Ireland (a division of Penguin Books Ltd.)
Penguin Group (Australia), 250 Camberwell Road, Camberwell, Victoria 3124, Australia
(a division of Pearson Australia Group Pty. Ltd.)
Penguin Books India Pvt. Ltd., 11 Community Centre, Panchsheel Park, New Delhi—110 017, India
Penguin Group (NZ), Cnr. Airborne and Rosedale Roads, Albany, Auckland 1310, New Zealand
(a division of Pearson New Zealand Ltd.)
Penguin Books (South Africa) (Pty.) Ltd., 24 Sturdee Avenue, Rosebank, Johannesburg 2196, South
Africa

Penguin Books Ltd., Registered Offices: 80 Strand, London WC2R 0RL, England

This is a work of fiction. Names, characters, places, and incidents either are the product of the author's
imagination or are used fictitiously, and any resemblance to actual persons, living or dead, business es-
tablishments, events, or locales is entirely coincidental. The publisher does not have any control over
and does not assume any responsibility for author or third-party websites or their content.

SOLACE GLEN HONEYMOON

A Berkley Prime Crime Book / published by arrangement with the author

PRINTING HISTORY
Berkley Prime Crime mass-market edition / October 2005

Copyright © 2005 by Susan S. James Mayer.
Cover art by Erica Tricarico.
Cover design by Joe Burleson.
Interior text design by Kristin del Rosario.

ISBN: 0-425-20636-X

BERKLEY® PRIME CRIME
Berkley Prime Crime Books are published by The Berkley Publishing Group,
a division of Penguin Group (USA) Inc.,
375 Hudson Street, New York, New York 10014.
The name BERKLEY PRIME CRIME and the BERKLEY PRIME CRIME design are trademarks
belonging to Penguin Group (USA) Inc.

PRINTED IN THE UNITED STATES OF AMERICA

10  9  8  7  6  5  4  3  2  1

# ACKNOWLEDGMENTS

Thank you, Christine, for good directions. Thank you, Mary and Jena, for starting me out on the journey. Thank you, Christie and Tim, for the gift of a traveler's tale and much laughter, one glorious night on a dock beneath a starry sky. Thank you, Jim, for sharing that sky with me.

# PREFACE

❈

THE MOSQUITOES PACK up in October, crashing into the taillights of fireflies in their rush to escape the first frost. You wonder where they go, all those flying insects— the biting pests and the alluring lightning bugs. A yearly mystery, as perplexing as the cicada invasion every seventeen years when Maryland is blanketed with crunchy, creepy crawlers. Great for fishing. Not too savory on a picnic.

Personally, I believe the mosquitoes go on vacation. They head to the Caribbean without need of suntan lotion or floppy hats. They converge on brackish inland ponds, staking out the same spot they held the year before, waving to that nice North Carolina mosquito clan who always camps out diagonally across from them, noting with disapproval that the pushy New York mosquitoes got there first, as usual, and snatched the best spot, the one with the most scum and shade. Perfect for cocktail hour.

This is what the Maryland mosquitoes do when the first chill sneaks in. This is where they disappear. I know, because last October, Tom and I went with them.

One thing I've learned in my twenty-five years of tidying up after people—two types of personalities run loose in the world, those who say, "Expect the unexpected," and those who say, "Don't expect a thing." Take my word, the town of Solace Glen, Maryland, is filled with folks who not only expect the unexpected, but mope for days if the unexpected lets them down. Small towns, whether in central Maryland or northern Minnesota, thrive on threats to the mundane. We may value our quiet lives, the lack of tall buildings and traffic, the comfort of familiar faces, but it's the laugh line furrowed into a cheek, the dips and crinkles in a forehead, that catch our eye and spark interest. The fissures in life unite us more than the smooth plains. The tremors keep us jumping.

Solace Glen has never experienced an earthquake, unless you count the two times Screamin' Larry, our criminally insane disk jockey, blew up the gas line. We've never suffered the winds of a tornado, unless you count Larry's airwaves battle with my cleaning partner, Ivory—all air, no harm. Hurricanes, even Isabel, never seem to stretch this far west of Baltimore to do much damage, and flooding is a localized event, restricted to a handful of basements that sit too close to streams that swell in springtime on their route to the Monocacy.

Since natural disaster is virtually unknown to Solace Glen, the community places special value on the unnatural manufacture of a scandal or two. Like an earthquake tremor, the rumblings of "he said/she said" keep us jumping. When Ferrell T. broke into homes, tampered with brakes, and almost killed Miss Fizzi about a year ago, tongues wagged so hard, we almost did produce our own tornado. When Stewart Larkin moved in months ago and brought along a stalker, the amount of hot air pushed through homes and gardens could have brought the barometric pressure low enough to amass another Isabel.

Not to say only negative or indecent incidents bring Solace Glen together. We celebrate the births and christenings of babies just like any other community. We throw parties for engagements, anniversaries, and high school sports accomplishments to beat the band. My own wedding to Tom, right before Halloween, brought the whole town out for one monstrous shindig. We wrote the invitation ourselves:

*Felicity Ann Paxton (Flip, of course)*
*and Thomas Henry Scott (her Tom)*

*request the honour of your presence*
*at their marriage (can you believe it?)*
*on Saturday evening, October twenty-third,*
*two thousand and four,*
*at six o'clock (black tie would be a hoot)*
*Solace Glen Presbyterian Church*
*Solace Glen, Maryland*

*Reception to follow at the home of Sam and Lee Gibbon*
*Dogs allowed if appropriately attired*
*(yes, that means black tie)*

Sometimes, when we're in the middle of a happy event, we find ourselves wondering when that big shoe's going to drop. We even find ourselves ducking. The moment is marred because we're so used to the daily output of bad news and headline tragedy that we don't savor the blessings right on top of us. Fortunately, that wasn't true of my wedding. I enjoyed every minute with the kind of incredulous ecstasy you'd expect of a forty-three-year-old woman who, in matters of the heart, held the attitude, "Don't expect a thing," until Tom and I discovered each other right where we'd always been.

I should have known, though. After the champagne and cake, after the music ended, I should have been more prepared for the unexpected. Shoes have a way of dropping off at the oddest times, in the oddest places. Sometimes, they're among the debris after a tornado, a child's sneaker snatched up and deposited miles away in someone else's battered home. Sometimes, they fall through a fissure in the earth and disappear into the darkness. Sometimes, they're lost in floodwaters, carried sadly, silently downstream and out to sea.

Shoes drop. Bad things happen. Wind. Fire. Flood. Murder.

Any time. Anywhere. Even on a honeymoon . . .

# PART ONE

✳

# The Dazzle of the Light

# CHAPTER 1

✻

MY WEDDING WAS everything a former Old Maid
could hope for, thanks to the Circle Ladies. The
women from all four churches in Solace Glen pitched in,
whipping up gourmet finger foods and brainstorming over
autumnal flower arrangements, wildly enthusiastic to
marry off the town drudge at last. Don't think I didn't hear
the whispers leading up to my happy event.

"Can you believe it? The lawyer and the maid. I never
thought either one of *them* would get married."

"I'd completely given up on Tom. When he turned his
nose up at my Sue Beth thirty years ago, I thought to myself, picky, picky, picky. Guess he ran out of women to be
picky about."

"Well, Flip's no slouch. She cleans up real good."

I took that as an honest compliment. I think being picky
about the person you mate with for life is a compliment,
too. All I know is, I liked the sound of Reverend G.G.'s
voice during the ceremony as she spoke our two names, the
consonants and vowels running side by side through the

litany until our hands clasped, our lips met, and our names linked together as tight as a Celtic knot: Thomas Henry and Felicity Ann. Better known as Tom and Flip Scott.

At that moment, my heart floated, a seashell wafting gently through water to settle safe at last on soft sediment. The church formality of my Christian name quickly distilled on my best friend Lee's irreverent lips as she and Tom's brother, Charlie, waltzed up the aisle at our heels. "Flip Scott! Flip Scott! Whoo-whoo-whoo! Let's party, people!"

As Margaret Henshaw says, Solace Glen does so love a good one. She and Lindbergh Kohl, her intended, presided over the festivities, filling the roles of host and hostess that my long-departed parents would have relished. Lee, along with her lanky better half, Sam, put on the dog at their house. The majestic, old, antebellum mansion probably hadn't seen such fireworks since the Civil War, when my newly discovered ancestor, General J.E.B. Stuart, marched through town.

The sugar maples around the house blazed under twinkling white lights. The patio out back reverberated with the big-band sound of a local jazz quintet, hand-picked by Screamin' Larry, of course. He occasionally grabbed the microphone and crooned, beer bottle in hand, an obese Frank Sinatra; but when "Strangers in the Night" sounded more like "Rangers Aren't My Type," the Eggheads, Jesse and Jules Munford, stepped in and guided him back to the oversized La-Z-Boy chair he'd brought along for his personal comfort. The Eggheads are good for something, at least, besides the occasional paramedic crisis, and they do enjoy cutting a rug. You couldn't miss their two shiny, bristly blonde heads bobbing around the dance floor. The single women could later brag of dancing several times.

I even saw Miss Fizzi, eighty-five years young, take a whirl. When she couldn't cajole her unresponsive nephew,

Suggs, into spinning her around, she started the orbit without him, breaking in between established couples to make a trio before moving on to the next station. Couples like Melody and Michael Connolly, and Sally and Wilbur Polk, didn't seem to mind, but the ones fresh to passion like Hilda Bell and Officer Sidney Garrett found the interruption a shade irritating.

What I found a shade irritating, if not downright distressing, was the casual remark Miss Fizzi dropped as she flitted by. "I planned your honeymoon, dear. You're in for such a treat. Happy Halloween!"

I slit eyes at Tom, but he feigned innocence and sprinted off to retrieve more champagne.

At one point, finding myself without an admiring crowd or a groom on hand, I sat back and drank in the whole scene of my wedding, savoring a moment I never thought would be mine. For forty-two years I'd lived and worked in this small Maryland town, cleaning the homes of friends, envying the family photographs I dusted, and the children's beds I made. Then Tom and I found each other exactly where we'd been all our lives. Alone, but here. Here in Solace Glen. Watching the same seasons change, sharing the same August month of birthdays, rooting for the same high school football team, breathing the same sweet air, serving the same faces we'd come to know and love.

Well, mostly love. There are always a few rotten apples in the barrel, like Roland Bell and Marlene Worthington, and C.C. and Leonard Crosswell. We'd invited them to the wedding if only for the sake of inclusion. Solace Glen is a pretty small potato, after all, and every calorie counts whether you want it to or not.

When it came time to toss the bouquet, the clan of single women I'd been Tribal Chief of for so long bunched together and eagerly raised their arms. Why the eagerness, I could not fathom, given the sorry choice of bachelors guffawing on the sidelines. I turned my back and hurled the apricot roses skyward, astonished at the mad scramble that ensued. Wouldn't you know, Ivory cheated. She brought along her giant schnauzer, Ebony, for the sole purpose of fetching the prize bouquet. She must have trained the huge, three-legged beast for months because Ebony shot up like a basketball player at tip-off. Before Hilda or her mother, Garland, or Tina Graham or Marlene could make a grab, the big, black dog had the roses clenched securely in her teeth and nobody had the nerve to pry them loose.

Ivory whooped and smacked her lips. "Good, pretty girl! You make your Momma proud! Looky here, Flip! Ebony and I are gonna be next!"

Screamin' Larry responded with a resounding belch, the bachelors' signal to cluster around his La-Z-Boy while Tom pretended to enjoy sliding my lacy blue garter off to toss into a pack of grown men, hands shoved deep inside their pockets. The garter fell unceremoniously at Pal Sykes's feet, and he scurried backward like it might explode, dumping beer in Screamin' Larry's lap and prompting Larry to sing "Praise the Lord and Pass the Ammunition"—a threat or a thank you; with Larry, it could go either way.

After the official cutting of the beautiful Lady Baltimore cake, a gift from Garland's Bistro, and more champagne, Margaret tactfully suggested she might keel over, she was so dog-tired. Sally poked an elbow in my side and popped her gum. "Come on, Princess Bride, time to get the hell outta Dodge. Lee and I will help ya defrock. Hair looks great, if I do say so myself."

She whipped a salon hairbrush out of her purse and hooked arms with Lee, the two of them stumbling up the staircase behind me, snorting at their honeymoon jokes.

"Laugh all you want," I groused. "For all I know, Miss Fizzi's got us booked at a Motel Six in Alaska."

Lee howled a little louder than necessary and a look passed between her and Sally that made me freeze in my tracks. "What? What do the two of you know that I don't?"

"Ooohhh, nuthin', nuthin', nuthin'." The cackling intensified, and they scooted up the stairs to transform me from Princess Bride into Honeymoon Queen. Assisting in the effort, Lee's life-size dolls, Plain Jane and Dear John, sat side by side on a settee holding hands, collecting my discarded wedding clothes. I'd found a nice aqua and navy blue wool suit in Baltimore as a going-away outfit. I tried to find a hat to match, in honor of a sepia photograph of my mother leaving on her own honeymoon, dark hair topped off by a little hat with a sophisticated 1950s veil netted across her face, but hats and I don't mix.

Like two style wizards in competitive fashion houses, Lee and Sally fussed over me. When Sally brushed a curl one way, Lee would take her comb and twist it the other way. When Lee buttoned the top button of my blouse, Sally reached out and popped it open. Gradually, my other "sisters" and "mothers" drifted into the bedroom and threw in their two cents about how a bride should look when she pirouettes away on her honeymoon.

With Margaret's stern nod of approval, spine stiff and straight as her classroom yardstick, Lee rebuttoned my blouse. "She needs to look more demure," Margaret instructed, cramming a bobby pin deep into her gray bun before giving me the once-over with a critic's eye. "She is marrying the town lawyer, after all. Tom might even be a judge one day."

"He's a good judge of women, already." Sally rearranged the blouse and exposed my neck. "But he's not made of paper. He's flesh just like the rest of us, and he enjoys seein' a little of it."

Ivory hugged the precious wedding bouquet to her ample bosom, rocked back in her chair, and whooped. "That's good advice, Flip! Sally ought to know, with all those husbands and bein' a former beauty queen."

Tina and Melody inspected my shoes. "Honestly, Flip."

Tina bent down as far as she could, given her girth. "Couldn't you think of something besides navy pumps? What do you think, Melody?"

Melody fingered a garnet brooch from her jewelry store, coffee bean eyes narrowing. "I think she could use a couple of gold buckles. I could kick myself for not bringing some along."

"Leave her alone." Garland swatted a piece of lint from my skirt while Hilda fluffed my hair with her fingers, making Sally's ears blow steam. "She's lovely. Just perfect."

"Where's Tom taking you on your honeymoon? Has he told you yet?" Hilda shimmied with excitement. "When I get out of college, and Sidney and I get married"—the ladies pursed their lips and raised both brows—"he said he'll take me wherever I want to go. I want to go on a cruise around the world!"

Sally slapped Hilda's hands away from my hair. "Ha. The way Sidney runs through his policeman's salary, buying you expensive dinners, chocolate, and flowers, you'll be lucky if he can afford a trip to the next county. I'm on my third husband, honey. Believe me, you can't eat flowers, and chocolate doesn't work in a tuna casserole."

I answered Hilda's questions the same way I had for weeks. "I don't know where we're going. He won't tell me. But I suspect, given the fact nobody in this room knows how to play poker, you and I are the only ones in the dark, Hilda."

"What! Mother, why haven't you told me? Why can't I know, too?"

Garland waved her away. "Because you can't keep a secret to save your life, that's why. Now, Flip," she swatted at another piece of lint and placed two hands on my shoulders, "you've never been anywhere but Ocean City, Maryland."

"That's not true. I've been to Baltimore, and Washington, and Frederick, and Deep Creek. I've been all over Maryland."

Garland glanced at Margaret, who glanced at Miss Fizzi, who glanced at Lee, who cocked her head. "Yeah. Precisely our point."

Garland's hands pressed into my shoulders until I felt the warmth. "All of us want you to know that you can call us *any* time, just like you always do when you go to Ocean City in the summer."

"Yes, dear." Miss Fizzi perched on the settee with Plain Jane and Dear John, all one happy family. She dangled a champagne flute precariously close to my wedding gown. "We want you to have a wonderful time, but we do have our concerns."

"What concerns?"

"That you'll feel . . . overwhelmed," said Margaret, always one to choose her words carefully, "and get homesick."

"On my *honey*moon?" Little did they know how good "overwhelmed" sounded to a woman decidedly under-whelmed most of her life, a woman more than ready to climb every mountain and ford every stream. "You know how much I've wanted to travel my whole life."

"Flip." Melody adjusted my new pearl earrings and necklace, a gift from Tom that she had helped select. "We know you. Even when you go to Ocean City, you always call home once or twice a day. You can't help yourself, you love us, and we love . . ." Melody's lower lip trembled. Her eyes welled up. "Oh, you look so pretty! I can't believe you're a bride!"

Margaret stepped in as Garland and Melody fell away, jerking lace handkerchiefs out of their sleeves like a couple of magician's assistants. "Heavens. This is turning into a crying jag." She spoke sternly, but dabbed her eye and hugged me tight. "We feel like we're sending our own daughter or sister off into the big, wide world. Your mother and father, and many others smiling down from heaven, would be so proud."

The tears sprang up, fat drops on the rims of my eyes. I looked around the room, so grateful for this circle of women. "You're all just trying to make me raccoon-eyed."

Garland pressed a clean handkerchief into my hand. "Just remember, wherever you go, at whatever time you feel the need, you call us. We need to stay connected."

"That's right, girl." Lee wore a wicked leer as she threw an arm around me. "*We'll* get you through this horrendous honeymoon! We can do it, can't we, ladies?"

With yips and yelps, the Belles of Solace Glen raised their glasses and hustled me out of the bedroom to the top of the stairs. Our guests lined up from the bottom of the staircase to the driveway outside the stately old house, ribbon-tied hankies filled with birdseed in each hand. Tom joined me at the top of the stairs, whispered for the twentieth time that day how lovely I looked (even with raccoon eyes), and we coasted down the stairs and outside, past all of Solace Glen. The birdseed lightly stung our faces and fell into our hair, sticking to the wool of my new suit. We paused at Tom's car to yell out thanks to everyone and shake off birdseed. Tom's brother, Charlie, stepped out of the car, motor running, and we grabbed hugs from him, Margaret, and Lindbergh before tumbling into the front seat. Tom slammed his door and we pulled slowly away, the sound of clanging cans tailing our happiness.

Giggly and breathless, mindful of savoring every moment of the most wonderful day of my life, I turned and watched as the waving crowd and twinkling lights grew small. The ladies were right about one thing. Except for the summer trips I managed to take to Ocean City each year, and the occasional foray into Baltimore or slightly beyond, this marked the first time I'd ever left Solace Glen heading for a beautiful, exotic, romantic destination straight out of my well-worn pocket atlas.

Then I remembered—Destination Unknown.

"Tom," I walked two fingers up his arm, smiling sweetly, the perfect new wife, "I know you said to pack for

June weather, but is that all you can tell me? Can't you tell me where we're going *now*? Especially since everybody else seems to know already?"

The perfect new husband grinned, and in the darkness, I could practically see the gleam in his searing, hawk eyes. "I could." The grin widened. "But I don't want to."

"Well, it's not exactly being nosy for a bride to want to know where she's going on her own honeymoon!"

"Mmm-mm-mm. Do I detect a note of exasperation? A hint of anger? The muted tone of a"—he gasped—"*shrew*? Good God, what have I gotten myself into?"

"Toy with me all you will," I huffed. "I just want to know if I get to use my new passport or not."

"Why, I don't know. Guess we'll have to refer to Miss Fizzi's instruction manual."

"Excuse me?" My stomach practically curdled. "Seriously, Tom. You did not let an eighty-five-year-old spinster plan our honeymoon, did you?"

"You know how busy I've been. Meetings. Moving into the new house. Court appearances." He flicked on the car light and reached into a breast pocket, pulling out a paper packet. In the harsh overhead light, I read Miss Fizzi's scratchy handwriting: "Honeymoon Instructions—Do Not Lose."

I groaned and sank into the seat. The Italian Alps and European cities, the Orient Express and sleek ocean liners fizzled into oblivion. I envisioned Miss Fizzi booking the same old room I always settled for in Ocean City, the whole town granting their stamp of approval: *We wouldn't want Flip to feel overwhelmed! We wouldn't want Flip to get homesick!*

Tom flicked off the light and buried the packet in his pocket again. "I don't know what you're groaning about. It's very reassuring for a man to have instructions on his honeymoon." The car picked up speed. "I wonder what Miss Fizzi suggests we do first."

* * *

LESS THAN TWENTY-FOUR hours later, the loud drone of a twin engine airplane kept conversation to a minimum, but the breathtaking sight of endless, sapphire blue water sprinkled with white crests filled my picture window. For a woman who'd never stepped foot on a train, a plane, or even a Greyhound bus, the second day of marriage proved magically transporting.

"Thank you, Miss Fizzi," I murmured, nose pressed to the windowpane. I squeezed Tom's hand. So far, my favorite daft old lady showed she knew a thing or two about honeymoons—and me.

We'd driven away from our wedding reception the night before, me wondering where in Alaska we'd pitch our tent. I couldn't have been more surprised. We ended up a short distance away in Taneytown, Maryland, at Antrim 1844, a nineteenth-century plantation home converted into a luxury country house hotel. In a nod to my newfound ancestry, Miss Fizzi booked us in the J.E.B. Stuart room, complete with queen canopy feather bed and double Jacuzzi.

Popping open a bottle of Taittinger, Tom boasted, "I approved her choice, of course." As if he had much say in the matter.

All in all, Miss Fizzi's arrangements exceeded expectations, and when Tom whispered in my ear at five A.M. the next morning, time to rise and shine, better have my passport handy, and, by the way, he'd added an extra day to the honeymoon, my screech of joy could have woken J.E.B. Stuart himself. After rushing to Dulles Airport to catch a flight to Miami, I proudly handed my new passport to a ticket agent for a second flight to Grand Cayman. Just when I thought I'd died and gone to heaven, stepping out on the tarmac of a real tropical island, Tom revealed we had just enough time for lunch and a rum punch before our third airplane of the day winged its way to the island of Little Cayman.

As the wheels of the twenty-passenger plane touched down on the grass runway, I couldn't imagine a more peaceful or tranquil spot on earth to spend a honeymoon.

Never had I been so wrong.

# CHAPTER 2

※

A FEW WEEKS earlier, Hurricane Ivan had torn through the Caymans, devastating a large portion of the main island. The airport itself evidenced some destruction, but when our small plane lifted above Grand Cayman, Tom and I stared down, awestruck at the power of wind and water. Mountains of debris pocked the landscape. Crashed boats lay sideways, swept from moorings to the middle of the island. Flat, concrete foundations lay exposed where once houses stood, where families sat down to dinner, children played with toys, teenagers talked on the phone with friends, and mothers wrote out the weekly grocery list in spotless kitchens. We marveled that the airport had even reopened, and wondered what lay in store at our final destination.

Thankfully, the huge storm spared most of Cayman Brac and Little Cayman, the sister islands, but clear indications of damage remained. As the plane glided down to the end of the grass runway of my dream honeymoon island, wouldn't you know the first thing I noticed was the clean-up?

A small truck or two whizzed past the airstrip loaded with palm fronds and planks of wood. A moderate-sized house presented challenge enough for me; I couldn't imagine scrubbing up an entire island.

We watched as our fellow passengers greeted friends or piled into vans, shuttling off to the three or four inns on Little Cayman. A couple took off for McCoy's Diving and Fishing Lodge, another three headed for the Little Cayman Beach Resort. A group of six piled into the Southern Cross Club vehicle.

"I read about that place in a travel magazine. It's supposed to be really nice." I picked up a carry-on bag and tagged after Tom like an eager puppy, unable to conceal my excitement. "Where are we staying, honey?" Surely, Miss Fizzi would not let us down. After the unexpected luxury of our wedding night, I held high hopes for a ritzy condo or private villa where a dozen servants would wait on us hand and foot, just like in the travel magazines. I would lounge by a pool day in, day out, bowls of fruit and kiwi sorbet at my elbow while Tom anointed my toes with coconut oil.

"It's a new place. Brand new. I called the owner a couple of weeks after the hurricane, and he assured me they'd be up and running by now." He hauled our luggage away from the plane, and we stood on the sideline as new passengers boarded the aircraft to fly back to Grand Cayman. "I guess our ride's a little late." He lowered his sunglasses, black pupils narrowing in the bright light, searching for a jeep or van.

The circles under his eyes matched mine, and I smiled dreamily, replaying our wedding night in my mind. The lack of sleep, the thrill of traveling so far, the sticky warmth of the air, the sweet, unfamiliar scents—I slowly sank down and nestled on our largest piece of luggage, breathing in a whole new atmosphere. "I think that rum punch at the airport finally hit me."

"No, no. It's not the rum. It's me." Tom plopped down at

my feet and wrapped one hand around my ankle. "I always have this effect on women, you see, when I go out of town. Solace Glen has a way of inhibiting its professional men. We have to be on our best behavior at all times. Straight red neckties, sensible haircuts. Crisp, white shirts. Charcoal gray suits. And no joking around or the Presbyterians will fine you. That is why," he rubbed my calf, thumb pressing into the muscle, "I asked Miss Fizzi to pick the most private, most relaxing Caribbean spot she could find. Within my budget, of course."

"Aha." I ruffled his thick, dark hair, the fringe of his scalp just beginning to gray. "I wondered how long it would take to hear the b-word. Maybe that's why we haven't seen hide nor hair of a van. 'Transportation of guests not included.' You'll have to tote me three miles just to reach the threshold."

Tom grunted in pretend agony and withdrew Miss Fizzi's honeymoon instruction packet. "It says we'll be picked up at the airport and transported to the resort."

"I like that word. Re-sort." I could almost smell the co-conut oil on my toes as two men rumbled by in a white jeep. We peered at the printed letters on the side. Police. "When we get back to Solace Glen, I'm going to talk everybody's ears off about my fabulous resort honeymoon. Especially to Lee. Payback for all the hours I've had to endure listening to her jabber about moonlight dinners, Finger Lake canoes, and historic inns where '*Wine* flows out of the tap, Flip, not water!'"

Tom chuckled. "She and Sam had quite a time last May, I know. But don't you fret, my lovely. Our honeymoon will make theirs look like a bus ride to Newark. Think of all the things you can brag about to the Circle Ladies. Snorkeling with iridescent schools of fish . . ."

"Ohhh."

"Lazy days on a white beach, with all the umbrella drinks you can handle."

"Ooooo."

"Candlelit, gourmet dinners served at water's edge."

"Ahhhh."

"Hours of fishing with your handsome mate."

"Excuse me?"

"Skin-diving lessons at Bloody Bay Wall."

"Bloody what? You know I'm petrified of . . ."

A small truck chugged toward us, creaking and swaying down the narrow paved road, a steady stream of exhaust in its wake. An arm stuck out the window and waved. A voice boomed, "Hell-ooo!"

Tom squinted. "I think he means us."

The truck, dusty and rusted, looked like something hauled out of the jungle of Okinawa sixty years after the Japanese surrendered. It ground to a halt in front of our luggage, and I gawked at the door with the sloppy, hand-painted name of our honeymoon "resort." CAMP IGUANA. Only then did I notice the tiny lizards painted in multi-colors beneath the dust, scampering across the dented steel frame. "Tom . . ."

He hugged me into his side. "Well! This is shaping up to be a real adventure, isn't it? Let's lock and load!"

Before I could flash angry eyes at him—*what have you gone and let Miss Fizzi do to us?*—a large hand grasped mine and shook hard.

"You must be Mrs. Scott! I know how you newlywed ladies like to be called Mrs. as soon as possible, but after this, we're on a first name basis at Camp Iguana. Hello, hello, there, sir! You're Tom, right? Jimbo. Jimbo Tull. Welcome, welcome! Sorry I was a little late in arrivin'. That truck picks the worst times to act up." The large hand belonged to a large man in his mid-thirties with a decidedly Southern accent and cropped hair the color of sunshine. He stood well over six feet tall, nearly six and a half, every inch muscle. "Here, lemme help you with that gear. We'll just throw it in the back and you two can jump in the front with me, OK? Here we go!"

Before I could say, *Not on your life, bucko,* Tom

pushed me into the center of the truck's front seat. Two doors slammed on either side, and I flinched at the grinding and squeal of gears. The duct tape holding the seat together scraped against my bare legs. I jerked the ratty towel under Tom's hip over to my side.

"So! Tell us about Camp Iguana!" Tom called over the din, clearly in the camp spirit.

"You'll love it!" Jimbo boomed. His wide mouth, teeth even and white, stretched almost the length of his enormous height. "You'll be downright crazy about it!"

"Downright crazy" did come to mind. Along with "no escape."

"How many guests do you have? Did you have a lot of damage? My wife and I can't get over the destruction we saw on the main island!"

I suddenly brightened and smiled at Tom as we bounced along, warm and fuzzy at the sound of that wonderful four-letter word—*wife*. All women must have the same reaction the first time their husbands say it, and I had to admit, "Mrs." gave me an equal thrill.

Jimbo nodded, bleached brows joined, and shouted, "The main island got hit pretty hard, but like I said on the phone, we lucked out. Took longer to reopen than I thought, though. Hard getting supplies. We've got eight guests, including the two of you, with two more arriving tomorrow." He shot us a broad grin.

"Only eight?" I tried to picture Camp Iguana. A rambling old house with cavernous rooms? A large tent crammed with bunk beds? Sleeping bags stacked along the shore? "Where are the other guests from?"

"North Carolina, England, and New York!"

"Wow. England?" I turned to Tom with saucer eyes, as if he'd thrown in a couple of cosmopolitan foreigners just for me. I couldn't wait to call and brag to Margaret, a true anglophile.

"Yep." His friendly voice suddenly turned sharp and edgy. "My partner, Jay, invited them, along with the New

Yorkers." The edge disappeared just as suddenly. "The Carolina couple are friends of mine from way back. So is our fishing guide."

"Is that where you're from?"

"Yes, ma'am, Raleigh born and bred, and a proud alum of N.C. State! I forgive you for bein' Terps. We'll let it pass for now."

"How'd you end up here?"

Tom pinched my cheek. "You'll have to forgive my wife. She's a fountain of questions with a nose as long as the Mississippi."

"Quite all right. That's how strangers become friends. I'm here by a twist of fate, I guess. After college, I got a job shuttling fancy boats from Maine to Florida on the Intercoastal Waterway. That led to shuttling boats around the Caribbean. Every island I stepped foot on, I wanted to stay and find a bit of land, but I was young and havin' a good time, and the money was nothing to sneeze at. Then one day, about five years ago, I stepped foot on Grand Cayman and met Laurie, my wife. Prettiest wisp of a willow I ever did see. That did it for me. We married in record time. Her folks weren't too crazy about the idea. Thought Laurie married beneath herself and shouldn't have to work for a living. We ran a little marina on the main island before this place came up for sale. Years ago, I'd been to the U.S. Virgins and come across Maho Bay, an ecological resort. Ever since, I dreamed of doing the same sort of thing, maybe a tad more upscale, and offering fishing and diving packages, to boot."

"Upscale is good." I could still imagine the faint scent of coconut oil.

"Yes, ma'am. Let's just say we're workin' on that part of the plan. Here's the camp road comin' up on our right."

The loud ten-minute drive along the main road ended, and we left the relative safety of pavement to bump down a dirt lane strewn with chunks of concrete and gravel, prone to jolting dips in the earth that seemed to suck all four tires into the jaws of hell. Hidden from view to the general public by a brace of wind-battered bamboo, silver thatch palm, and Casuarina trees, our "resort" offered a painful first impression. I almost expected to see a ragged sign nailed to a tree with the grim warning, "I'd turn back if I were you."

"Hurricane Ivan did a number on our driveway!" Jimbo shouted, his short blonde hair glistening in the humidity. "This is actually the second full day we've opened to visitors, so you'll have to bear with us. Might be a few kinks to iron out!"

I clung to Tom as the truck lurched forward. "A few kinks?" If the road looked like a moon crater, what about the hotel? Assuming, of course, Camp Iguana-for-Breakfast-Lunch-and-Dinner *was* a hotel. I pictured fallen plaster, water-stained walls, soaked mattresses, live goats and chickens in the dining room. To spare Miss Fizzi's feelings, we would have to lie and swear the place looked like the Taj Mahal.

Around a bend in the crater, trees and shrubbery opened up to a surprising vista of one long, thin expanse of sand running along gorgeous blue water. Two workers raked seaweed and palm fronds on the beach, another two hammered at an expansive new dock where a large boat and a smaller one sat tethered. Further down, stationed forlornly between two massive palms, their bushy tops reduced to ragged slivers, a dirty white concrete building stood. Green shutters hung precariously off window casements, and potted, red hibiscus trees partially hid open doors. As we pulled in front of this sad structure, I discovered the reason for the potted trees. The doors weren't doors at all, but mismatched planks of wood nailed together, leaning unhinged against the outer walls.

"We lost our doors in the hurricane," Jimbo explained, sliding out of the truck, "so we picked up what blew in on the beach until our supply shipment arrives. We're not exactly first in line since the big island got hit worse. The potted plants are brand new, though. Come on, Laurie will get you checked in at the bar, then I'll take you to your hut."

"Hut? Did he say hut?" Miss Fizzi's ritzy condo and private villa sank into the sea like Atlantis, along with a vat of coconut oil.

Tom pulled my jangled body from the truck and gave my neck a brisk rubdown. "How about that ride? Invigorating, huh? This is gonna be great, really great!"

He sucked in a huge breath of sea air, grinning like his old Labrador retriever, Eli, catching his first whiff of the Thanksgiving Day turkey. I couldn't decide if he'd slipped into courtroom theatrics, or truly loved the idea of knocking around Camp Shambles for the next nine days.

We followed Jimbo into the concrete structure, and I was pleasantly surprised by the colorful, tropical décor of the open-air lobby. A mahogany ceiling fan moved air lazily over a set of rattan sofas and chairs. The green, blue, and yellow parrot print of the pillows perked up my spirits, and my silly lust for condos and villas began to wane. On the left, a dining room held a few simple but brightly painted tables and chairs. Sounds of supper preparations filtered through the kitchen door—clanging pots, muffled voices, laughing, and shouted orders.

Jimbo led us to the right of the lobby where a long bar dominated the room, the wood dark and glistening, reminiscent of a sleek sailing vessel. Through an open side door, a patio with an eclectic collection of plastic and aluminum outdoor furniture faced a small swimming pool. A striking young brunette, probably in her mid-twenties, with Audrey Hepburn eyes and silky hair stylishly twisted into a knot, leaned against the counter. She laughed at the comments her customer made, a well-tanned, good-looking man seated at the bar, cradling a drink. When we entered the room, she visibly jumped, a guilty tinge to her frozen smile.

"Laurie." Jimbo spoke her name in the tone of a preacher catching a member of the church gone astray. "These are the Scotts. Remember? Tom and Flip. Our very first honeymooners?"

"Oh. That's right." She stood up straight and in hurried, birdlike movements, stacked a row of glasses along the bar as if completing a test before time ran out. She added unenthusiastically, "Good thing the honeymoon suite didn't wash away."

Encouraging news.

Jimbo's normally loud voice dropped significantly. "And this guy at the bar is my partner, Jay Carruthers. He's also our dive master, if you go in for that sort of thing."

As Tom stepped forward to shake Jay's hand, Jimbo pointed at the full glass. "Jay, isn't it a little early for this? Thought you were taking a group out for a sunset dive."

"Welcome aboard." Jay leaned from his barstool to shake Tom's hand. He spoke in a clipped, polished British accent, like a stage actor or a top salesman. Fortyish, handsome to a degree of suspicion, Jay's skin gleamed a burnished copper and his eyes shimmered sky blue, with barely a hint of crow's feet. He combed his sun-streaked, sandy hair straight back. "I am doing a sunset cruise, old boy. That lovely twit, Tootie, is setting up the *Tyrol* as we speak. But what's a sunset without a bit of lubrication?" When Jimbo failed to respond, he turned to us. "Well, nice to meet the two of you. Tally-ho, enjoy your stay. I daresay I will." He held up his glass and winked at Laurie, who returned the gesture with a sultry, Mona Lisa smile. She absently wiped the bar counter and watched him skip away from Jimbo's glower.

"Bet he didn't pay for that drink, either," he growled. "We have a gentleman's agreement, ya know."

She shut her eyes tight, lips clamped, irritated, as if she'd heard the complaint a thousand times. "That drink came out of his own stock." She clenched her teeth, but in the next instant, addressed Tom and me politely, the charming hostess. "Don't mind us. We squabble like this all the time. It's called the New Owner/Operator Disease."

"Jay's an operator all right," sneered Jimbo, but he

changed his tune when he caught Laurie's warning eye. "Say, where are my southern manners? You two haven't experienced our special Iguana Igniter. Laurie, fire up a couple of shot glasses. On the house, folks. Welcome to paradise!"

Laurie immediately popped a couple of small glasses on the bar and poured a green concoction from a cold pitcher.

"What's in it?" I politely searched my glass for talons.

"Something with rum in it, I'm guessing." Tom threw his head back, downing the thick green liquid.

When his eyes didn't throw off sparks, I followed suit. "Oh, wow. That's good. Mint?" I asked Laurie, and she nodded at each guess. "Lime? Cointreau? And something I can't quite put a finger on."

"And you never will; that's the secret. But I'll give you a hint. It's native." She reached under the bar and placed a hotel register in front of us. "Now, if one of you two lovebirds will sign here, we'll get you settled in, and the honeymoon in paradise can commence. Right over there is a bulletin board with diving and fishing excursions to sign up for, along with daily weather predictions and meal information. Snorkeling gear is free, just sign it out at the lean-to where the bikes are located. Supper's at six-thirty tonight. Cocktail hour begins upon arrival and never ends."

"About this diving business." Tom ignored the horrible face I made. "How do we go about learning?"

*We?*

"Jay and Tootie can get you started in the pool. When you're ready for the real thing, they'll hold your hand the whole way."

*I wouldn't care if they strapped me to their backs. Not going, not going.*

"Does everyone around here dive?"

*My worst nightmare.*

"Sure seems like it, especially after the hurricane." Laurie laughed, such a pretty young woman when she did. "I grew up on Grand Cayman and Barbados, so I went from playpen to tank pretty quickly."

Jimbo rocked on his heels, pride in his loud voice. "My wife plays it down, but Laurie's an expert on open-water dives, and knows the Wall like the back of her hand. She's a much sought-after private guide. Even has her own groupie."

"Oh, Jimbo, stop it." The irritation returned, marring her lovely features. She crossed her arms, vexed for some reason at the sincere compliment.

"What about Picky Jiffers? Him and his oily goatee, not that anybody can get close enough to touch it. He's kind of a reclusive Howard Hughes character," he explained to us. "Rented a new villa on the east end a couple of weeks after the hurricane. Got a fancy, fast cigar boat. The handful of islanders who've met him weren't impressed, I hear, but he's none too impressed with us, either. Except for Laurie."

"That's enough. Drop it."

Jimbo either ignored the peevishness or didn't understand it. "It's true. He can't seem to get enough of Laurie, and diving the Wall. Me, I can take it or leave it. I'd just as soon go fishin'."

Tom did an about-face. He would have zoomed off on his favorite subject, but I halfway feigned exhaustion and allowed my knees to buckle.

"OK, Jimbo," Laurie instructed, all business, "that's our cue to take care of these folks and their luggage."

After the unexpected pleasures of the main house, anticipation for a decent room began to swell. "Tom," I stumbled to his side, woozy, "do you think Camp Iguana really has a honeymoon suite? I mean, a real suite with bedroom furniture and a bathroom and everything?"

"We're about to find out, my pet. But so far," his eyes sparkled mischievously, "I got noooo worries."

*Poor thing,* I thought. For all the years I'd known him, Tom rarely took a vacation. His idea of time off meant a good snore on the lounge chair while a football game on TV passed him by. Then it hit me. Tom didn't care about the trappings: fancy furniture, gourmet meals, gambling casinos, glamorous entertainment. And neither should I. He was here; I was here; and there were plenty of fish in the sea. Literally. I stood on the tip of my toes and kissed his cheek, which was somewhat rough from lack of shaving. "I love you."

"And I love you." He kissed the top of my head. "Don't worry. This will be a grand adventure, just like the rest of our lives together."

We piled into the truck for a short ride over smooth grass and sand to a cluster of structures scattered among royal palms and sea grapes, each little building steps away from the lapping sea, each one well screened and private.

"Tom," I leaned in to his ear, "they do look like huts."

"They're tent-cabins," Jimbo interjected, "very ecological. Ten of 'em, but we hope to expand to fifteen or twenty over time. I have big plans for this place. Big plans. Right now, four cabins are still undergoin' repair, but they're all good wood with canvas roofs. The rest held up surprisingly well during the storm. The community bath is right here, the concrete building. Men on the right, gals on the left. Septic should be fine by now."

"Should be?" The gleeful anticipation began to dwindle. "Which one is the 'honeymoon suite'?"

"The one at the very end. Has a little more privacy than the others, and," the sun-bleached eyebrows wiggled, "its very own outdoor shower."

"Well, now!" Tom slapped my knee. "All the trimmings! Just like home!"

The beloved image of our new house—House Beautiful—popped into my dizzy head, a home built with love and care, great skill, and a sharp eye for detail. The most up-to-date kitchen. The most handsome pine floors. The widest porch with a generous assembly of rocking chairs where we could admire our blossoming pear and cherry trees.

I stared glumly at our honeymoon hut with its patched canvas roof, canvas curtains, and recently replaced mosquito screens, fondly recalling our central air and heat, large stone fireplace, and luxurious whirlpool bath.

Then my eye caught Tom's, and we burst out laughing. Our grand adventure. Our new life together. Joys and obstacles, champagne and lemons.

The exact same words poured from our mouths. *"Thank you, Miss Fizzi!"*

# CHAPTER 3

※

N<small>O ADVENTURE IN</small> paradise should begin without proper nutrition, rest, and a call to Miss Fizzi. She toasted us long distance with her afternoon glass of sherry. "I vaguely remember something about a hurricane. Was there much damage?"

"Not as much here as on Grand Cayman. Oh, Miss Fizzi, we're already having a *wonderful* time, thanks to you. The inn at Taneytown was the most fabulous place I've ever stayed, and you couldn't have picked a more beautiful island. It takes your breath away. We're soooo grateful!"

I could practically hear the flutter of her heart. "You are so welcome, dear! I'm thrilled to my toes. Everyone here has been on pins and needles to hear how the honeymoon is going. I'm so honored you'd report to me first. What about the camp? Are the counselors nice? I told Tom I had my doubts about sending the two of you off to camp at your age, but when he saw the price, he insisted."

I finished off a pack of cheese crackers from the plane and glanced around our simple digs. Our cots—not quite beds, yet close enough—did possess frames of wood. The mattresses, on the thin side, felt shockingly comfortable, and didn't spout seawater, at least. The cool, crisp white linens, soft and divinely scented, stretched beneath an even softer aqua coverlet. In the corner, shelves held the clothes Tom had quickly unpacked, and a round plastic table and four white, plastic chairs decorated the small deck overlooking the sea. Blooms of pink and lavender spilled from large, terra-cotta pots. A cool breeze blew through screened windows on all sides, and a pole rolled with canvas anchored each sill, a ready-made curtain. One bare bulb on the ceiling provided what light we might need after sunset, along with hurricane lamps and candles. "It's fascinating," I said, trying to choose my words as carefully as Margaret during a lecture on English literature. "I can't wait to explore. And tell Margaret a couple of people staying here are from England!"

"No! Really? How swank! Are you the only Americans?"

"No, there's a couple from North Carolina and another from New York."

"Oh, dear. Rebels and carpetbaggers. I hope they don't come to fisticuffs. That's the nice thing about being from Maryland. You can claim both sides." In a persistent nineteenth-century mindset, Miss Fizzi urged us to take a nap, the answer to every ill, to recover from the wedding hoopla. She ended our conversation with a strange lilt in her voice. "Have fun! Call Margaret and Lindbergh in a day or two, and remember, Flip, expect the unexpected . . ."


THE CLANG OF a dinner bell woke us from an hour's nap, refreshed, excited, incredulous at our surroundings. I hopped out of bed and drank in the scene from our deck.

"Oh, Tom." He slipped behind me and wrapped his arms around my waist. "It's beautiful, isn't it? I never dreamed. I never dreamed."

"Yes, you did." He squeezed tight. "We both did. Now, let's eat. I'm starved!"

As we walked hand in hand to the main house, I teased him. "Really, tell the truth. Fess up. How did Miss Fizzi come up with Camp Spartan? You must have said something to lead her to this. What did you say—that *camp*ing would be fun? That you loved *camp* as a boy? That you're a longtime supporter of the *Camp* Fire Girls of America?"

Tom pressed his lips together, as if wrestling with a dense legal point. "Perhaps she heard me quoting Thomas *Camp*ion. Or speaking of the presidential *camp*aign."

"You're impossible."

"I think I have all kinds of possibilities." He kissed my hand. "Truth be told, Miss Fizzi found Little Cayman all on her own, following my request for a small, somewhat isolated Caribbean getaway. When she shocked me with the cost of flying here from Maryland, I insisted she find the most affordable accommodations she could. Cheap is my middle name. As soon as I saw the name of this place, I knew we were in for a treat."

"Or trick, maybe. Halloween is only a week away."

"Come on. I know you." He swept his arm out. "Cloudless blue skies, the beginning of an amazing sunset, azure seas, the scent of tropical flowers, warm, white sand. We can go barefoot every day, and never have to wear a tie or spiked heels. The start of the perfect honeymoon, peaceful, uncluttered, and quiet."

"I know, and I can't believe it." I could have cried, but instead twirled around and skipped backward like a schoolgirl. "No phones! No TV! No cooking or cleaning or clients with emergencies to ruin our fun. Miles away from the nosy noses of Solace Glen. Though, I must admit, my nose is the nosiest. Plus, we do have our own shower."

"That's the pioneer spirit, my little campfire girl. Who knows what other delights lie in store?"

"Yes," I threw my arms in the air, "who knows? First thing I'm going to do is drill every bit of information I can from that English couple. Maybe I'll even learn to speak with a *Brrrrr*itish accent. Margaret would be impressed. She likes to think she looks like the queen, only taller. Oh, what if these English people *know* the queen!"

"Just tell them you do, that you're a distant cousin or something." He bowed low. "Now I'm even more amazed you agreed to marry me."

I dipped my knees in a little curtsy. "You should be."

"In all seriousness, this is a beautiful place to start our married life together, isn't it?" He pulled me in to his side, his handsome, magazine features animated. "We deserve a break, darn it! An honest-to-God, get-away-from-it-all break from the daily routine. Savor the moment, my love, savor the moment." He twirled me around the dance floor of sand, ending with a low dip and a toe-curling kiss.

Our spirits high, we ambled toward the outdoor bar and patio. A new face greeted us with a ready smile, smooth, tanned skin, and a sharp, angular nose. Tall and lanky, he wore sunglasses and kept his straight brown hair on the longish side, tucked behind flat ears. He waved us over like an amiable old pal.

"Evenin'. You must be Tom and Flip." My ear took in another Southern accent, the dialect slightly different from Jimbo's, but my pitiful travel experience didn't allow for an exact distinction. "I'm Fa-Fa. The name's funny, but the story of the name's mighty borin'. What'll y'all have? We've got a good supply of fire water."

"I'll have whatever you've got on tap. The lady would like a gin and tonic. Heavy on the lime."

"The lady is a kindred spirit."

While Fa-Fa mixed and poured, we fell into an easy conversation about the island, how he got from the Carolinas to his current job as bartender and fishing guide, and who else held temporary residence in the beachside bungalows. I rattled off questions and listened, enthralled at every word, soaking up this new person, this amazing new life Heaven surprised me with in mid-life. "How long has the camp been open? What was it before?"

"Just a homestead, but the family decided to sell. Jimbo and Laurie bought the property late last winter. Everything in the islands costs more in the end than you think it will, Camp Iguana being no exception. It's been a struggle. In May, Laurie flew to Grand Cayman to visit friends and ran into Jay." His voice dipped the way Jimbo's had. "Jay's an old beau of Laurie's."

I remembered their easy manner with each other at the bar, Laurie's guilty reaction when we walked in, Jimbo's tense words, and Laurie's open irritation with her husband. Maybe Jay amounted to more than an "old" beau. "So Jay decided to invest?"

"You've seen Laurie." Fa-Fa grinned, tan skin setting off teeth that gleamed white as beach sand. "She sets her mind on somethin', there's no stoppin' her. She wanted Jay as a partner, and got him to invest a pretty substantial amount. Things were lookin' up for all of us. Had a real strong opening in September with plans on the board to expand. But you know the story. Hadn't been in operation a month when the hurricane knocked us for a loop. Underinsured and overextended. Despite an avalanche of cancellations, we finally reopened to guests the day before yesterday. Four cabins occupied, four couples. Henrietta and George came all the way from London. He's OK, kind of a talker, but she's a little high-falootin'. You know how the British are."

I didn't, but couldn't wait to find out.

"I believe they met Jay in Barbados. Then we've got Frank and Renata from New York, also acquaintances of Jay's. And Buddy and Dempsie are from North Carolina. Buddy is Jimbo's oldest friend. No lie, they met at birth in the hospital. I didn't enter into the picture until years later when I met the three of them at N.C. State. When we opened last month, we had a healthy number of folks from Carolina, but people came from all over, even with little advertising and a pretty lame Web site. You're our first Maryland couple, though. Never been to Maryland, unless you count I-95. What's it like?"

Tom responded, dry as toast, "The frantic mid-Atlantic. Not like here."

"Oh, pooh, it's not frantic where we live." I delighted in describing Solace Glen to Fa-Fa, from the fountain in front of the drug store to the white spire of the Presbyterian church. "We're right in between Baltimore and Washington, only further west. Ever heard of Solace Glen?"

Tom nearly choked on his beer, but Fa-Fa smiled. "Naw, can't say that I have. Ever heard of Duke, Alabama? No? You're kidding. My hometown."

"I thought you said you came from North Carolina."

"I did, but what self-respectin' member of the Wolf-pack's gonna admit he was born in a place called Duke? My old man moved to Raleigh when I was a teenager. Been grateful ever since. By the way, most of our meals are buf-fet style. You can eat inside or out here on the patio, weather permitting. When the dock's finished, we'll throw a proper party out there one night. Always nice under the stars. Keep in mind, you're on island time now. When you hear the din-ner bell clang, that's merely the signal to have another gin and tonic, heavy on the lime. Food is but an afterthought."

"Spoken like a true member of the Wolfpack." Tom leaned toward his best new fishing buddy. "Be forewarned. I'm a Maryland Terp, a lawyer, and a guest here. Make sure I catch the most fish or I'll sue. Well, Mrs. Scott, shall we dine?"

In the excitement of the day, I'd only nibbled food like a tadpole. "Lead on. I could eat a whale."

The dining room contained four or five tables of differ-ent sizes, each painted in brilliant, tropical colors and sport-ing various motifs. Hummingbirds, frogs and bugs, iguanas, flowers, and fish. Two couples sat quietly talking at a table for six, while at another table, a man ate silently, his nose in a journal. He did not raise his head when Fa-Fa joined him, obviously another member of the staff. I spotted Laurie through a swinging kitchen door, chatting with the cooks and idly arranging flower blossoms around a cake.

"Oh, Tom, wouldn't Garland and Hilda have the time of their lives running a place like this?" I whispered. "No big crowds, and after work they could dive into that beautiful, clear water. I wish everybody in Solace Glen could see this place, but I guess pictures will have to do."

"Frankly, I've decided to tell the other guests we're from Paris."

"Don't include me. I'm a distant cousin of the queen."

Nothing fancy, Camp Iguana's kitchen nevertheless knew how to make the most out of fresh, simple foods. The buffet brimmed with kiwi, apples, oranges, bananas, and wonderful smelling grilled vegetables, properly seasoned. One meat offering of lamb kabobs and one fish offering of pecan-encrusted red snapper anchored the meal, with sauces arranged in small, bright yellow bowls. Various breads lay piled in attractive, handcrafted baskets.

The layout struck me as so lovely, in fact, I found myself burbling, "This is so nice! What a great idea! Look at that. I could do that. Wouldn't it be phenomenal this winter to give a Caribbean party when the whole town of Solace Glen is . . ."

Tom placed a finger across my mouth. "Weee are from Pa-ree. Pa-ree, Frawnce. We hate your nasty 'amburgers and fries."

Jimbo sauntered into the room and announced a couple of wine choices (obviously, islanders would run out of sea-water before they ran out of alcohol). Plates full, we made our way to the two couples at the hummingbird table and introduced ourselves. As the usual get-to-know-your-neighbor talk unfolded, our different backgrounds came to light, causing me to wonder how we managed to vacation on the same small spit of land, at the same little resort, at the same time. I could hardly eat from firing off questions, as if frozen for a century and, defrosted at last, I had a lot of catching up to do.

Dempsie and Buddy, Jimbo's dear friends, resembled jumbo-sized Kewpie dolls. Buddy proudly claimed a friendship with Jimbo stretching back to diapers. "There's nuthin' I wouldn't do for that guy," he bragged good-naturedly, round face already sunburned. His curly brown hair, neatly brushed, showed the first signs of receding on either side of his temples. "He's like a brother to me, and godfather to our two boys. There's nuthin' he wouldn't do for me, either."

"Jimbo even gave up dating me when he found out Buddy had a secret yin for my company." Dempsie patted Buddy's arm, face just as round and red, framed by shiny, chin-length, black hair cut in a pageboy style. If the Pills-bury Doughboy had a wife, Dempsie would fit the bill, every inch of her puffy and soft. I liked her immediately, and knew she'd fit right in with the Circle Ladies, if ever she traveled our way. She and Tina could compare notes and complain about their latest diets. "I met Jimbo and Buddy, and Fa-Fa, too, at N.C. State at a frat party. Lord, those were some wild days!"

"One can but imagine," Henrietta drawled in a thick, London accent that brought to mind cold rain and fog. Thin to the point of worry, she'd stretched her beautiful titian hair so tightly into a chignon, it acted as an instant facelift, not that she needed one. Henrietta (no nicknames, please) sat in her chair like the ruling monarch she claimed to have met—several times, in fact—showing deference to no one, not even her spouse, George, whom she unaffectionately dubbed Georgie, like a small terrier. "Georgie, run and fetch me another ba-naw-na . . . Georgie, pawss the sawlt . . . Georgie, must you go fishing *again* tomorrow?"

Despite the bossy snobbery, I hung on every word, fascinated with the accent and description of her life in London, and completely intimidated by the woman. When Tom started to crack a joke about my royal distant cousin, I kicked him under the table. A woman as sophisticated as Henrietta would not see the humor. She might even take offense, and I would spend my nine days in paradise trying to hide behind palm trees at the sight of her. George, a.k.a. Georgie, seemed nice enough, if more than a little henpecked. He wore sunglasses atop his floppy teak-colored hair, which should have turned gray years ago, after being married to Her Royal Attitude. But somehow, he'd managed to retain an attractive boyishness as he approached middle age, causing him to act and look younger than the sour-faced Henrietta.

As soon as Tom heard the word *fishing,* his ears perked up. "George, what sort of fishing have you got planned for tomorrow?"

"Deep-sea, maybe. Today I did a bit of barracuda hunting with Fa-Fa over there. Evil looking fellows. Not Fa-Fa, of course; the barracuda. Truly evil." He bared his teeth at us. "Pretty good fighters, though. You really must go out with Fa-Fa. Splendid guide, excellent fellow. I'm afraid I bombarded him with questions all day. I'm the curious type, you see."

Fa-Fa raised his head at the sound of his name and waved at Curious George. The fishing guide left his companion (who never took his eyes off the journal in his hand), and approached our table. As comfortable as an old sweatshirt, Fa-Fa reminded me more and more of our good friend, Sam Gibbon. He eased into a chair, sunglasses removed, a little bleary-eyed, a crooked smile, pure affability. "Did I hear my name taken in vain?" In answer to a fresh barrage of questions from Curious George (offering my nose a rest), he ran through the story of the eco-friendly Camp Iguana, and how Jimbo sought his help and services. Fa-Fa, who made his living traveling the globe, guiding fishermen in and out of various bodies of water, told one fascinating tale after another. I sneaked a peek at

Tom. His dark, intelligent eyes swirled with wanderlust. Floating down Brazilian rivers, fly-fishing in Alaska, stalking fishy prey with a wooden spear in the Solomons. No one back home would ever have guessed that the mind behind so many boring Last Wills and Testaments harbored such Technicolor visions.

The women in the group sank back in their chairs, outnumbered and forgotten in the surge of this passion for a scaled, pop-eyed species. In no time at all, Fa-Fa had three men signed up for deep-sea fishing the next morning, and two out of three wives who refused to stay home and knit.

Henrietta's face screwed up. "I'd rawther do something else. Anything else." She took a sip of Merlot, shuddering as if she'd drunk sewage, and waited for Curious George to cancel out, but he didn't, emboldened by the high turnout.

Just as we received the happy news we'd shove off at six-thirty in the morning, voices rang out in the barroom. The sunset divers made a loud entry into the dining area, Jay leading the parade, fresh beer bottle in hand. He sent a cursory salute to Jimbo, who grunted in return, and marched straight toward Laurie, loitering around the buffet. "Good news, everyone! The last section of the dock is repaired and ready for all three boats and dinner parties! Did you hear that, Laurie?"

Her wide, doe eyes locked onto his. "I heard." She remained motionless as he moved embarrassingly close, their two bodies almost connected. No one could miss the electricity.

"At last. You can retrieve your boat from Brac tomorrow. Picky Jiffers will be thrilled. I know how Daddy Moneybags abhors using his racer for your little jaunts to the Wall."

I expected Laurie to bristle at the mention of her mysterious client as she had with Jimbo. But her smile catapulted into laughter. She tapped her hand lightly against Jay's chest, as if they shared a private joke.

Before Jimbo could close in, Jay slid toward our table,

changing the subject. "Fa-Fa, old boy, what are you up to? Marketing yourself again?"

"Marketin' is somethin' I leave to you and Jimbo, Jay. I'm just a poor, fly-castin' fool. You two are the boss men."

"You? Poor? From what I hear, your family could buy all of England and reduce the rest of us to serfs. Hail to the Joneses of Alabama!"

Something in Jay's manner grabbed my attention— sarcasm, coldness. A definite disdain. Fa-Fa ignored the comment and glanced over Jay's shoulder. He greeted the divers by name, his way of introducing the guests to each other. Tom rose and shook hands while I nodded sweetly, desperately trying to employ mental crutches, like rhymes or celebrity faces, so I would remember these new arrivals, plus our table companions. Miss Fizzi's words popped into my head. *We want you to have a wonderful time, but we have our concerns.* If my lack of social grace didn't make the list, it should have. At that moment, I could have crawled out of the room—overwhelmed—but the man by my side drew close, and over and over again referred to me as his wife. My Tom. He put me right at ease.

The surname of the New York couple, Renata and Frank, flew over my head, but I knew immediately what celebrity face I could match with Frank's; he was the spitting image of Aristotle Onassis. A slightly misshapen man, stoop-shouldered, with facial scars, his gray eyebrows seemed to explode. His wife, Renata, carried no celebrity stigma whatsoever. Her dark gray hair frizzed out in the humidity, and the lines in her face bore proof of a hard life, the lovely Roman nose unpowdered and shiny. She equaled Frank's short stature, and hung behind him, shy and unsure of herself. I empathized completely, but unlike my gallant Tom, Frank ignored his wife, immune to her discomfort.

"What a sunset! Magnificent! Oh, how do you do! What's the name? Well, Tom and Flip, I hope you didn't miss the most fantastic sunset I've witnessed in years! Got in a little diving, too, thanks to Jay and Tootie. That Tootie, what a knockout in a wet suit! Do you dive? Everyone around here dives! I love it! It's great! Great! What do you do, Tom?"

As Frank pulled Tom away, I continued to nod and smile sweetly at the two new women in our group, Renata and Tootie. Tootie flopped into a chair to reapply her lip gloss. A beautiful, long-legged platinum blonde with a lion's mane of hair, she epitomized what the Beach Boys sang about for years. She couldn't have been more than a couple of years out of college. With golden skin, lucid blue eyes that seemed to favor Jay, and an obvious awareness of her iconic California looks, Tootie sat contentedly on the sidelines, accepting the admiring gaze of men and the envious eyes of the other women. When Laurie nudged her to come help in the kitchen, though, she shot a look at Laurie's back equal to a stabbing. Maybe nobody else noticed, but I did.

The new arrivals descended on the buffet, and the rest of us settled in to get better acquainted. Since the camp only held eight guests for the evening, and the whole staff, including the cooks in the kitchen, couldn't have amounted to more than seven or eight, it was impossible to blend into a crowd the way you might on a cruise ship or at a sprawling hotel. The discussion almost immediately centered on the sunset dive, with Frank raving about the clarity of the water. Like Renata and Dempsie, I quietly smiled. The dive and fish talk bore all the markings of a foreign tongue, a language I was determined to learn at breakneck speed, anxious to fit in and make Tom proud.

"Did you dive, too?" I whispered to Renata, in a mild attempt to participate.

She shook her head, and softly replied, "No, I stayed in the boat. I'm happy to watch from a safe distance."

Dempsie and I murmured our approval, members of the same club, but Henrietta looked down her nose at us with a pitying expression, as if we'd confessed to cutting our own hair.

Fa-Fa poured the wine and threw in a geology lesson.

"Little Cayman is only ten miles long and one mile wide, mostly bluff limestone and ironstone—porous, so water absorbs quickly. Plus, there are no rivers or streams clouding up the dive sites with runoff."

"We missed you out there today, Fa-Fa of Alabama/ Carolina," Jay slurred. "You know, our fabulous Fa-Fa here used to be a superb diver on top of his many other skills. But a nasty boy named Ivan came along. How's that bad back? Need a painkiller?" He lifted his beer bottle and winked.

Oddly, a darkness fell across Fa-Fa. Jay snickered.

"How many dive sites are there?" Dempsie piped up. "Not that I want to try any. I'm a hopeless landlubber."

"Amen, sister." I hoped to send Tom a message. Surely, he had not forgotten my recurring nightmare of drowning. Dempsie smiled back at me, the same stripe running down her spine when it came to deep water.

"There are forty-one named sites, but probably more than fifty in all." Fa-Fa quickly regained his light footing. "And if you've never dived, you really should try a resort course. Jay and Tootie will teach you the basics here in the pool, then later in the day take you out to Bloody Bay Wall. Starts at eighteen feet, plunges to over a thousand. Not to worry, ma'am, we won't push you over the edge of the Wall until the second day."

I nervously laughed along with the others. The thought of hovering above an ocean cliff in a wet suit made my palms sweat, but Tom, almost giddy, announced we might accept the offer. I zapped high eyebrows and tapped a foot, but he ignored me, happily sipping Merlot.

"You know," Frank croaked, his voice strong but naturally hoarse, "I've dived all over the world, and I'm damned impressed with this place. Hear that, Jay? Damned impressed. It's so well protected. Your laws must be very strict, am I right?"

Weaving in his chair, Jay pointed a thumb at the man sitting alone at the far table. "There's the robot to ask. Ahoy, Dirk! Come over here and give your standard, bloody boring lecture on the law! Dirk's a marine biologist, studies grouper sex or some such alarming thing. He's up on what you can and cannot do under these waters far more than I. Or so he tells me every damned minute of the day."

Dr. Dirk Gutenberg set down his journal, annoyed at the interruption, but slowly rose and moved toward our group of curious newcomers. Of average height and with buzz-cut hair, drill-sergeant eyes, and an astonishingly large chest, he looked as if he could hold his breath underwater for hours. Black-framed glasses perched on the end of his bulbous nose. "Someone has a question about Cayman's environmental laws?" Even to my untraveled ear, the German accent came through unmistakably. "They are among the strictest in the world."

Frank again launched into raptures on the clarity of the water, peppering Dirk with questions about what a diver could and couldn't do. After every answer, brisk and to the point, Dirk's harsh eyes drilled into Jay. He ended the question and answer time by adding, "Each offense carries a fine of up to six thousand U.S. dollars and one year in jail. So be careful. The darkest secrets are always exposed to light." With that, he rotated abruptly and left the room.

"Brrrrrr!" Curious George shivered. "Something of a brusque fellow, I must say."

"I'd be brusque, too," Buddy quipped, "if I had to watch a bunch of ugly groupers having sex all day."

Dempsie howled, her laugh loud and infectious. The conversation lightened, back to the important topic of rods and reels and flies. After a few minutes, Tootie emerged from the kitchen and beckoned Jay with sweet, robin-egg eyes and pouty, coral lips. But he hesitated, and Frank clamped a hand around his arm. "Jay, tomorrow I want to take up where we left off. I really am interested in your offer. I've been looking for a place like this for quite a while."

I heard a gasp across the table, barely audible. Every line in Renata's face creased deeper. "Frank . . ."

Jay dipped his head and rose, suddenly anxious to leave the table. His eyes darted at Jimbo, who stopped pouring wine in midstream.

Just then, Laurie stepped through the swinging kitchen door, nearly colliding with Tootie, who spoke for the first time, her beauty instantly dimmed by a voice that sounded like squealing tires. "Damnit! I spent two hours on this manicure! Now it's ruined!"

"Excuse *me*," Laurie gritted her teeth and watched Tootie swish away, hands in the air like a surgeon before a delicate operation. She slammed a tray of coffee cups on a table, ignoring Jimbo when he called her name. In the next few moments, she managed to gather herself, as if dealing with reality meant shutting it off temporarily like a faucet. The tension in her facial muscles gradually relaxed. She regained graciousness, along with the mask of the charming hostess, making sure we had all we needed before her exit.

Fa-Fa and Jimbo remained in the room with the guests, fielding more than an hour's worth of questions (most of them from Curious George and me). Questions about Little Cayman, boating, fishing, the hurricane, what paths led them to a life in paradise.

By the end of the evening, though, I wondered, *what kind of paradise was this?*

# Chapter 4

OUR HALF-DAY INTRODUCTION to deep-sea fishing ended before noon. I found myself sitting on Tom's lap, congratulatory beer in hand, sun on our faces, the warm wind whipping my ponytail into a frenzy as the boat headed back to Camp Iguana's new dock. Our two "keepers," very commendable king mackerel, lay stored in a large icebox, supper for the evening. Dempsie gripped a soft drink and held on to her floppy hat, doughy skin a little green, padded stomach a bit queasy. She sat across from Buddy, who busily smeared more sunscreen across his burned nose, grinning like a lunatic at the icebox where his trophies rested in peace. Thrilled at his own success with a swordfish, Curious George stood near the bow, yelling questions at Fa-Fa as he steered the boat for home.

Tom raised his sunglasses, smiled his magazine smile, and kissed my cheek. "It doesn't get any better than this."

"That's what you said last night."

He kissed the other cheek. "I think I'll say the same

thing every day for the rest of our lives. *'Stop this day and night with me . . . '"*

". . . *'And you shall possess the origin of all poems.'* See? You've even gotten me reciting poetry. Pretty soon I'll have expensive taste in wine, and won't want to read anything but legal briefs and nonfiction."

"Plenty of legal briefs I've read could count as fiction, believe me. But no shop talk."

"Right, no shop talk. Speaking of talk, I'm *dying* to call Margaret and Lindbergh, and Lee and Sally, and Tina and Melody, and Garland and . . ."

"I get the picture. I'll take the cell phone out of the locked box, I promise. I do like having you all to myself, though. Along with a few polite fish."

"There's that four-letter word again. To prove what an understanding woman you married, I'm going to learn fish talk if it kills me. Whoa!" The boat hit a wave and I sloshed beer on my handsome groom. "Good thing I took those seasick pills."

Dempsie squealed, but immediately laughed at herself. "I'm afraid I'm not much for water sports!" she called. "Where are the life preservers again? My two boys really would miss me."

"Not the teenager." Buddy's belly, the shape of an oak cask, shook when he laughed.

All in all, the campers in our group proved an easy lot to get along with. Even George, who definitely wore his curiosity on his sleeve, displayed a mischievous, charming side when out of the company of his snobby wife. Naturally witty and self-deprecating, he'd kept everyone in the fishing party entertained from the moment we stepped aboard. Puzzled at his match-up with Henrietta (myself the curious type), I had wormed my way next to him while fishing.

"You know," I began with a compliment, always a stealthy way to yank out information, "I love listening to you and Henrietta talk. You have such lovely accents!"

"You're very kind to say so. I, uh, I like hearing you talk, too."

"You are *very* kind to say so." I watched his method with a rod and reel and found something nice to say about that, too, before fishing for something other than fish. "Did you and Henrietta grow up together? You sound so much alike, I wondered."

"Oh, a sort of Henry Higgins, are you? Guessing what county and street people live on based on their diction?"

"No." I had to laugh. "Far from it. This is my first real trip anywhere. It's my honeymoon, you know."

He registered the appropriate amount of surprise at discovering a middle-aged honeymooner, as if he'd started a book and thirty pages later realized he'd read it before. "You don't say."

" 'I do.' That's a little bridal humor. Anyway, speaking of brides and grooms, how did you and Henrietta meet?"

"The usual way." He stifled a yawn. "Through work, about eighteen years ago." He opened his mouth to say something else, but thought better of it.

"Tell me." I tossed a line into the waves. "To pass the time."

"Righto. Well, I run a fine art auction house, or rather, my family does. One of the largest in London, actually. One day, I came in to work, and there was Henrietta at the receptionist's desk. Very attractive girl. Good phone voice, you know, and excellent carriage."

*Henrietta? Snooty Henrietta a receptionist? A working girl??*

"Was it love at first sight?"

George frowned. "I suppose I thought it was. What did I know?"

"I'm sort of surprised. I mean, I don't know either one of you, but I would have guessed Henrietta came from a prominent family, and never lacked for anything."

George scoffed. "Good Lord, no! Just the opposite! Her father is a church organist and music teacher in Dover, and her mother, rest her soul, was a shop clerk for a millinery. To hear Henrietta tell it, she lacked everything growing up. Scrounging around for loose buttons to sew on sweaters. Potatoes and bread at every meal. A seamstress job here and there to make ends meet."

The cover on Henrietta's book changed drastically. "I never would have thought."

"Then her devious plan is succeeding," he said wryly. "She has become a different person from when we first met. Very different, indeed."

Before poaching on personal territory, I backed away. "So that's how you met—the 'usual way.' What I like to hear are the unusual ways." I fooled with the reel as if I really knew how to deep-sea fish. "What's the most unusual way you've ever met someone?"

I posed the question as an offhand remark, a way to continue a conversation with someone I happened to be on a boat with for a few hours. But George lit up. "By jove, I must say . . . well, I will say. I met someone about five months ago at a park. She'd been rowing and first one oar slipped away, then the other, and there she was in the middle of an empty lake, calling out like a wingless bird. Lovely thing, lady of the lake and all that. I'll never forget."

"And you happened by?"

"Yes, this occurred in a rather secluded area, you see, at an odd time of day, and I had gone walking to clear my head of . . . things."

"How did you manage to bring her to shore?"

"I swam out, grabbed the oars, and climbed into the boat with her."

"Wow! I'd have fallen madly in love with you on the spot!"

His cheeks blushed redder than Buddy's sunburn. "On the spot. Yes. Well!" He abruptly reeled in. "Must try the other side. No bites here."

The book cover I'd envisioned for Curious George as a

mild-mannered lap dog disintegrated, my first impression well off base. A romantic first meeting. A hot affair carried on behind Henrietta's back all across London. Even here, on a Caribbean vacation, he could only think of *her,* his mistress, the Lady of the Lake. I alone knew his torrid secret. When I turned to Tom, aglow and atwitter, he wrongly attributed my flushed face to the joy of fishing.

Now, as the boat sped toward Camp Iguana, I mulled over George's revelation and the dinner conversation the night before with the other guests and staff. I poked a finger in Tom's diaphragm. "Do you get the feeling the co-owners of our merry little camp can't stand each other?"

"Oh, good Lord." Tom jerked his knee so I'd slip. "Does that nosy brain of yours ever take a rest?"

"No. Get used to it." I regained my place on his lap. "Jimbo is itching to knock Jay into outer space because Jay is trying to slither out of their partnership and into Laurie's bed. If he's not already in it. And Laurie and Tootie aren't the best of friends, either. Tootie's the newest fly in the ointment."

"Flip . . ."

"You find out all kinds of things if you ask the kitchen staff the right questions. Anyway, Tootie arrived right after the hurricane because, with Fa-Fa hurt, Jay needed another diver, and the resort she worked for on Grand Cayman went under. Do you know she's a part-time swimsuit model, and have you noticed how she looks at Jay? I think she's falling for him, and it's driving Laurie crazy. Even in the most exotic places, people act the same."

"I see no change in you whatsoever. Except for the sunburned nose."

"But aren't the people here so *interesting?* How they ended up here, for work or pleasure. What their histories are, what their relationships are . . ."

"Flip . . ." A familiar warning tone.

"Don't worry. I'll behave. I'm only speculating."

"Your 'speculations' usually lead to trouble."

I wrapped an arm around his neck and struck the pose of a Camp Fire Girl, wide-eyed and innocent. "I have no idea what you're talking about. Think we'll have s'mores for lunch?"

THE BOAT PULLED up to the dock a little after noon. We stumbled onto land with wobbly sea legs to wash up and change clothes for the midday meal. I began to appreciate the private outdoor shower attached to our tent cabin. The fresh, trickling water ran like a cool balm over dry, salt-stung skin.

The coconut and royal palms rustled in the light breeze as we made our way to the main house. I stopped in my tracks and slowly rotated, taking in the wonderful scene, carving a memory. Tom watched with empathetic eyes. He knew exactly how I felt. We had arrived on Little Cayman less than twenty-four hours before, but the island had crept into our hearts forever. The site of our Grand Adventure.

Everyone opted to eat outside on the patio, the blue sky and sunshine too wonderful to waste. No s'mores greeted us at the buffet table, either. It brimmed with luscious fruit, three kinds of salad, and sandwich fixings with homemade bread. Laurie's latest cake, ringed with white and violet blooms, perched on a plate above a row of oatmeal raisin cookies. Just as we sat down at a table with Buddy and Dempsie, the harsh bark of angry voices rose inside the barroom.

Buddy grimaced at his mound of pasta salad. "Sounds like Jimbo and Jay are goin' at it again."

"Oh? What have they been arguing about?" I noticed Curious George alone at the next table, tilting an ear our way.

"Well, I . . ." Buddy hesitated, but the whole situation made him so mad he had to blow off steam. "Jimbo poured everything into this place. I'm a VP for a large property management company, so I know what some folks have to go through to grab their piece of the rock. In this case, Jimbo came to me for advice. I told him it looked like a good deal and to go for it, even made a modest investment on behalf of my company. He and Laurie depleted their savings to buy this property. They knocked most of it down and started from scratch. Jimbo has real vision, ya know? He has a strong sense of where he wants to go, what he wants to make of this place. It's been his dream for years. Then Laurie had to go and run into Jay. He's ruined everything."

I wondered if part of the "ruin" included Buddy's company investment. "Jay's an old beau of hers, right? That's what Fa-Fa said."

"Yes, that's true," Curious George leaped into the discussion. "They almost married, in fact, about six years ago, but Jay developed cold feet."

Buddy sucked in a deep breath. "Let's just say some things never die, even when they should."

Dempsie raised her chin. "Buddy . . ."

"Well, honey, we both know it's true. It kills me, it just kills me to see Jimbo go through this. I'd do anything to keep him from hurting so bad, you know that. That damn Jay. If it weren't for him . . ."

"Buddy! Lower your voice," she cautioned. "Both you and Jimbo have got the worst tempers! You better watch yourself."

"Tell me more about Jay." I propped elbows on the table as George scraped his chair closer.

Buddy followed instructions and lowered his voice. "He's from England, but spent most of his life in Barbados. That's where he met Laurie. She couldn't have been more than nineteen, fifteen years younger than Jay, at least. He was her first love, and she's never gotten over him. What can I say? Bad habits are hard to break. Anyway, she ran back home to Grand Cayman, brokenhearted, and met Jimbo on the rebound. I think she settled for him. That's the word—settled. But to him, that woman is the sun, the moon, and the stars. No matter what she's done to him, he'd do anything for her."

"Except let her go?"

The question struck a nerve. Buddy stared straight ahead. "Jimbo's not the type to let another man steal his wife. He'd kill first."

I shivered at the coldness of his words. "What about the business end of things? Jimbo and Jay are partners, after all, because of Laurie."

"Yeah, it's a fine pickle, isn't it? Laurie shouldn't have pushed the two together, but Jay waltzed in and convinced Jimbo he needed a major investor, and he had all the connections around these waters to get things done. So Jay kicked in a hefty percentage, brought in the first customers, and did some advertising. But then the hurricane hit and now he wants out, but not at a loss. The camp is underinsured, and Jay pled poverty when it came time to make major repairs and fix everything. Now he's brought in some of his well-heeled contacts, the New York people . . ."

"Frank and Renata," George said, "and myself and Henrietta. Yes, Jay was keen for us to see the resort. Not at all what we expected, though."

"Yeah. Looks like Frank is the only one who wants to invest, but his idea of a resort is golf and glitz. You know, the Atlantic City of Little Cayman. Jimbo doesn't want him as a partner. He wants to buy Jay out himself, which is his right under the deal, but can't afford it after everything they've been through. So Jay's balking, tryin' to renegotiate what he's supposed to kick in, and tryin' to suck as much money as he can out of Frank in the meantime. When all is said and done, I hope to God he sails off into the sunset, and Laurie regains the good sense God gave her. She's not the toil-and-sweat type, doesn't take to the innkeeping business naturally, but she used to be kind, at least." His jaw twitched. "She's changed. She's nervous and cranky. She snaps at Jimbo about every little thing. It's

all Jay's fault. Everything he touches rots. Laurie's changing for the worse right before our eyes, and it's all his
fault."

We sat uncomfortably still, listening to the shouts we
couldn't ignore. "Sounds pretty heated back there."

Dempsie attempted a joke. "Yeah, that's our boy, Jimbo.
He'd stand his ground even with the whole Georgia Tech
line comin' down on him."

"Yeah," Buddy said gruffly, "he won't back down for
nothin' or nobody."

Renata and Frank walked up from the beach. In a good
humor, Frank greeted us with a wide smile, but the pleasant mood vanished when he caught wind of the argument,
especially Jimbo's adamant refusal to take on a different
partner, and the sky-high numbers Jay flung around.
Renata touched Frank's arm and shook her head em-
phatically, but he bulldozed past her toward the angry
voices.

Dempsie watched him enter the barroom. "What's
that man thinkin', jumpin' into the middle of a private
disagreement?"

"I wouldn't exactly call it private," Tom set his napkin
beside his plate. "I think I'll step inside and ask them to
take this show on the road so we can eat in peace."

But he didn't have to. The moment Frank tried to insin-
uate himself into the white-hot battle between the two partners (no doubt hoping to swing things to his advantage),
Jimbo had had enough and stormed out. Flying off in the
opposite direction, Jay entered the dining room just as Laurie exited the kitchen. She froze, a question mark in her
large eyes. Jay opened his mouth to speak, but stalked out.
Laurie crossed into the barroom and whispered with Fa-Fa,
who'd witnessed the entire scene. When she pressed a hand
against Fa-Fa's arm, he blushed.

"Poor Laurie," Dempsie sighed.

"Poor Laurie, nothing." Buddy gripped a roast beef

sandwich between two fists as if readying for a long pass. "If I was Jimbo, I'd . . ."

Frank returned, shaking a weary head. When he realized the number of eyes watching, he heaved stooped shoulders. "So what are you gonna do? It's business. Businessmen argue. I'll talk to them individually. Maybe I can help out."

He forced a tight-lipped smile, as if nothing unsavory had happened. The worry lines in Renata's face deepened. "Frank, please. Don't do this." She struggled to maintain composure. "I can't take any more!"

"What are you . . . hey, leave me alone. Just leave me alone! You wouldn't know a good deal if it bit you on the nose! I know what I'm doing."

"Frank, are you forgetting what happened last time? Didn't you learn anything? Do you want to put yourself and me through *that* again?" She drew herself up to her full height of five feet, four inches. "I won't have it. I won't help you this time if you insist on being a fool!" She hurried away just as Henrietta arrived on the scene. Surprisingly, Henrietta turned around and followed her.

Frank shrugged and motioned to George. "Mind if I join you? I'll buy you a drink. I could use one."

As vacationers are prone to do, serious discussion gave way to lighter topics. The argument between Camp Iguana's partners sank beneath the weighty issues of fishing lures, best suntan lotions, and favorite brands of rum. The Eggheads would have fit right in, arguing over product brands. *Hawaiian Tropic. No, Captain Morgan's. No, no Coppertone. No, no, no, Ron Rico.*

Despite the turbulence, Laurie put her best foot forward. At the end of the meal, she carried the cake plate from table to table, her slender hips wrapped in a triangular kitchen tea towel. Fa-Fa trailed behind with the cookie tray, a worshipful disciple, sunglasses covering his eyes, as usual. He reminded guests that Jay and Tootie planned to take a dive party out that afternoon. Tom and Buddy responded by claiming the nearest hammocks. Dempsie and I yawned into our hands and stumbled toward the cabins, looking forward to the feel of cool sheets and open breezes.

By the time we woke up, the boat had magically disappeared, leaving Camp Iguana as quiet as a cemetery.

# Chapter 5

I lay on the small, wood-frame bed, its length parallel to Tom's bed where we'd shoved the two together. A bottle of spring water stood on a side table and I reached for it, cotton-mouthed. The afternoon projected a hazy, lazy aura, the air slightly thick from the harsh sun, still high in the sky. But always there was the breeze. The delicious breeze that made the treetops dance and cooled the surface of the brilliant water. I tried to imagine myself in that world beneath the waves, conjuring up watery images from the countless movies and documentaries I'd seen over the years, plunked down in front of a *National Geographic* special or curled into the fetal position as *Jaws* played out. Somehow, I couldn't quite see myself in a slick, black wet suit with a breathing device strapped to my back, chasing fish or vice versa. Horror, horrors, and more horrors, as Margaret might say. I would call her the next day, when Tom and I had explored more of the island. I would tell her that the wonderful time the Circle Ladies wished for me was in the works, and they could drop their concerns because I'd married the right man. After forty-eight hours away from Solace Glen, though, I did miss their sweet, familiar faces.

I gave in to temptation, but dialed Sally, instead, knowing Margaret liked to grade papers at that hour. My favorite beautician answered the salon phone almost immediately, the chatter in the background akin to a flock of songbirds.

"Everybody, hush up! It's Flip on her honeymoon!"

"Hey, Sally! Who else is there? Sounds like every female in town."

"No, only Tina, Melody, and me, but you know us. Welcome to the yak factory. How's tricks? You miss us?"

"Of course, but not enough to leave my handsome husband."

"You kinda like that word, don't ya, girlfriend? What have you two been doin' to occupy your time?"

Screeches of laughter followed the question, and I quickly ran through the list of our tropical activities. "Oh, my." Sally popped her Wrigley's. "You must love that man something awful to go deep-sea anything. Can you even swim? Did you hear that, girls? Flip went deep-sea fishin'!" Her hand covered the mouthpiece of the phone. I heard a muffled question-and-answer period. She removed her hand again. "What time is it there? Wait. Never mind. It's early yet."

"What?"

"Never mind, I said. Oh, Miss Fizzi just walked in for a touch-up. Gotta go. You call us later, OK?" She hung up before I could say good-bye.

I stretched from head to toe, yawning, and slowly shed the laziness. Grabbing a pair of sneakers, I tossed bathing suits, towels, and two sun hats into a backpack. Time to explore Little Cayman so I'd have something new to tell Margaret.

The spirit willing, if not wide awake, Tom forced himself

out of the hammock. "I don't know when I've slept so hard during daylight hours. I think I've found a whole new vocation. What do you think?"

"I strongly rule in favor of power naps." Buddy's loud snore punctuated the sentiment. "But my clients and yours wouldn't put up with the practice back home in you-know-where."

We grabbed a couple of cold water bottles from the bar, and chose two bicycles beneath a lean-to behind the main house. Gathering snorkeling gear, we set out on a leisurely trek. Not quite three-thirty in the afternoon, we pedaled slowly, both of us shaking off the sandman.

Fa-Fa assured us we'd never get lost, since Guy Banks Road, the one main thoroughfare, encircled the island with only one or two roads cutting through the middle. With barely one hundred and seventy residents, traffic didn't pose a problem, either. No red lights or DO NOT WALK signs flashed; electricity had not even come to the island until 1991. We meandered along, a jeep or truck sputtering by on occasion. We rode past Blossom Village with the one grocery store, a car rental agency, real estate office, and a restaurant. We rode past the one church, the one museum, and the Booby Pond Nature Reserve, home of the famous red-footed booby, covering over two hundred acres with its mangrove pond and scores of birdlife. We rode past the tiny building of the Edward Bodden Airport, and the grassy landing field we'd floated down to the day before. Near the lighthouse, at the southwestern end of the island, we veered toward Preston Bay, a spot Fa-Fa pointed out as a nice, private place to relax and snorkel. The relaxing part came easy, but the snorkeling proved a different story.

"What do you mean you don't know how? You mean you brought me all the way to the Caribbean for a fun-in-the-sun honeymoon and you can't even teach me how to put these flippers on?"

"I know they go on your feet." Tom examined the long pieces of plastic. "It's this long tube thing that worries me."

"At least we're doing this in private." I sat uneasily on a rock and looked up and down the empty beach.

"You know," Tom said as he slid a foot into one black flipper, "the water doesn't look all that calm to me. Will you be able to save me if I get into trouble?"

"*Me* save you? You always said you loved water sports."

"From a fishing boat, I do." He pulled on the diving mask and positioned the mouthpiece between clenched teeth. "How-oo-why-wook?"

"Oo-wook-illy." Together we slogged our way across the rocky beach to the water's edge. "Oo-irst."

Tom nodded and plunged in, completely forgetting to keep the breathing tube above water. He came up gulping for air and tore the mask off. "Whoo! That was exhilarating! What say we head for the nearest pub?"

I took my mouthpiece out. "Nothing doin'. We will not be the only campers who don't get their feet wet. I may be too chicken to scuba, but the least I can do is conquer four feet of water with a breathing tube. Come on, now. Nice and slow."

Somewhere between giddiness and fear, we managed to ease our faces into the waves. I nearly choked. Not from fear, but amazement. Never could I have imagined such a world. I wanted to shout, even sing, at the beauty that lay before me through a clear plastic mask. *I-can't-believe-I'm-doing-this-I-can't-believe-I'm-doing-this-I-can't-believe-I'm-doing-this!* Small schools of silvery fish flashed by. Behind coral boulders raced electric blues and sun-streaked yellows. Like nothing I'd ever seen before, black, spindly sea urchins waved with the rhythm of the tide.

I reached out and clutched Tom's hand. Our eyes met. That was it. That was the moment I would cherish and keep in a golden box for the rest of my life. That moment where we both knew without a word spoken. *Look at the world*

*you have given me. Look at what we've given each other.*
*Without you, it simply could not be.*

The Whitman poem Tom loved to quote instantly
sprang to mind and filled a moment already brimming:

> *Stop this day and night with me and you shall possess*
>     *the origin of all poems,*
> *You shall possess the good of the earth and sun, (there*
>     *are millions of suns left,)*
> *You shall no longer take things at second or third hand,*
>     *nor look through the eyes of the dead, nor feed on*
>     *the spectres in books,*
> *You shall not look through my eyes either, nor take*
>     *things from me,*
> *You shall listen to all sides and filter them from your*
>     *self.*

We floated in this ecstatic state for a good half hour,
rarely breaking the surface or breaking contact. When we
finally turned inland and washed ashore, perched on the
edge of the sand and the water, breathing heavily, flippers
off, masks dangling around our necks, Tom said what we
both felt.

"The vacation has officially begun!" he gasped. "We did
the wedding. Got through that with no broken bones or exploding gas lines. We dutifully fulfilled our respective
spousal obligations—no broken bones there, either. But I
knew something was missing. And this—this is it!" He
threw his arms wide. "Vacation!"

Our breathing gradually returned to normal. We sat still
as seashells, listening to the gentle splash of the breaking
waves, our faces wearing the red outline of the diving
masks. Quietly approaching twilight hours, the sky allowed
the blazing, orange burden it held to slip lower. Large,
fluffy white clouds cavorted in the trade winds. Between
the sun and the wind were we, two fish out of water, laid on
the sand to dry until supper time.

Tom cleared his throat, a signal that the moment required special notice, usually in the form of a verse or two of poetry.

"I hope you have something new for me." I nestled against his chest. "When it gets to the point I've learned a poem myself, it's time to move on."

"As a matter of fact, I do have some new material." Which he recited:

"'Long enough have you dream'd contemptible
    dreams,
Now I wash the gum from your eyes,
You must habit yourself to the dazzle of the light and of
    every moment of your life.

Long have you timidly waded holding a plank by the
    shore,
Now I will tell you to be a bold swimmer,
To jump off in the midst of the sea, rise again, nod to
    me, shout, and laughingly dash with your hair.'"

"Am I the one laughingly dashing my hair?" To illustrate, I shook my shaggy locks like a wet puppy.

"No." He caught my shaking head between two hands and kissed me. Lightly, insistently. My Tom. "You are 'the dazzle of the light.'"

What could I do but melt into the earth, and pull him into my heart?

A LITTLE AFTER five o'clock, we heard the far-off drone of an Island Air plane engine. A quick dunk into the water, a quick rub of a towel, and we packed up and climbed onto our bikes.

Tom hunched over like Lance Armstrong. "Let's watch the plane land. Come on, I'll race you!"

"I'd beat the pants off you, then I'd feel guilty and you'd feel grossly inferior. Not a good start to a marriage." I straddled the bicycle, awkwardly plowing along. "You know there are no shopping malls or casinos on an island when the big event for tourists is to watch the plane land."

"There might be a rock star on board."

"And who would you like to see parade off—Britney Spears?"

"No, then I'd feel guilty and you'd feel grossly inferior. Not a good start to a marriage."

"I myself would like to see Ben Affleck or Brad Pitt dance off the plane, and I would not feel guilty in the least."

"Yet, somehow, I would feel grossly inferior."

We pedaled slowly along the road to the side of the landing field, pausing near an IGUANA CROSSING sign. The twin-engine airplane looped around the end of the island and headed down for a landing, gently setting its wheels on the grass and smoothly easing into a parked position.

"Let's see if Brad brought a hottie starlet along." Tom pushed off. "There may be hope for me yet."

"If you're hoping for a harem, keep dreaming. Your wife may have something to say about that." *Wife*—such a pleasant word, on my lips or his.

We rode toward the end of the runway and stopped to watch the dozen or so tourists disembark. The same jeeps and vans from the local resorts stood ready to load up the newcomers and carry them away, with Jimbo's Camp Iguana truck nowhere in sight.

"Didn't Laurie say we were getting a couple of new faces today?"

Tom nodded. "That's the plan. Why don't we wait and see who ends up without a ride so we can assure them help is on the way."

"OK, that's a good . . ." I gasped in midsentence. "Oh, my Lord."

A familiar voice rang out. "Hey! You two didn't have to meet us at the plane! That's so sweet!"

Lee Jenner Gibbon leaped off the plane with Sam's assistance and galloped toward us.

"Tom," I said with gritted teeth, "did you . . . ?"

"No. No, I swear I didn't."

As Lee bowled me over with her hug, I couldn't hide the disappointment. "Well. Gee. What are you two doing here? A twenty-four-hour visit, maybe?" Under my breath, "Jeezeree, Lee. We *are* on our honeymoon!"

"Nice to see you, too." She threw her arms around Tom's neck. "So how's it going? Don't you love Miss Fizzi's honeymoon plans?"

"Did she come, too?" Tom glanced anxiously at the plane.

"Of course not." Sam gave me a quick hug and slapped Tom's shoulder. "She says she's traveling vicariously through us. We're supposed to deliver a full report." He stared at Tom's blank face. "You mean, she didn't tell you? You really had no idea we were coming? You didn't expect . . ."

"The unexpected?" I stuck a hand on my hip. *Now* I understood the strange lilt in her voice on the phone. *And remember, Flip, expect the unexpected . . .*

Sam rolled his eyes and squinted tight. "Oh, man. We thought . . . she told us . . . oh, man."

The four of us, the best of friends until that moment, stood soundless and lobster-faced.

Lee decided to give it a stab. "Flip, Miss Fizzi thought, and everybody else agreed, that since you've never been out of Maryland, and hardly out of Solace Glen, after a couple of days you'd feel lonely and homesick for friends."

"On my *honeymoon?*"

Sam took a turn, voice starting at the high pitch of a choir boy, sinking with each word. "And she thought Tom would appreciate a fishing buddy. And you know, since you've known each other all your lives . . . you might get bored . . . and it would be more fun to vacation with friends. More lively."

Tom removed his sunglasses, revealing the blackest pupils. "On my honeymoon."

"Tom, I swear, she told us you knew we were coming because she'd written it down in that packet of plans she gave you more than a week ago, and if you had a problem with it, you would have told her, or we'd have gotten a call."

My turn. "Tom. Did you see anything in that packet?"

"N-no."

"Did you read everything in the packet?"

His mouth opened. His shoulders rose. "Oh, boy."

"For heaven's sake!" A short hour before I would have died for him. Now I wanted to kill him.

Another embarrassing, red-faced silence. Then Lee snorted. She bit her lip. She snorted louder.

Both hands rose to my hips. The snort turned into raucous, uncontrolled, hysterical laughter. Sam, holding his breath until then, exploded with her.

Tom and I stared at each other, and read the same thought. We burst out laughing with them. *"Thank you, Miss Fizzi!"*


WE FOLLOWED JIMBO'S dilapidated truck at a distance. Lee and Sam sat in the front seat with our host, Lee hurling questions at Jimbo, reminding me of myself. The initial shock had worn off. Time to discuss the game plan.

"I think you better dig up that packet, *sweet*heart, and double check if anybody else is going to honeymoon with us. My only concern, of course, is how we're going to fit the Eggheads in one twin bed, and Screamin' Larry in the other."

"We'll just sleep out under the stars, darling, with the no-see-ums."

"You mean *you'll* be sleeping out under the stars. What in the world was Miss Fizzi thinking!"

Tom tried in vain to muzzle a grin. "Her heart's in the

right place. She thinks of you as a small-town babe-in-the-woods who'll disintegrate in any atmosphere other than Solace Glen's. You know how protective all the Circle Ladies are of you. You're their very own Little Orphan Annie. The whole town's probably in on it."

"I'm sure they took a vote at the last Circle meeting." My eyes crossed. "Now I know what Sally and Lee were guffawing about at the reception, and why Sally acted so preoccupied with the time when I called her. I mean it, Tom, you better take a good, hard look at that packet and make sure there are no more Halloween tricks in store for us!"

Tom kept grinning, sunglasses askew over his aristocratic nose. "Yes, dear. Right away, dear." He swerved close and gave my shoulder a quick shove. "Come on, Flip, you have to admit it's funny. And what should we do, send Sam and Lee back to Maryland? Destroy our friendship and humiliate every soul in Solace Glen? You know darn good and well the entire town is basking in its glory, slapping each other on the back at what a good turn they've done, sending Ginger and the Professor to attend to us." His voice choked melodramatically. "I think I'm going to cry."

"Oh, hush up." But I smiled gently. "Do you really think Lee's more like Ginger than Mary Ann?"

We parked our bicycles under the lean-to and returned the snorkeling equipment while Sam and Lee received the welcome treatment. As we walked back to our cabin, we spotted the *Tyrol* on the horizon making its way to port in time for dinner.

"What do you think?" Tom pointed at the boat. "Should we try that resort course now that we've conquered snorkeling?"

I shuddered. "I don't know. The thought of going deeper than four feet with nothing but an air tank between me and a watery grave is pretty scary."

"Fraidy-cat."

"Absolutely, and proud of it. I've managed to survive forty-three years as a card-carrying fraidy-cat, thank you very much."

"Oh, come on," he joked. "What do we have to lose but our lives?"

"My point exactly." But I wasn't joking.

# CHAPTER 6

❋

T HE CLANG OF the dinner bell brought hungry campers
     scampering toward the main house like a pack of
Pavlov's dogs. The guest tables divided up with George,
Henrietta, Renata, and Frank at one, while Tom and I sat
with Dempsie, Buddy, Sam, and Lee. No more than the
ten of us were expected during the length of our stay, and
fortunately, Miss Fizzi's packet contained no other surprises. No need to fear Screamin' Larry doing cannon-
balls in the pool. No cause for alarm if the mechanic bent
over Camp Iguana's truck didn't wear Pal's name tag
stitched onto his shirt pocket. No reason to suspect the
Eggheads to materialize at the sound of an ambulance
siren.

Our old friends quickly adapted to our new friends.
Sam and Buddy, both natural storytellers of the first order,
regaled us with one tall tale after another. Dueling liars,
Tom called them. Fa-Fa and our hosts served drinks and
side dishes, giving Lee the opportunity to practice her flirting skills on southern prey, and Sam the opportunity to act

jealous. Dirk ambled in for supper, unimpressed with the beautiful new auburn-haired guest. He hunched over a science journal, oblivious to the dining-room chatter. The mood grew light, wine flowed, the shrimp creole delighted, but when Jay and Tootie strolled in, almost connected at the hip, the chatter dropped to a dull drone. The mood darkened from gray to black when Laurie purposefully dropped a glass that shattered at Tootie's bare feet.

"How clumsy of me." Her lips tightened as she walked away. "You might want to clean that up." Jimbo followed her into the kitchen, none too pleased.

"Who are they, and why the frowns all of a sudden?" Lee whispered. "He's attractive, but who's the bimbo?"

"Don't act ugly, and don't hate her because she's beautiful. That's Tootie. She works as a diving instructor here. The good-looking guy is Jay. He's part owner of the camp, but wants out of the deal at a hefty price. I'll fill you in later." You could accuse me of gossip, but never indiscretion.

Jay, bottle of wine under one wing, topped off his glass and perused the room. The tanned face lit up when Lee entered his sights, prompting me to wonder how Laurie could stand to rerun an affair with such an unredeemed ladies' man. "You heard Laurie, Toots. Clean it up." He skipped away from Tootie's astonished face and made a beeline for my best friend. A glint of amusement sparked in Lee's hazel eyes, full of mischief, so aware of her power, so willing to have a little fun with it. She turned a frosty shoulder just as Jay swooped in.

"Hell-o! You must be Lee Gibbon. I'm Jay, the dive master and part owner of the paradise you find yourself in. I saw your name on the sign-up sheet for the resort course."

"Lee!" I blinked. "You signed up to dive?"

"I signed you up, too." She beamed bright as an ocean sunrise. "And Sam and Tom."

"What?!"

"You heard me." She ignored the hovering Jay. "And don't try to weasel out of it. Look at Tom, grinning ear to ear. You wouldn't want to disappoint the love of your life, would you? On your *honeymoon?*"

Jay repositioned himself so Lee couldn't possibly ignore his handsome face. "That's the spirit! Dive into adventure. Take a chance, I always say."

At this point, Sam rose, stretching to his full height, over six feet of Married Man. He stuck a hand out. "I'm Sam. Sam Gibbon. Lee's husband."

Jay forced himself away from the Altar of Lee long enough to extend a limb to shake, but the lecherous, toothy grin never left his face. Apparently, husbands—no matter the size, shape, or devotion—posed little obstacle or concern.

"Oh, dear . . . if *you're* going, Flip," Dempsie stammered, "I—I guess I'll throw caution to the wind, too. What d'ya think, Buddy?"

I didn't think Buddy heard her at first. He drew a bead on Jay with the intense eye of a hunter, finger on the trigger. "I think we're all plum crazy," he finally relented. "Yeah, count us in, too."

Jay gleamed, smooth as the glass in a mirror (an item I suspected he used with some frequency). He absently placed a hand on Lee's shoulder. "That's wonderful. The more the merrier, and the more loose change in my pocket."

Lee shuddered his hand away, hazel eyes on fire. She tossed me a look that said, *Can you believe the nerve of this jerk?* A glance at Sam revealed everything on his mind. *Who does this lowlife think he is, laying his greasy paw on my wife right in front of me?*

Tootie, unwilling to play maid or second fiddle, stepped over the shattered glass at her feet and sidled close to Jay. He twitched, irritated, when she slid a bronze hand flirtatiously across his back, marking new territory. Lee took note of the obvious and sniggered at the California beach goddess.

"So what's the schedule?" Tom sat on the edge of his

seat. I half-expected him to pull out a palm pilot and enter a string of dive appointments. "Flip, isn't this great? This is going to be fantastic!"

I moaned in answer. Jay's wandering hand found my shoulder, but gave it a brotherly pat. "You'll be surprised at how easy it is to scuba. And how stunning." The roving wolf eyes landed on Lee again, no doubt picturing her in a thong bikini. "We'll meet at the pool tomorrow morning at ten. The instruction period should last about an hour, then we should have time for a few Bloody Marys. Pop down to the dock around threeish and we'll shove off for the Wall."

"How deep will we dive?" Dempsie anxiously fiddled with her shirt collar.

"Not too deep. Thirty feet or so."

"Thirty feet," I gulped. "Sounds deep. Doesn't that sound deep to you, Dempsie?" But our whines met loud resistance.

"OK, OK, OK. But if I do this," I said, turning to my laughing husband, "you're gonna owe me big time. Furs. Jewelry. A few SUVs."

Suddenly, a voice cracked like a whip through the laughter. "Jay! I want a word with you! Right now!" Boiling mad, Dirk broke away from a powwow with Fa-Fa and strode across the room.

"What now?" I murmured into Lee's ear, suddenly grateful for her familiar company.

"Dirkie," Jay coolly toasted the air with his wineglass, "what's got your knickers in a bunch this time?"

Dirk came close to thumping his chest against Jay's. "Fa-Fa tells me you've been at it again."

"Did he, now?" Jay's steady gaze fired an arrow in Fa-Fa's direction. The fishing guide leaned against a wall, arms crossed, sunglasses blocking all expression in his eyes.

"I warned you, what you're doing is illegal, and you're using my boat to do it! I could lose everything! My boat, my license, my livelihood, not to mention my reputation as a scientist. You know how I despise the authorities. Who wouldn't, born under a Communist regime? But I promise, I will call the police myself and turn you in. You won't think it's so funny when they throw you in jail. Spearguns, Jay? Gill nets and poison? Not to mention the pounds and pounds of coral you've hammered out of these waters."

"What proof do you have?" Tootie squeaked in Jay's defense. She flicked a newly polished fingernail against Dirk's massive chest, and flipped her long hair behind one ear. "Just the word of a bartender."

Fa-Fa took no offense, only turned the tables. "A bartender's word is no better or worse than a preacher's, Tootie. We have a way of seein' and hearin' an awful lot, just like you've seen and heard an awful lot. Don't let him use you."

"Tootie," Dirk spoke roughly, "you haven't been here long enough to know this man. Don't be a fool. Don't allow him to manipulate you the way he's . . ."

Jay cut him off. "My, my." He puckered his lips and took a generous sip of wine. "You're frightening the guests with this little morality play, Dirkie. And you don't really think *you're* going to testify against *me,* do you, Fa-La-La? Not really."

Whatever point Jay intended to drill home obviously hit the mark because Fa-Fa's countenance changed in an instant. He slunk out of the room like a frightened dog.

"Come on, old boy." Jay wrapped an arm around Dirk's ox shoulders. "You know how things are between Jimbo and me. He set that Alabama hound loose to have a go, that's all. You know I play on the up and up."

"No. I don't know that. I only know what I constantly hear from others and what I've seen myself."

"What did you see? One little bag of coral I found caught between some rocks. Trust me." Jay raised his glass in the direction of the bar. "I'll buy you a drink. What'll it be? Sky's the limit."

But Dirk threw the arm off his neck. "I'll see you in hell first. You've had your last warning." He stalked out of the room, pausing briefly to have a word with Jimbo, who turned three shades of purple.

Jay turned to us and said jokingly, "Someone really ought to lock me up and throw away the key." He headed for the bar where Laurie was unloading clean glasses. Between sips of wine he called to Tootie, "Hey, babe, go fetch the expense log so Laurie can have her weekly heart attack."

Brown eyes sad as a spaniel's one moment, fiery the next, Laurie clanked the glassware angrily as Jay leaned over the bar to soothe her.

"You know," Frank said loud enough for all to hear, "he's flamboyant, Jay is. And I've certainly never known him to be anything but honest. As a diver, he's unequaled. Unequaled."

"Oh, Frank, you think every cloud only hides a rainbow." Renata eyed Jay suspiciously. "Sometimes a cloud is nothing but a cloud. You can't believe everything you're told. We've hardly known the man six months."

"Really?" Henrietta stabbed a yellow toothpick through an olive in her martini glass. "He led us to believe the three of you were lifelong friends. George and I only met him six months ago, too. In Barbados, in April."

"Really?" Renata raised her chin high, suspicions confirmed. "That's where we met him. He told us he'd known the two of you at least fifteen years!"

Suddenly, both couples realized that Frank's "anything but honest" comment meant exactly that. Renata wore the somber expression of a company CEO contemplating bankruptcy. "Frank, tell me you didn't give that man any money yet."

The sallow cheeks turned beet red. The cheerful expression dried to a crisp. "A deposit. A deposit, that's all."

"Oh, honestly! Not again! With no contract, I suppose! No lawyer?"

"It was just a deposit!" Frank erupted, enraged, forced to reveal his bad judgment not only to his wife, but in front of perfect strangers, as well. He tried to mask the anger and humiliation with a plastic smile. "No strings attached. I'll get it back. It's no big deal."

But I could tell it was a very big deal. Frank threw his dinner napkin on the table and hustled toward the bar. When Jay spied the New Yorker steaming his way, he pointed at a bottle of cognac and motioned Laurie to set out a snifter the size of a cantaloupe. He snapped into Hail-fellow-well-met mode, and slapped Frank on the back.

"I have some questions," Frank began tersely, but in no time at all, he was chugging cognac and roaring with laughter, the sunny disposition revived.

Not so sunny, Renata shoved her chair away from the table. "That man!" On the verge of tears, she turned to Henrietta. "I don't know what I'm supposed to do. Just when things are finally going our way, he gives money away on a whim. You have no idea what I've been through!" She fled the room with Henrietta at her heels.

"Whoo," Lee flattened a palm against one cheek. "What an operator that Jay is."

"You're certainly right about that." Curious George drew a chair up to our table, eager to observe and comment as Jay turned the charm on Frank. "I hope the old boy can recover his deposit. I fear it amounted to a pretty penny."

"What do Frank and Renata do in New York?" I asked, not one to squander the resources of a fellow gossip.

"Oddly enough, they run a franchise of laundromats."

Dirty laundry. Right up my alley. "You don't say. I would have thought they owned restaurants or nightclubs. You know, something that would better parallel a resort."

When George shook his head, his soft hair flopped up and down, reminding me of a college boy as opposed to a sophisticated art auctioneer from London. "Righto. That would have been my guess, too. Renata told Henrietta they've been at it for years, building up a little empire of washers and dryers. They've only been able to travel in the past year, thanks to her hard work. In truth, Renata is the one with the good business brain and work ethic, not Frank. Apparently, his special talent is going from one financial mess to another, leaving poor Renata to clean up after him. Notions of grandeur, I'm afraid. It's landed him into terrible trouble." He leaned forward, lowering his voice. "The latest scrap resulted in a bit of jail time, I'm afraid. Assault and battery when a deal went sour. He was on some sort of probation for months. Renata is frantic to keep him out of trouble, another good reason to travel. I think the man is swept up in the romantic notion of owning a little piece of the Caribbean, but even if he did, Frank would destroy this lovely, peaceful place with his awful Las Vegas ideas. Something to brag about in New York, you know."

"I'm sure if we asked Jimbo and Laurie," ventured Tom, "they'd tell us the reality of ownership is far less than romantic."

"You can say that again," Buddy growled. "I don't get how some people can fool so easily. Look at Frank, five minutes ago a bull ready to charge, now Jay's got him twisted around his little pinkie. I don't get it."

I studied the man at the bar. "Frank's a real Jekyll and Hyde, isn't he? I never would have thought, but where money is concerned . . ."

Tootie returned, toting the expense log Jay had asked her to fetch. She caught his eye and a silent message flashed between them. She slowed down, hips swaying rhythmically in a tie-dyed sarong. She allowed one bikini strap to fall off her shoulder just as she reached the bar. Her smile nearly knocked Frank off the barstool.

"Good heavens!" George clucked in astonishment. "He's using that girl to . . . well, he's obviously using her as . . ."

"As bait," Buddy blurted. "It's what he does best—use people."

"Why, yes. And he's so *open* about it. The same way he's so open about Laurie." George blinked at us. "Well . . . I mean to say . . . haven't the rest of you noticed?"

Buddy allowed the question to pass, but muttered, "Pretty thing like Tootie would be a hell of a lot better off with a decent guy like Fa-Fa."

"But would Fa-Fa be better off with her?" Lee plucked a butter knife off the table and pretended to file her nails and admire herself in its reflection at the same time.

"You're just jealous." I knew her all too well. "You never trust any woman as pretty as yourself. You turn into a cat at the very sight."

"Mee-ow. My point is, Fa-Fa seems like a man with brains and taste."

"Well!" Sam slapped his knees and stood up, stifling a yawn. "I've got brains and taste, too, but both are worn out. It's been a long day, puddin', and we have a busy day ahead of us trying not to drown each other. You'll all excuse us, I'm sure."

"You know, sweetie." Lee took his hand. "This is our second honeymoon in five months. How about a swim like we did in Lake Canandaigua?"

Sam's tired eyes threw off the baggage and glittered. "Oh, yeah. Lake Canandaigua. That was a mighty refreshing swim, as I recall."

With that, they broke into adolescent giggles and wandered away side by side, hands sliding comfortably into each other's back pockets. I watched them head for the shoreline, the lapping water beneath twinkling constellations. "When I see how happy those two are, I can't be mad about them showing up on our honeymoon, can you, Tom? At least now you have your old fishing buddy to spin a reel with."

"And you have someone to root around in other people's dirty laundry with."

The sound of raucous laughter erupted from the bar. Frank, one end of a red sarong in his fist, gleefully pulled the fabric as Tootie spun like a toy top in the opposite direction. She tumbled into Jay's lap, unveiling a matching red bikini bottom.

"Laurie!" Jay gasped. "We're going to need another bottle of cognac!"

Stone-faced, Laurie slammed a bottle on the table and stomped out of the room. At the door, she wheeled around. The stone expression softened into such anguish, such longing, it broke my heart.

Jay did not see it. He was too busy.

Frank tried the sarong on for size, "Hey, when I own half this place that means I own half the bar, too, right?"

"Quite right. Ownership does have its privileges." Jay replenished Frank's glass.

"What else will I own half of?" The businessman leered at Tootie and her red bikini.

The laundry in paradise just got dirtier and dirtier.

# CHAPTER 7

❈

THE NEXT MORNING, a glorious Tuesday, those who
had not partied into the wee hours (like Jay and Frank)
found their way to the hot Jamaican coffee and scrambled
egg buffet. Fa-Fa and Curious George plotted the best route
to cruise for bonefish, while Henrietta, sick of the wind
slapping her London coiffure into a frazzle, suggested Renata accompany her to the little spa down the road. "It
would do you a world of good. Oh, please, do come with
me, Renata. My treat. I'll take care of everything."

My initial impression of Henrietta began to shift.
Haughty and proud, Henrietta hid her modest background
by one-upping the upper class. Maybe she thought she had
to, thrown into the exclusive world of art and antiques at an
impressionable age, where everything—and everyone—
carries a price tag. Maybe she believed you're judged by
how high you can stack the stuff you collect, and the poker
face you show the world. She'd taken very good care of her
own face, hardly forty years in the making, not a laugh line
to be found.

Renata wrestled with the simple decision. "I don't know. Frank doesn't like it when I change my appearance. He says it's unnatural."

Henrietta's jaw fell. "What's more natural than a woman making the best of her assets? Come on, Renata, you're a savvy businesswoman. Use your assets!"

"Well . . . when you put it that way, I . . . OK. Why not?"

I silently cheered, disgusted with Frank's sleazy behavior the night before, as if a girl as stunning as Tootie would give him the time of day without an agenda.

"Hey, Laurie." Buddy caught her as she whizzed by with a fresh pitcher of orange juice, his grip a little tight. "Where's Jimbo this morning?"

She tilted under the strength of his pull. "He and Tootie are preparing the tanks for the dive trips today."

"Isn't that Jay's job?"

"Normally, but he's a little under the weather this morning."

"Big shock." He relaxed his grip slightly, but spoke in an even tone. "It's just that Jimbo has enough on his mind lately. He doesn't need to be foolin' with diving equipment."

"He's never been very comfortable with it," she jerked herself upright, annoyed, "but when we bought this place, he figured he'd better get certified and know enough to help the dive staff. I just hope he hurries because we have to get to Brac today. I need my boat so I can take a regular out to the Wall."

"Is it Picky Jiffers again?" Curious George honed in on the conversation. "That gazillionaire with the villa, the black goatee, and the fancy cigar boat?"

"Yes," she answered slowly, wary of George's constant questions and intrusions. I started to wonder myself. "How do you know about Picky?"

George pointed at Fa-Fa. "I'm driving the poor man insane. That's what I do when I'm not catching fish, you see. I entertain myself with the local color. Fa-Fa told me about Picky Jiffers. He dives with you at least three times a week? Very picky fellow, hence the nickname? Only wants you as a friend and guide, and every detail must be so-and-so and such-and-such?"

"Yes," she snapped, turning away, "and I certainly don't want to be late on a dive appointment with him. Isn't that what most of the customers come to Little Cayman for?"

"Not us!" Dempsie and I sang in chorus, chickens-of-the-sea.

"Don't tell me you've had a change of heart, Flip." Lee shuffled barefoot into breakfast with Sam, their shirts and shorts wrinkled from poor packing. "Gosh, look at all this food!" She scooped up a couple of muffins before hauling in some bacon. "My theory is, if I practice having a big stomach, the baby will naturally follow."

Dempsie examined her doughy midriff. "That used to be my theory, too, but two kids later, I can't seem to stop practicin' the big stomach! I keep sayin' someday I'll join a class or get a job that keeps me hoppin'. Seems all I'm good for lately is pushin' a grocery cart up and down an aisle and doin' laundry." She spoke with the usual bright smile, but I caught the melancholy in her voice.

Buddy said between bites, "That's job enough, honey," completely missing the sadness.

We finished breakfast and lingered over coffee, listening to the stories Sam and Tom and Buddy traded like a pack of boys' baseball cards. I could have lingered all day in the dining room, or on the beach, or in a hammock, but within an hour the six of us dangled our feet in the pool, waiting for Jay to show up for the dreaded scuba lesson. The butterflies in my belly fluttered all the way up to the dryness in my mouth.

Jimbo and Laurie passed by on their way to the dock. "Jay's not here yet?" Jimbo checked his watch, face cross, and started to veer away.

"No, you don't!" Laurie grabbed his arm. "You don't have time to get into another battle with Jay. I will *not* be late for Picky Jiffers!"

Twenty minutes later, I held out high hopes that the whole diving experience had collapsed, but Lee spotted Jay and Tootie hauling equipment from the boathouse. "There's our drunken sailor now, finally awake. Probably has his eyelids propped open with pink umbrellas. From the looks of it, he fell out of the wrong side of bed, too."

Sure enough, the man snarled and shouted at Tootie. He chugged on a bottle of colored sports water, rehydrating. The closer he drew to our waiting group, though, the mask of camaraderie reappeared. "Hello, hello, hello! I hope everyone had as lovely an evening as I enjoyed." The lovely red-shot eyes lingered on Lee. "Mrs. Gibbon, you look ravishing this morning. Paradise must agree with you."

"And I thought it was my husband." She looped an elbow through Sam's arm. "You do agree with me, don't you, dear?"

"Ninety-seven point six percent of the time."

Jay handed her a pair of flippers as if presenting flimsy lingerie. "But you have yet to experience all we have to offer. OK, listen up, everyone! Stand, please, so Tootie and I can fit you with a tank."

Thus, the lesson began. As his cohort did most of the heavy lifting, none too cheerfully, Jay wove among the six of us, pointing out the purposes of this confusing new attire. "I know it feels impossibly bulky, but in the water it's a different story. Now, everyone in the pool! Lee, let me adjust that for you."

He reached toward her, but Lee leaped into the pool, splashing him with a decent cannonball learned from years of rope swinging into the Monocacy. Jay gleamed as if she flirted with him, and wiped his sunglasses dry with a shirttail. Sam plunged in with equal force. The friendly smile evaporated.

Buddy and Dempsie eased in with Tom, who decided to embarrass me into the water. "Why, bless my soul. Do my eyes deceive me? Is this a mermaid I see before me, her goggles toward my heart?"

"That's no mermaid," Sam joined in. "It's a sea nymph. Tom, you remember the canoe trip we took about a year ago? I could hardly keep that woman in the boat she was so keen to leap in the river."

"Hush, both of you." I inched toward the edge of the pool. "A fear of drowning is a healthy fear. One I've carefully nurtured all my life."

"It's impossible to drown in these waters." Jay snapped on his gear, gracefully sliding into the pool. Tootie draped herself across a lounge chair and removed her bikini cover to bolster her tan.

Unable to resist a dig at the other pretty woman, Lee hissed, "Does she do anything besides toast in the sun and swish her bottom?"

I hissed back, "Pay attention to the lesson! And scrape that green monkey off your back before he drowns you!"

"Jay, what do you mean, 'it's impossible to drown' here?" Dempsie clutched her mask.

"I mean just that. I've never lost a diver yet. Tootie, why don't you rise off your lovely duff and instruct our group on their masks? I'll meander about offering vital assistance where needed."

"Where needed," of course, meant Lee, but the meandering didn't get too touchy-feely in close range of Sam. Lee jutted her chin out, the perennial high horse, and two-stepped around in the water at arm's length. Tootie huffed loudly and began a series of shrill squeaks and yips designed to relate proper mask usage. I held on to every word Jay and Tootie said, executing their instructions to the letter. How to clear the mask at the surface, put it on, clear it underneath the water, how to read the air gauge, how to breathe and not panic.

Not panic. Easier said and done in four feet of chlorinated water. Through the fogging mask, I swept my eyes across the sea and imagined it drained dry and safe. Safe as Center Street running neatly through Solace Glen. Safe as Garland's Bistro, or Connolly's Jewelry Store. Safe as the cherry wood conference room in Tom's law office, or the picnic grounds at the fire station. Safe, dry, familiar places with comforting names. Not names like Bloody Bay Wall, Windsock, and Harlod's Holes.

"Ironic, isn't it?" Tom glided over.

"What is?"

"That you have spent your whole life leafing through travel books and atlases, yearning to travel, and when you finally find yourself on a gorgeous, exotic, tropical island, you get homesick."

"How did you do that?"

"Do what?"

"Read my mind?"

"I just know you. But remember the poem— *'wash the gum from your eyes . . . habit yourself to the dazzle of the light.'* And don't be afraid. I'm right here. I wouldn't let anything happen to you, above or below sea level. The Circle Ladies would never forgive me."

I floated into his lap and clamped my arms around his neck. "Thank you. You're right, and I love you for it. So bring on the dazzle of the light."

Fifteen minutes later, the lesson ended and Jay cheerfully suggested we reward ourselves with a batch of Bloody Marys. "Then after lunch and a short snooze, we'll meet down on the dock for our jaunt to the Wall. Trust me, ladies and gentlemen, you will not be disappointed. Now, on to the bar!" He barked at Fa-Fa, approaching from the boathouse, "Bartender! Start mixing those bloody Bloodys! Tootie, pick up this equipment and haul it to the *Tyrol!*"

Tootie's starlet features crumpled in confusion and humiliation. The suave, handsome man she'd thrown herself at, the man who'd used her sex appeal for financial gain, treated her, in the end, like a servant girl unworthy of kindness or respect.

To my chagrin, Lee blithely remarked, "So that's what she does besides toast and swish. Not that she looks too happy about it."

Indeed, at second glance, the hurt in Tootie's liquid blue eyes crystallized into the purest form of hatred.


LUNCH HAD ALMOST ended when Laurie and Jimbo puttered up to the dock in their two boats, back from Cayman Brac.

"Guess Laurie can get back to business now. That's good news." Buddy buttered a roll, more butter than bread. "The hurricane set her back, but the boat looks in good shape. If you didn't know, Laurie's a really popular dive guide. People fly over here from Grand Cayman for the day, and she charges them an arm and a leg for a more personal diving experience than they get from the large operations."

Frank interrupted from the next table, enjoying a meal with Curious George, and no wives. "Hey, what's that about Laurie? I knew she dived, but I didn't know she raked in big bucks for it. Jay never mentioned it."

"Why would he? He likes to believe he's the only game in town."

Frank pursued his favorite subject. "This money she makes, is it part of the resort's income, or her own?"

Buddy shifted in his chair. "Excuse me, Frank, but even if I did know such a thing, why would I talk about it? Where I come from, you don't discuss another person's income."

I could practically hear Tom and Sam say, "Here, here."

"No offense, no offense." Frank raised open palms in peace. "Just trying to get a handle on my new partnership, that's all."

Dempsie quit eating. "You mean it's definitely a done deal? Jimbo didn't say anything about it this morning."

"Yeah, well," Frank beat around the bush, "I'm still working on Jimbo. But he'll come around. He'll see the business advantages of me as his partner."

"Not while Jay's still in the picture," said Buddy. "I'm tellin' ya, Frank, Jimbo expects Jay to live up to his end of the deal and kick in his fair share, or do like the contract says and sell exclusively to him and Laurie at *fair* market value."

"Contracts are fluid creatures," Frank argued with a smile wide enough to reveal a gold molar. "Contracts change with the circumstances. Jimbo will see this. I think Laurie sees it already."

"Maybe Laurie's more fluid than Jimbo," Buddy snapped. "I tell you this right now, when that man makes up his mind, there's no changing it. So you better concentrate on getting your deposit money back from that slimy, smooth-talkin' con artist."

Frank's wide smile dissolved into his jowls. He threw his napkin on the table, thick eyebrows wild. I thought he might actually take a swing at Buddy for throwing ice on his tropical dream, but he mumbled something to George and stomped away.

Curious George squeezed a lemon into his teacup and whistled. "I'd pay to be a fly on the wall. Our friend Jay is about to hear an earful from our New Yorker."

Lee scoffed. "Yeah, right. Remember what happened last night? One slip of the strap from Miss Tootie and Frank will believe anything Jay tells him."

Jimbo appeared with Laurie and Fa-Fa, checking on the guests. He clapped Buddy on the back and helped himself to half a biscuit. "What's wrong, bro? Somebody get eaten by a shark?"

When Buddy explained Frank's little explosion, Jimbo turned crimson. "Damnit! I told Jay to keep Frank out of this! It's between him and me, and nobody else. Now I've got to wrangle that deposit money out of Jay, set him straight on this coral business, and who knows what else! Honestly, if he's not the death of me, I'll be the death of him," he muttered, stalking away.

"Look, Laurie," Fa-Fa lightly touched her shoulder, "you've been under a lot of stress lately. If you need me to run interference . . ."

"No, no. Thanks, anyway." Voice high as a sparrow's,

she shifted her focus to the guests as if, somehow, we offered relief from the tension playing out in her personal life. "I do apologize. It seems the hurricane destroyed more than a few buildings and trees. I hope our continuing saga doesn't ruin anyone's vacation."

"Don't you give it another thought, Laurie. As a matter of fact," Dempsie boasted, "we're all going diving this afternoon with Jay."

"Good, I'm glad to hear you're enjoying yourselves despite our running battles. Jay's a good dive master." She added bitterly, "I'll give him that."

"What else do you give him?" Buddy jabbed, deathly cold.

The color rose in Laurie's swan neck. "He's a really good diver," she repeated. "Speaking of which, I have to leave for Picky Jiffers's villa." She directed her last comment at Buddy, as if they were alone in the room. "I have many sins, but being late isn't one of them."

Not exactly a confessional, but no one could have missed the inference. Jay aside, I puzzled over Laurie's strange sensitivity and protectiveness toward Picky Jiffers.

Now, where did the sin lie in that?

# CHAPTER 8

✳

"WHERE'S MY BLOODY tank?" Jay barked at Tootie from the captain's chair of the *Tyrol* as six nervous divers waited on the dock to come aboard.

Tootie silently counted the line of tanks in front of her and cursed. "I thought *you* brought it from the boathouse."

"Noooo, lovey, *you* were supposed to, so why don't you run fetch it?" He spoke to her slowly, as to someone mentally handicapped. "The one with the big red X on it, remember?"

Her back stiffened. When he barked again, Tootie spun around and headed for the boathouse.

"Ooooo, where's the love?" Lee smirked.

"Looks like Jay tossed it overboard, along with his sobriety."

"Flip," Dempsie's voice shook, "are we really gonna do this? I mean . . . really?" Goose bumps covered her trembling flesh.

My chest heaved, heart pounding. I knew exactly how she felt. At Jay's signal, Tom herded the two of us toward the boat where Buddy reached out a hand to help. Our captain instantly flipped from ogre into game show host. "Welcome aboard the *Titanic*, ladies and gentlemen! A little black humor from your friendly captain. As you know, this fine vessel is the *Tyrol*, which the thrifty Camp Iguana rents from Dirk, our marine biologist and Eco-Snitch. She's a very nice-sized lady, a little more than thirty feet, sturdy, big-boned, and true, like an efficient German nanny." He drew an aspirin bottle out of his windbreaker and washed a couple of pills down with a beer, the bottle open and waiting beside the steering wheel.

Tom said in all politeness, "Frank was looking for you earlier. Did he find you?"

Jay's upper lip twisted, and he tapped his temple. "Yes, he did. The reason for the headache. Tootie! Where is that lovely twit?"

Within seconds, the California beauty burst out of the boathouse with the missing tank, but slowed down perceptibly en route for Jay's benefit. For her benefit, he fired up the motor and gunned the engine.

Sam and Lee settled into padded seats across from Tom and me, with Dempsie closer to the stern. As soon as Tootie stepped into the boat, Buddy threw the docking ropes in, jumped aboard, and we puttered toward the reef. At the wheel, Jay mumbled something about needing a traveler, and threw his empty beer bottle in a trash bin. He unscrewed the cap off a fifth of rum and poured a generous splash into a large plastic cup.

"Yo-ho-yo-ho, a pirate's life . . ." Lee sang in my ear.

"He never seems to quit, does he?" What effect an ocean of alcohol might have on a diver, I had no idea, but it couldn't be good.

The *Tyrol* picked up speed and cut across the clear water, taking the same route Fa-Fa had taken on our deep-sea fishing expedition. Dempsie and I confessed a fondness for motion sickness pills after that jaunt, the only reason we could look on the rolling seas with confidence. Lee, on the other hand, could perform somersaults on a moving Ferris wheel. She and Sam sat hip to hip, poking each other's ribs to see which one would giggle first.

Once we cleared the narrow passage through the reef, Jay pushed the power button and the boat flew across the waves toward the nefariously named Bloody Bay. Fa-Fa told us the name originated in the nineteenth century when the British ambushed a fleet of pirate ships, and the waters of the bay turned red with blood. Tootie checked our oxygen tanks for the umpteenth time, lined up like lemmings against the side of the boat, waiting to jump off a cliff. Meanwhile, I snuggled against Tom, reminding myself as the fear of the unknown burbled up, what a lucky woman I was, in this beautiful place, with this loving man. I stared at the island's shoreline as we zipped along, taking in the intermittent green and hurricane-damaged foliage, the white sand, and the occasional pastel of a house or a cluster of buildings. How often had I dreamed of a place like this? Of moments like this?

I looked up at Tom, his face relaxed, his hair puffed full in the wind, the slight, white trace of sunscreen below one ear. For a second, a twinge in time, I imagined our lives filled with such moments. Lives of leisure and relaxation, color, tropical flowers, and strange scents. Every single day a pleasure cruise. Surely, I wouldn't have to needle him into the next vacation. Then I remembered Solace Glen, and his host of needy clients. The desk that never cleared of paper. The piles of documents neatly stacked in his home office. The incessant ring of the telephone. Thoughts that naturally led to my own work images: Miss Fizzi's Victorian living room, Lee's antebellum house, Margaret's hallway of books, Reverend G.G.'s manse, the strains of Mozart as I dusted Lindbergh's sleigh bed.

"I'm going to call Margaret right after the dive. She won't believe how brave I am."

"I'll confirm the truth," Tom promised. The boat whopped

down hard over a foam-topped wave. Jay tumbled off the
captain's stool.

"Need some help up there?" Tootie yelled, no kindness
in her voice.

Jay raised his hand and swiped it, as if erasing her from
sight. He repositioned himself on the stool, cursing at the
spilled drink, and tore a paper towel off a roll, clumsily
mopping his chest.

"Hey, Tootie." Tom pulled her aside. "Is he OK to dive?"

"You'd be surprised." She glared at Jay's back. "He
shocks me every day." When she saw the real concern in
our eyes, though, she remembered her job. "Oh, don't
worry. He's a good diver, even if he is a mean, drunken
louse, and I'll be right there with you. We'll get you home
in one piece. Haven't lost a guest yet."

Not reassurance enough for me.

With our pirate ship holding a steady course, Tootie
seized the moment to change into her wet suit, a show designed to catch Jay's eye, but he paid more attention to the
bottle. Not so the other men on board. She slowly peeled
away the sarong that swaddled her hips, daintily dropping it
into an oversized, plastic yellow beach bag. The antennae of
the First Wives Club zinged in the same direction. Lee
ground a heel into Sam's foot as he swiveled around to catch
a better view. I could practically see her eyes spit green.
About the same time, I caught Tom drooling and jabbed an
elbow into his midriff just as another elbow caused Buddy to
groan.

Jay didn't bother to turn around, too engrossed in mixing
himself another cocktail. Despite the cruel neglect of her
target audience, Tootie went on with the show, ever hopeful.
She spent an inordinate amount of time gathering her long,
blonde mane into a tight braid, flexing her biceps and chest
muscles as she twisted each strand. That important task
done, she drew a small mirror from the beach bag and
set about applying lipstick. She pouted and puckered and
rolled her tongue from side to side, totally consumed with

the project. Just as she achieved perfection, popping her mouth like a cork, the boat jerked to one side. She spent a good five minutes squawking words more suitable in a foxhole, scrounging around in the bag for another tube of lipstick.

"Almost there!" Jay called out, Tootie's cue to spring into action. She suddenly slid into her wet suit with lightning speed, a piece of attire well-designed for her statuesque shape. Gradually, the boat slowed and Jay circled a buoy, our pinpoint location to jump overboard. He cut the engine, and he and Tootie went about the business of mooring the *Tyrol*.

"Well," Lee couldn't hold the envy in check to save her life, "now that you're all so hot and bothered, a cold, refreshing dip is just what the doctor ordered." She stepped on Sam's foot on her way to a pile of flippers Tootie tossed our way.

"Owww. Hey, Tootie," Sam said, rubbing his toes, "my wife would kill for one of those wet suits. Don't you think she'd look fantastic in a red one?"

Tootie frowned and scraped her eyes across Lee as though a sickly iguana had crawled into the boat.

"Everyone gets a wet soup," Jay slurred. "Part of our genrush service package. So, spit-spot. Less get goin'."

He set down his plastic cup long enough to weave toward the row of tanks. While he suited up, Tootie handed out masks and flippers, instructing the whole time, reminding us of what we'd learned in the pool that morning, building our confidence for this exciting, scary, first-time diving experience.

"What the hell you think you're doing?" Jay knocked a mask out of Tootie's hand.

"I'm getting ready to dive, of course."

"No, no, no." He waved his hands in the air. "You stay in the boat today. I'll do this alone."

Tootie's mouth fell open. Her squeaky voice dropped an octave. "Oh, no. That is a really bad idea. We'll go down together, as planned. Even better, Jay, maybe you should stay on board for this one. I can take the group down myself."

"Hell, no! Won't hear of it!" Jay leered at Lee like she'd offered him something besides the diving fee. "Been looking forward to this all day."

"Then you go. Just go! Drown for all I care! You're already drowning in alcohol! But I'm not staying on board. It's not safe. You go on in, but I'll be a few minutes. I have to help these people suit up."

Jay slid his mask over his head. "No rush. I'll slide spit-spot down the rope and wait for our happy little campers at the bottom. Then we'll enjoy a nice, leisurely tour along the edge of the Wall."

Buddy cleared his throat. "Um, Jay, back at the pool I thought you said we'd go in first, then the instructors would—"

"That's normally—" Tootie began, but Jay cut them both off.

"Forget the pool. Forget what I said at the pool. This is here. This is now. This is what we'll do." He squinted at his oxygen monitor. "I'll go down first. Tootie will get you suited up and plunge in with you. Then one by one, you'll follow the rope down to the bottom where I'll be conversing with the local mermaid. Got that, Tootie? Does all that intricate information fit inside your tiny little brain? You bring up the rear. Your only asset. Got it? Everyone on the same page? Good. Then I'm off." He staggered to the side of the boat, swayed a moment on the ladder, and splashed backward into the water.

Tootie exploded. "That bastard is going to get his! Damn him! I'm so sick of his act!" She suddenly realized she had six customers staring at her, growing more and more nervous by the minute. And reluctant. "Hey, look, I'm sorry. Don't mind me and my big mouth. I just get so mad when a boss treats me like I'm his personal Sherpa!"

"Surprised she knows what the word means," Lee meowed in my ear. "Such a big word for such a small brain."

"That wet suit really got your goat, didn't it?" I shot back. "What's wrong, can't compete?"

"You have nothing to apologize for, Tootie," Buddy said with surprising tenderness. "Not the way he treats you. The guy's a jerk and everybody knows it. He'll get what's coming to him sooner or later."

Tootie shrugged. "Whatever. He is the captain, and what the captain says, goes. Law of the sea. OK, people! Step lively! I'm the only help you've got!"

We offered ourselves up to her, fumbling with wet suits, tanks, and masks.

"How long will we be down there?" Dempsie gripped her mask against her face, afraid to let go. "There aren't any sharks, are there?"

"No, sugar," Buddy patted her head. "Sharks are just a myth, like Bigfoot and saving social security. There's nuthin' down there but teeny, tiny little watery elves and fairies."

"And drunken pirates," Lee added, "and mermaids."

Tootie grew serious. "A word of advice. When you get to the bottom, which is about thirty feet or so, a nice, sandy spot between two coral formations, wait till we're all together before paddling anywhere with Jay, even if he's tearing your arm off to go with him. Give me time to plant my flippers on the floor before we start the tour, OK?"

We promised to honor and obey, reading between the lines.

"Go ahead and jump in the water the way we taught you this morning. Swim around the boat a bit. Get used to the equipment. I'll be set in a flash and we'll start our descent."

Sam and Lee, the brave idiots, couldn't wait to immerse themselves in Bloody Bay. They clambered to the side of the boat and pushed each other into the water like eighth graders. Tom had a more difficult row to hoe.

"Come on, Flip." A flat palm pushed into my backside. "Remember the poem? *'Long have you timidly waded holding a plank by the shore, / Now I will tell you to be a bold swimmer, / To jump off in the midst of the sea, rise again, nod to me, shout, / And laughingly dash with your hair.'* Come on, scoot, scoot, scoot. Start with the laughing and dashing."

Tootie listened to this conversation as if we spoke Chinese. She helped us into the water. I clung to Tom's hand until I realized I needed all four limbs to stay afloat and make any headway. Like the snorkeling adventure, the moment my head dipped under the water and I beheld a whole new brilliant, beautiful world, I wanted to crow. The six of us paddled around on the surface, masked eyes finding other masked eyes that reflected the same glistening wonder. A few minutes later, Tootie appeared and motioned us toward the buoy rope, a forty-five degree connection from the surface to the bottom. When we descended to the sea-floor, she promised, we'd really start to see spectacular fish in and around the coral formations. She pointed at Sam to lead the way, then Lee, followed by Tom and me, and Buddy and Dempsie. I figured with Dempsie on the tail end, if she started to panic, Tootie could calm her down, take her back up, or stomp on her head.

We floated toward the rope and Sam eagerly started his descent, head first, one hand lightly pulling him to the bottom. Lee followed and I could practically see the tingle up her spine, the electricity firing her hazel eyes. Tom tried to look cool, like he scuba dived to the office everyday, but proved himself as big a kid as anybody. No Ladies First for him. He practically knocked me into a tailspin racing for the rope. I waited a moment, counting heads, and tried to view the bottom where Jay flirted with mermaids, but only saw coral heads pocked with fascinating, waving plants, fish darting everywhere. I took a deep breath, checked the oxygen monitor for the tenth time, and threw myself into the role of bold swimmer.

The weights on my belt made the descent surprisingly easy, and I swallowed every few feet to clear my ears. My head swiveled back and forth and, at times, all I wanted to do was stop and stare, suspended in the water like an undulating jellyfish. The sun played along the sandy bottom and across the backs of bright yellow and incandescent blue fish, with slices of silver and black. Nothing stopped moving, and yet, for all the motion and activity, tranquillity enveloped the scene. I decided when I died, rather than the usual tunnel of light leading to heaven, I'd ask the angels to take a different route. "Ladies," I'd say, "maketh me to float down through green seas. Leadeth me inside the still waters."

Behind me, Buddy gave a thumb's up and pointed over a shoulder at Dempsie who, thankfully, had conquered her fears, too, and groped her way to the bottom with the rest of us.

As the end of the rope neared, Sam and Lee came into view, kneeling on the sand, alien creatures in their diving gear, Lee's hair floating above her like seaweed. When Tom joined them, clouds of white kicked up as he settled down like a spaceship on the moon. I glided over and realized at once that all three twisted their heads around, searching for something. Then it hit me.

Jay was gone.

# PART TWO

❉

# The Eyes of the Dead

# CHAPTER 9

✳

THE SIX OF US knelt in a semicircle on the sandy bottom of Bloody Bay, a hop, skip, and a tumble away from the edge of the Wall with its deadly drop. Tootie signaled the group to remain together, and ascended a few feet above us. She began a spiraling rotation, swimming in a tight circle that gradually expanded until she easily covered a search area well beyond the edge of the Wall and across the more shallow depths. We watched, mesmerized, occasionally glancing around us, expecting Jay to pop from behind a column of coral or suddenly rise from the deep abyss with a mermaid on each arm. But he did not appear.

We shook heads at each other, eyes magnified in the masks, shoulders rising and falling in helplessness. What could we do but watch and wait, a small herd of inexperienced divers? Meanwhile, Tootie searched, and the clock ticked.

Fifteen long minutes dragged by until she finally stopped circling our heads and swam as fast as she could to our bewildered group. She pointed to the surface and one by one we slowly ascended, following her lead, clearing our ears every few feet. By the time I broke the surface, I heard her screechy voice. "We've got to call for help on the radio! The flag! We've got to hoist the diver down flag!"

Lee paddled over, gulping sea water. "Omigod. I can't *believe* this! Can you believe this? What do you think happened to Jay?"

Sam and Tom dog-paddled to us. "I swear," Sam rasped, "I was the first one down there, and I didn't see a thing. No Jay. Nothing. I thought maybe I'd gotten mixed up about what he said, but then Lee reached the bottom, then Tom, and we all had the same look in our eyes like, *Where in blazes is this guy?*"

Directly in front of us, Buddy steered Dempsie to the ladder and Tootie, already on board, quickly counted heads and started hauling us out of the water. She shook uncontrollably as she radioed for help, the "diver down" flag clutched in her hand.

"Tootie—ugh!" Hauling myself out of the water and onto the deck, I grunted under the weight of the diving equipment. "Did you see anything? What could have happened to him?"

"It can't be good, whatever it is. There should be some dive boats close by until the police boat arrives."

To a landlubber, the idea of police in boats sounded strange, and I tried to picture Solace Glen's Officer Sidney Garrett cruising around the fire pond. Tootie threw the flag up and restated our position to the voice on the radio. We unzipped wet suits and helped each other out of the heavy oxygen tanks with Tootie's intermittent assistance. Between aiding the dumbfounded tourists, trying to talk on the radio, and running up the flag, she didn't have a moment to catch her breath, but somehow managed to hand out bottled water.

"I can't believe how thirsty I am after bein' in that water!" Dempsie exclaimed. "I mean, it's not like we actually did anything except sit around on the bottom."

"What else could we do?" Buddy squeezed a water bottle into his mouth. "That drunken fool probably tottered right over the edge of the Wall. He's long gone." He almost sounded pleased.

"Unfortunately, that's as good a guess as any," Tom said. "You're always reading about experienced divers, even sober ones, who lose their lives through one mishap or another."

"Thanks, sweetie." I patted his cheek. "Certainly makes me want to try this again."

"I'm with you, Flip." Dempsie waved a hand across her flushed face. "I've had all the scuba diving I care to have in one lifetime! How long do you think it'll take for the police to arrive?"

We shaded our eyes from the sun and scanned the horizon on both sides of the *Tyrol,* the sea vast and empty in every direction. Presently, Tootie spied a boat coming toward us from the east. A voice cracked the silence over the radio, and she spoke to the captain of the oncoming vessel. Luckily, the group of divers aboard the *Mystified* proved highly experienced, and did not hesitate to volunteer in the search for Jay. As the boat drew close, the captain and Tootie yelled information back and forth. Until the police arrived, Tootie would stay on the surface with us, but the six new divers would spread out by twos and cover a wider area than she could manage alone.

"I don't know why they're wasting their time," Buddy said, vexed. "He's shark bait by now."

Dempsie's pudgy face crinkled. "Buddy! He could be down there, passed out, trapped on some coral or something. There's still a chance they'll find him before . . . you know."

"Before his air gives out and he does become somebody's supper?"

I blinked at the callous remark. At least forty-five minutes had passed. "How long will his air last?"

"We usually make sure to have at least sixty minutes for

this type of dive," said Tootie. "I think that's what he had."

"You *think?*" Lee cocked her head and raised one skeptical brow. "You're the one who brought his tank from the boathouse. Didn't you fill it yourself or check the gauge?"

"No!" she exploded. "I didn't do a damn thing to his tank! He said to get it and I got it. That's *it!*"

"Whoa. Chill out." Lee spoke with unnecessary sharpness. "I'm not accusing you of anything."

"Could have fooled me. Just because he treated me like dirt all of a sudden and started flirting with you doesn't mean I killed him. Get over yourself."

Lee gaped. "All I wanted to know was if you checked his gauge!"

"Hey, Tootie?" Buddy rubbed both hands on his knees to warm up, hesitant to ask the question. "Didn't you and Jimbo fill the tanks this morning?"

She didn't answer, but brushed past him, jamming a hand inside her beach bag. She jerked out a pack of cigarettes, which scattered across the deck, and spent the next few minutes cursing, scrambling to find a tobacco stick that wasn't soggy.

Soon, the radio blared again and we watched as a police boat approached at top speed. Tootie sat on the edge of the stern, arms crossed, legs jangling, pouty mouth puffing smoke like the tailpipe of an unmuffled car. Lee watched her every move, jaw firm as concrete. I'd seen that look before.

The police boat carried two divers who immediately set to work. The captain told Tootie word had spread to Cayman Brac and Grand Cayman, and other police boats would arrive soon with more divers.

"Thanks. Look, I've got to get these people back to camp, but we'll hold off another fifteen minutes. I have to let Jimbo and Laurie know what's happened, then I'll come back and join the search, if that's OK with you. I can bring extra flashlights, too."

"Thanks," the voice replied, calm and efficient. "Everybody else on board healthy? Good. I'm going to need to talk to all the divers, including you."

"Sure, not much to tell, though. Jay was a little worse for wear when he went under, if you get my drift."

"Oh, yeah. I get your drift."

I did, too. A small island's nothing but a small town, where every little sin is amplified. I knew exactly how many sherry bottles Miss Fizzi threw away in the garbage, testament to the number of evening soirees she enjoyed with her friends, and how much C.C. and Leonard prized a good scotch, while Lindbergh preferred Irish whiskey.

Tootie hung up the radio receiver and lit another cigarette, concentrating on a long drag, suddenly as calm as if she lolled around at a cocktail party. "So you heard. We'll give it another fifteen minutes, see if they find anything."

"You mean wait until all hope is gone." Lee spoke bluntly, as always, but with the slightest trace of judgment. For us, the moment held a sort of *Wizard of Oz* quality, where, trapped in the castle, we anxiously watched the sand slip to the bottom of the hourglass.

Tootie settled into the captain's chair and casually glanced at her watch. She wiggled her toes to pass the time, catching rays of light on her silvery nail polish. The rest of us gravitated to the two sides of the *Tyrol* and stared into the water. No one spoke a word. The late afternoon sun threw bolts of light off the peaceful, blue sea and the sky showed the first signs of changing into its red robe. The three boats bobbed quietly on the surface, the silence broken only by the occasional crackle of voices across the police radio. Meanwhile, below, eight divers swam frantically about, searching for a man running out of time.

So still and quiet on the surface. Beneath the quiet, a beautiful world gave up none of its secrets.

* * *

THE SURPRISE OF tragedy is how the normal things still
happen. We take showers, we eat dinner, we talk and share
a bottle of wine. Granted, the talk revolves around the terrible event, but human nature longs for the familiar, the
regular, the uninterrupted rhythm of our lives.

So it was we returned to Camp Iguana, took our showers, ate our dinner, shared our wine, and naturally, the talk
revolved around Jay's disappearance. Tootie delivered the
news to Jimbo, and headed back to the dive site to help in
the search. He showed no reaction, as if told a meat shipment went missing in transit, but when Laurie returned,
cheerful after depositing Picky Jiffers at his villa, she could
barely orchestrate our supper. She floated mindlessly around
the dining room, pretty face vacant and spectral. Minute by
minute, she withdrew, responding to little more than a request for more water.

Most of the staff wore the same blank face. Fa-Fa ate at
his usual table, sunglasses covering his eyes, the ever silent
Dirk at his side. Jimbo wandered in and out, replenishing
bowls and plates of food, normally Laurie's job. Whenever
he asked her a question, she wafted away.

The guests did their best under the circumstances.
Frank picked at his rice pilaf as if it contained shards of
glass, no doubt wondering if he'd ever see his deposit
money again—who to sue? who to sue? He hardly noticed
Renata's lovely transformation. She sat across from him,
stunned at the news, but beautifully coifed, the gray hair
magically gone. She looked years younger with her ash
blonde highlights, thanks to Henrietta's guidance. Her new
English friend radiated with the pleasure of doing a good
deed. Henrietta had enjoyed her day at the spa even more
than Renata—her proud creation—delighted to present the
new and improved businesswoman to Frank and the other
guests as the main course of dinner conversation that night.
But Frank's gruff indifference, and Jay's disappearance,

ruined the moment. Defeated, Henrietta sawed at her lamb chop, complaining about everything from the weather to the taste of her mineral water. Now and then, George attempted a mild reminder that a man's life had ended only a few hours before, and couldn't she find it in her heart to respect the dead?

"I didn't respect Jay when he was alive. Why must I respect him now that he's drowned? Drunken fool brought it on himself."

Though most of us shared Henrietta's uncharitable opinion, I wondered. If Jay habitually dove under the influence, why did things go so terribly wrong this time? Why did Tootie fly off the handle when Lee and Buddy asked a couple of simple questions about the tank? Did she do something to it in the boathouse or earlier, when she and Jimbo filled the tanks? Did Jimbo? Who else had access to the diving equipment?

Was Jay's disappearance really an accident? *Or was it murder?*

# CHAPTER 10

✖

EARLY WEDNESDAY MORNING, Lee and I sat side by side on the edge of my bed, talking into Tom's cell phone. We needed to pick Margaret's brain. Margaret always has an opinion if you gave her enough facts. Cheek to cheek, we held the phone between our two ears.

"What?!" We heard the clunk as Margaret dropped the phone.

"Can you believe it!" Lee nearly split my eardrum, and I forced the phone away from her.

"Margaret, I would have called earlier, but the arrival of you-know-who threw me for a loop . . . Oh, yes, we were *very* surprised when we saw them get off the plane . . . No, he didn't bother to read that part of Miss Fizzi's packet, so you can tell her and the usual suspects that we didn't expect a thing! It's worked out well, though. Just think if Lee hadn't signed us up for those diving lessons! . . . Well, I'm sorry we didn't call last night, either . . . I know, I know, it's not like me, but it *is* my honeymoon! You shouldn't have worried. Anyway, the other guests wanted to talk about what happened to Jay, and we didn't want to miss anything."

Lee forced her head against mine so she could hear Margaret's excited voice. "I completely understand, dear! To think, all this drama occurred when you were brave enough to scuba dive! Mercy! And here we were in a tizzy, thinking you wouldn't try anything new, and Tom would get bored without some other company. Wait till I tell the other Circle Ladies!"

Such faith they had in me. "You do that. So what do you think happened, Margaret? You may refer to your notes. I know you've been writing everything down. Do you think somebody murdered Jay?"

Before Margaret could render a verdict, Lee grabbed the phone and announced her own theory of the case. "I think the bimbo killed him . . . Yeah, Tootie. She certainly had reason to, and opportunity. She worshipped the ground he stumbled on, but he flirted with me outrageously, *and* was having an affair with Laurie . . . Oh, yes, we're positive. Plus, Jay started treating Tootie like a slave. If Sam treated me that way, I might put a little something extra in his eggs, too. I'm *sure* she messed with his tank."

I pulled at the phone. "Margaret, Tootie's not a bimbo. She's a diving instructor, and she looked after us very well under extreme circumstances. You know how Lee gets around women who are prettier than she is. And younger. Remember how she acted when Stewart Larkin moved to town?"

Lee stomped one foot. "If you recall, I was right about her all along! Stewart is now a convicted felon." She crossed her arms. "You think Tootie's prettier than I am? Really?"

Margaret finally got a word in edgewise. "It sounds like an accident to me, and Lindbergh is nodding his head in agreement as I speak. He says hello to both of you . . . and stay out of trouble. Where was I?"

"An accident."

"Oh, yes, but as anybody in Solace Glen will tell you, some 'accidents' happen on purpose. If I were you, I'd keep one eye open at all times. Especially on Tootie, the man who runs the camp, and that friend, I've got it written down someplace . . . Buddy?"

"That's right."

"And Dirk, the scientist who argued with Jay. Oh, and the New Yorker who gave Jay money. I suppose anyone could have gone into the boathouse and fooled with the oxygen tank, even a guest, if he knew what he was doing. What do the police think?"

"We'll find out soon enough. We've been summoned for a breakfast interrogation."

"What an exciting honeymoon! Lindbergh and I will never be able to live up to it! Keep us posted!"

Lee and I promised to do exactly that. At lunch time, after our grueling police interrogation, the next call would zing straight from the private confines of Camp Iguana to the well-known public address system known as Garland's Bistro.


POLICE CONSTABLE NETTLES, formerly of Sunbury-on-Thames, currently Little Cayman's senior police presence, readjusted our timetable of fishing and swimming. During breakfast, he and a protégé appeared. The constable, a bald, handsome man with skin the color of creamed coffee and a voice made for singing ballads, wore khaki shorts that touched his kneecaps and a crisp white short-sleeved shirt. Tall and muscular, he could have hoisted Lee and me above each shoulder with little trouble.

The young man beside him wore the same casual uniform, but there the similarity ended. Topping his head like a circus clown poked the most unusual hair—yellow, cotton-candy puffs divided into three distinct peaks.

Twenty-something, a tad overweight, his fleshy cheeks resembled two grapefruits, pink and freshly scrubbed.

Laurie and Jimbo affirmed that all guests and staff were
accounted for, whether they'd participated in the fateful
dive or not, and offered the floor to the constable. He rose
and cleared his throat. "Good morning, and thank you. I
apologize for the intrusion on your valuable vacation time,
but we do have a few questions. I am Constable Nettles.
Allow me to introduce my new assistant, PC Arnaud
Fitzgerald, who completed his training a few days ago."
He prodded the young officer to say a few words about
himself.

Arnaud took one giant step forward, swelled up like a
blowfish and spouted, "I'm French/Irish! Single! Age
twenty-four! Hobbies include shell collecting and birding!
Graduated second in the class! I look forward to interrogating you all!" He turned three shades of pink and stepped
backward, offering his new boss the first clue that Arnaud's
talents did not lie in public relations.

Constable Nettles, forehead folded into ridges, assured
Arnaud he would not be interrogating anything. He
smoothly took over the meeting and informed us that up to
thirty-five divers and seven police boats had joined in the
search for Jay.

"It's definitely a search, not a rescue?" Curious George
couldn't wait to pose the first question.

"Yes, we are fairly confident we will not find Jay alive at
this point. But miracles are known to occur."

"What could have happened to him?" Sam, the college
professor, was used to asking questions. "I mean, he just
disappeared without a trace. It was the darnedest thing."

"And you are?"

"Sam Gibbon. This is my wife, Lee. We were the first
ones to reach the bottom where Jay said he'd be."

"This is unusual, is it not?" PC Nettles zeroed in on
Tootie as Arnaud furiously recorded every word in a little

notebook, eyes bright. So much more fun than the stale classroom. "Isn't it your policy to have the dive master descend with the guests, especially on a resort course dive?"

"Yeah, but like I told you yesterday, Jay was a little worse for wear." Tootie withdrew an emery board from her bag and filed her nails like her life depended on it.

"You mean flat out drunk," Buddy interjected.

Tootie didn't deny it, and filed harder. "So what else is new? At the pool lesson, he told me we'd both descend with the students, but at the last minute insisted on going down first. He even ordered me to stay on board, but I'm not a *complete* idiot." She directed this last comment at Lee, who defiantly scrunched her mouth sideways, convinced of Tootie's guilt. "I insisted on bringing up the rear. He made a nasty comment about it, but what the hell."

"You did not question him on his decision to go down alone?"

"You can't argue with a drunk, plus, he's the captain."

"But surely . . ."

Tootie's words came hurriedly, "I had to consider the safety of the guests. You get that, don't you? We would have been better off without him on a first descent, him in that condition."

"Better off without him. I see. He was alone in the water for how long?"

"By the time I got everybody suited up, a good ten minutes. No more than fifteen."

"And no one saw anything on the bottom?"

We all shook our heads while Tootie continued. "Nothing. I swam around in circles over a pretty wide area, too. Took a good sweep. I would have spotted him. He had a big red X painted on his tank."

"You could have 'overlooked' it." Lee sniffed.

PC Nettles studied the ceiling a moment. "We have three possibilities, none of them pleasant. First, that this is a terrible accident. This is our first assumption, but my years in police work have taught me never to stop at the first assumption."

"And the second possibility?" I asked, although I knew the answer.

"That someone negligently—or intentionally—caused harm to come to Jay Carruthers."

Jimbo almost burst into laughter. "Aw, come on, Constable! You don't really think somebody here would kill that jerk, do ya?"

The constable replied in a polite, if cool, tone. "As you say, Jay was . . . or is a jerk. We need to explore how many others besides you held the same opinion."

I spoke up again, so willing to inject myself into the investigation. All the while, I could hear Tom tapping his toe. "You said Jay 'was or *is* a jerk.' Is that the third possibility? That he faked his disappearance?"

PC Nettles smiled at me as a patient, third grade teacher might at the class bigmouth. "Precisely, Miss . . . ?"

"Paxton. I mean, Mrs. Scott. Flip Scott." Just the simpleton who can't remember her own name. "I'm with him." I pointed at the man tapping his toe.

The patient smile widened ever so slightly and the constable leaned forward to shake Tom's hand. "You and your wife participated in the dive, also?"

"Yes, we did. Good morning, I'm Tom."

"And you saw nothing, either?"

"No, we . . ."

"Constable," I interrupted, so excited to use such a British term, "getting back to the first possibility that this was an accident? Other than being so full of rum that he passed out and toppled over the Wall, sliding thousands of feet to a gruesome death, what else could have happened to Jay?" Tom stepped on my foot, but I sweetly shoved him away.

"Flip," PC Nettles's lips twitched, "are you a gothic romance novelist?"

Little did he know how flattered I was. "Oh, no, I'm in the cleaning business. I deal in messes."

"I think you mean to deal with this one as well. But to answer your question, yes, Jay could have lost consciousness from the alcohol and slipped over the edge of the Wall. Or he could have fallen over, drunk but conscious. He may have taken ill, had a heart attack or some other trauma, and lost buoyancy. He could have been stung by a jellyfish and suffered *Irukandji syndrome,* an allergic reaction to the sting. Strong underwater currents, just before you descended, might have swept him out to sea or catapulted him into boulders, knocking him unconscious. His equipment might have failed, a valve or the wrong gas mix, throwing him into convulsions. A shark may have attacked him, but we've seen no sign of that. No gear has floated up. As you can see, there are any number of possibilities."

"That seals it for me." Dempsie's eyes grew wide as doughnuts. "No way I'm gonna dive again."

"Now, darlin'," Buddy said as he patted her shoulder, "don't let this one tiny incident destroy your career as a deep-sea treasure hunter. I was bankin' on it."

Dirk harrumphed in the background. "That's exactly how Jay pictured himself!"

"Oh?" The constable moved toward the scientist. "What do you mean by that?"

The color rose from the gruff scholar's chin to the top of his head, all eyes on him. Dirk regarded the constable with distrust, as if men in khaki shorts made up the bulk of the KGB. "I simply mean that one of Jay's many peccadilloes included collecting marine specimens and rare, protected coral. All for profit. Personal gain. Fa-Fa and I threatened to tell the authorities on more than one occasion."

"Why hadn't you done so already if you knew he acted in flagrant violation of the law?"

"You may not believe this—and I don't care if you do—but because of our concern and respect for Jimbo and Laurie. Jimbo and Jay were partners, you know. The resort could have been held liable for Jay's illegal actions. These two could have lost everything just at a time when they were forced to dig deep into their own pockets after the hurricane. We had hoped Jay would stop his stupidity after a warning or two, but he didn't."

"Did you argue with him about this? Did Fa-Fa?"

"Yes. Fa-Fa and I. A couple of times. Maybe more."

"His response?"

"Pure arrogance." Dirk spat the words. "I tell you, I had no use for the man. Any more than I have use for police investigations. The drunkard drowned. Leave it at that, will you?"

"You rent your diving vessel to the resort, do you not?"

"Yes, I do."

"So, with your knowledge of Jay's illegal activities on your own boat, you could have lost much, too. Perhaps everything?"

Dirk's silence answered the question, but his angry words of the previous evening flashed across my mind. *I could lose everything. My boat, my license, my livelihood, not to mention my reputation as a scientist.*

"You have access to your boat when the resort is not using it, correct?"

"Yes, of course. I use it for scientific dives. I am on staff here as an environmental lecturer. I don't participate in the diving lessons."

"But you have access to the diving equipment in the boathouse?"

Dirk hesitated. "I do. But every staff member has such access. We all dive, you know. This is, after all, a fishing and diving camp. Are you going to arrest everyone who dives?"

"Fa-Fa," PC Nettles turned congenially to the fishing guide, "you are a diver, too?"

"I can," he replied succinctly, like a practiced witness, "but prefer not to."

"You're certified?"

He dipped his head in affirmation. "I helped Jay out before the hurricane, but suffered an injury. I pretty much stick to fishing now."

"Have you access, also, to the boathouse?"

"As Dirk told you, all members of the staff have access. I store fishing equipment there." I wanted to observe Fa-Fa's eyes during this exchange, but he never removed his sunglasses.

Constable Nettles continued to play cat and mouse, scratching for information from each of us in turn. Meanwhile, his sidekick flew through the pages of his notebook, sweat breaking out across the wide forehead, causing tufts of yellow hair to flatten and wilt. His moldy old textbooks could never compare to this kind of thrill.

Henrietta and Renata pled Ignorance By Virtue of Spa, having strolled into camp just as Laurie had passed by in her boat and waved, returning Picky Jiffers to his villa. When pressed, Laurie reluctantly revealed that she had taken Picky to his favorite dive spot, a good two miles west of the site where Jay disappeared. "He gets very angry when another boat is even within sight," she explained. "He pays for complete privacy. I hope, Constable, you'll respect that privacy and leave him alone. He's got nothing to do with this." A comment that sounded more like a nervous plea.

Curious George and Fa-Fa had wiled away the afternoon hours fly-fishing, ignorant of Jay's plight until their return to camp. When PC Nettles turned his attention to Frank, he had to endure the New Yorker's rants and raves about the money he'd lost to Jay. We all pursed our lips and whistled at the amount.

Renata did not whistle. She slapped both hands across her cheeks, almost hysterical. "You told me ten thousand, and now I have to hear in front of all these people that you handed over *fifty thousand* dollars to that con artist! Frank! How *could* you?"

"It's a partnership! It involves pricey real estate, for God's sake! You've never understood how men do business! Stay out of it, woman!"

As Renata crumpled against Henrietta, I gauged the constable's reaction to this new figure in the equation. Jay, he plainly saw, could have used a calculator to count up his number of enemies.

Throwing fuel on the fire, and despite his "shark bait" comments the day before, Buddy snidely suggested that Jay did fake his disappearance, and at that very moment wined and dined a harem of gullible women on some other island. His eyes slid ominously toward Laurie, but he did not reveal the affair. "He played around. He was a good-time Charlie. Who's to say he didn't swim to a secluded cove and slither onto land? He could have hidden a stash someplace, rented or stolen a boat, and poof! He's home free."

But Laurie vehemently argued, "No! He wouldn't do that! He wouldn't! He slipped over the edge of the Wall. That's what happened. High as a kite. I warned him. I warned him so many times. And, anyway, I was to the west of you. If he'd crawled out of water onto land, I'm sure I would have spotted him." Her sad eyes flew to the sea. "I would have seen him."

"But, honey," Jimbo countered, unusually quiet until then, "you were under the water with Picky most of the time, and further out. Even if he'd gone west, Jay could have easily slipped past your line of vision. Or he might have gone east."

Laurie conceded that truth. She also conceded, along with Jimbo, the recent tension between the partners, large eyes darkening as her husband related their business relationship. "The slimeball couldn't live up to a deal to save his life! I really started to hate the guy."

"Enough to wish him dead?"

"Oh, now, Constable," Jimbo sputtered, unwittingly glancing in Buddy's direction. "I . . . I don't know."

"Miss Tootie," the constable completed a sweep of the circle, back to his starting point, "may I ask you a few more questions before we go?"

Tootie replaced her nail file with a cigarette the length of a ruler. She poked it in her mouth and torched it with a lighter. "Sure. Shoot."

"Was your relationship with Jay close?"

"What do you mean 'close'?"

"Platonic?"

The creases in Tootie's forehead took a turn for the worse. "What?"

Lee buzzed around my ear. "Pla-ton-ic. Too many syllables, too many syllables."

I waved her away, mouthing the word, "Jeal-ous."

PC Nettles slowed his speech down a notch. "Were you friends? In love with Jay? Living together? Engaged?"

Tootie sucked on the cigarette. "God, what a laugh. Engaged to Jay? Ha! No getting that man to the altar. Like Buddy said, he was a good-time Charlie, that's what he was." She seemed very comfortable with the past tense.

"So you were, for lack of a better word, sweethearts?"

That evoked an even bigger squeal. "Yeah, right! Sweeeeet-hearts." Her voice sank. "Let's just say I had some unreasonable expectations. Lucky I found out in time."

"What do you mean? What did you find out?"

"Nothing." She swept her blonde hair off one shoulder and flicked cigarette ash on the floor directly in front of Laurie, causing her to flinch. "It doesn't matter now. I don't want to talk about it."

Although the constable took this to mean Tootie suffered greatly, in too much pain to talk about the happy future she'd hoped for with Jay, I suspected a darker meaning. Laurie and Jimbo now owed her something for keeping silent about the affair, unless someone else spilled the beans. Furthermore, if Tootie swam in cahoots with Jay in his marine-life-for-profit scheme, not to mention his desire to wiggle out of the deal with Jimbo, the two of them could have plotted to take off. Take the money—including Frank's deposit funds—and run.

Or maybe just one of them did.

# CHAPTER 11

✤

OUR FISHING TRIP postponed, Tom and I spent the time between interrogation and lunch biking to our favorite, out-of-the-way snorkeling spot where we took a brief swim and walked along the short strip of beach, completely, blissfully alone.

"This has turned into a rather atypical honeymoon," he opined. "Although I should have expected the atypical, with you as a bride."

"That's right. When things get weird, blame me. Story of my life."

He kicked sand at my legs. "You certainly showed your true colors with your new best buddy, Constable Nettles." His voice rose ten octaves. " 'Oh, Con-sta-ble, you wouldn't believe all the big, bad messes I've had to clean up, and how many criminals I've swept off to jail just this past year. Ohhhh, *Con*-sta-ble, you really need *me* leading your investigation! Let's run through all the possibilities and theories and suspects one more time!' "

"Why are you so mean to me? If I'd only known. Come on, let's head back for lunch." I turned on my heel.

"You're not interested in lunch." He tugged my pony-tail, halting me in midstep. "You just want to see if anything else has happened that you can stick your nose into. Am I right, or am I right?"

I kissed his cheek and jerked the ponytail from his grip. "You're *always* right. Wanna race?"

Back at Camp Iguana, tranquillity reigned. Most of those with diving skills had joined the search for Jay, and police boats zipped around like water bugs, attracting our attention now and again. Music hummed from a radio in the kitchen while the staff prepared the dining room for lunch, but without Laurie's input. She'd accompanied Dirk on the grim underwater mission. Fa-Fa, unable to dive, took the opportunity of an open time slot to escort Sam and Lee on a fishing trip to Tarpon Lake. The three other couples lounged around the pool or on the beach, catching up with a good book or snoring under straw hats.

Tom skirted around the outdoor bar and pulled two cold beers out of the refrigerator, signing our names on the honor list. I hopped up on a barstool and propped an elbow on the counter, observing our fellow guests. We'd only arrived four days ago, but time seemed to have doubled. The six strangers I stared at through polarized sunglasses seemed oddly familiar after such short acquaintance. "I guess tragedy has a way of bringing people together."

"I wonder," Tom reflected, "if we're free to leave the island. Like the constable said, Jay's disappearance could be an accident, or he's in hiding, or . . ."

"Slow, foreboding drum roll, please—murder."

Tom absently peeled the label off his bottle. "Anybody could have tampered with Jay's oxygen tank, I suppose, and he was known to dive under the influence."

"Less likely to pay close attention to the equipment. I doubt he could even read the gauge before he toppled into the water. Did you see his eyes? Pretty blurry."

"Yeah, we may never know the truth. Then again, they might find his body any moment."

"Ooooh, yuk." I couldn't imagine. A weather report cut into the music over the radio, the announcer's words half lost to me. "What was that? More sun? More moon? More stars?"

"No, something about a system in a couple of days."

"Wonder what the weather's like in Solace Glen. Lee and I forgot to ask Margaret this morning."

"Probably an outbreak of autumn, followed by a rash of winter." He smiled indulgently. "OK, it's about lunch time at the Bistro, isn't it? Go ahead and make the call. Here's my cell. Be sure to thank everyone for peopling our honeymoon with poor, self-sacrificing Sam and Lee."

I squealed and grabbed the cell phone, fingers flying. "Lee will be so mad I called without her, but I can't wait!" The phone rang no more than twice before someone picked up. "Hello? Hilda? Hey, it's Flip! And Tom's right here! Put your mother on! . . . Yes, we're having fun . . . Yes, this is a beautiful island . . . Hilda, put your mother on . . . Hilda . . ." I turned to Tom. "She's screaming at the customers to hush up, we're on the line. I can hear chairs and feet. Sounds like a stampede."

"Flip! It's Garland! Is that you? Margaret and Lindbergh are here. Margaret brought her notes. They told us about the diver disappearing! It's all anybody can talk about! I'm putting you on the speaker so people can hear. We're all dying to know, have they found his body?"

The sound of the stampede suddenly ceased. I could picture the wide-eyed, curious faces of friends and neighbors gathered around Garland's phone, waiting for my answer. "No, they haven't. The police constable questioned the camp guests and staff this morning, and

police boats are everywhere." I waited for the surefire reaction.

A community moan followed. "Oooooh, wow, oooooh."

"Did anybody confess to anything?" Miss Fizzi chirped.
"Confession is good for the soul, you know, even if you're
hauled off to go to jail."

One Egghead yelled, "I'd bet money the scientist did it!
Probably was lying in wait like an octopus and pushed the
jerky guy over that Wall."

"No, no," squawked the other Egghead, "it was Jimbo,
the husband! He did it out of jealousy as sure as I'm standing here."

"I think it was the New Yorker," croaked Pal. "Couldn't
get his money back, so he fooled with Jay's tank."

"Flip!" I heard Ivory's booming voice. "How you doin',
girl? Your wedding bouquet is still fresh. Ebony's teeth
didn't hurt it a bit, and . . ."

"Who cares! Sit down!" a bigger voice boomed.
Screamin' Larry injected his own opinion. "The guy's
brain exploded from the booze, that's all. He's d-e-a-d.
You're all idiots. Especially you." I knew he was pointing a
bloated finger at Ivory.

"Flip, it's Garland again. Call us Friday at dinnertime
when more people are expected. We're taking the weekend
specials off the chalkboard so Pal and Suggs can start a
betting pool like we do during the Super Bowl."

"You mean you're placing bets on whether Jay was
murdered?"

"Oh, no, we're way beyond that. The bets are on who
murdered him. The vote came in as murder, so now we
have to decide who did it. You're going to have to give us
more information, though. Margaret took down the names
and general descriptions of the suspects, but she got so excited, her handwriting's terrible. Promise you and Lee will
call!"

"Of course we will, but I think you're going through a

whole lot of hoopla for nothing. They're never going to find his body. No one will ever know what really happened."

At first, I thought the line had gone dead, until Pal's voice broke the silence. "You wanna bet!"

I hung up to the sound of raucous laughter.

# CHAPTER 12

✳

THURSDAY BROUGHT ANOTHER sunny, gorgeous day, perfect for spin casting the flats with Fa-Fa, and enjoying a picnic. We motored off immediately after breakfast in his seventeen-foot boat, looking forward to a few peaceful hours of chasing bonefish and barracuda. In the distance, not so peaceful, police boats flew across the water, the search area growing in width and intensity.

"Think they'll find him, Fa-Fa?" I flicked a line out, copying Tom's smooth rhythm.

"I doubt it. He's miles from here by now."

"Yeah, but dead or alive?"

Fa-Fa stuck a minnow on a hook, his brown, chin-length hair topped by an Atlanta Braves baseball cap, trademark black sunglasses hiding his eyes. "I'd bet my boat he's dead as driftwood. I agree with Laurie. He got ill or passed out, and lies at the bottom of Bloody Bay Wall."

"How *is* Laurie, really?"

"She's upset, but . . . I don't know. It's more nerves." He kept his head bowed low. "We're pretty tight, and I flat out told her she's better off without Jay, maybe she ought to wake up and work on her marriage. Things happen for a reason, especially the things that make us unhappy. Seems the only time I see a light in her eyes anymore is when she's diving, or Picky Jiffers calls."

"She's very protective of him."

"She can't afford to rock his boat. He's a major source of income lately."

I wondered if he'd become more than that, but I let it drop and picked up the topic we started with. "So you don't think Jay ran off?"

"Nope. Not that smart. And I honestly don't believe—at this point, anyway—that he'd leave Laurie behind."

"I guess that's the secret everybody knows except the constable. If he did find out . . ."

"It wouldn't look good for Jimbo, I know. Especially since he and Tootie filled the tanks that morning."

I ignored the nibble on my hook. "Fa-Fa, do you think either one of them would kill Jay?"

He chose not to respond but said instead, "That's just what George wanted to know."

"George?" No more nibble on the hook. "George is certainly interested in everything."

"You mean every*body*. I can't figure him out. Most tourists ask questions, but with him, it's like a CIA mission. He never lets up."

I reeled in a naked hook. Fa-Fa caught the line in midair and held it over the bait cooler. I tried again. "Do you think Jay was murdered?"

The hook in his hand slipped and dug into a finger. He grimaced and dipped it in the salt water, washing away the blood. "Like Buddy and Tootie said, Jay was a good-time Charlie. He could turn any situation around to his own advantage. As much as he 'loved' Laurie, he would have lost interest in her sooner or later, and moved on to greener pastures. You saw what a charmer the guy was. He would have schmoozed a business deal with Jimbo and Frank, too. Then Jay would have split, out of Laurie's life, and Dirk's hair, and Jimbo's."

"And yours?"

"Fish-ing," Tom muttered, "fish-ing."

"Yes, dear, I'm loving it. Fa-Fa, you were saying?"

"I wasn't exactly saying." He tossed my baited hook into the water, and I heard Tom's chuckle.

"Dirk said both of you knew about Jay's coral business, right? And you said you helped Jay with diving trips before the hurricane?"

"I saw more than enough of Jay's antics, if that's what you're getting at."

"Then why wouldn't you testify against him? Unless," I reeled in slowly, "Jay was holding something over your head?"

Fa-Fa pretended to concentrate hard on the bait in his hands.

"What did he have on you? Not that it matters now," I coaxed.

Poor Fa-Fa. Trapped on a small boat with a nosy woman who wouldn't shut up. He knew I wouldn't leave him in peace, but struggled with something.

"Come on, Fa-Fa. Tom's a lawyer and I'm a lawyer's wife. We are the soul of discretion. Plus, if there's a problem you're worried about, Tom can give you free legal advice."

"How kind of you to waive my fee, dear."

"Think nothing of it. Well, Fa-Fa?"

"This is not something I'd want the constable to know, you understand?" When Tom and I nodded, solemn as two priests, he relented. "I had some bad breaks in the past. Literally. In between jobs as a fishing guide, I worked places where the top priority wasn't exactly worker safety. Physically, I'm pretty messed up. After one stint on a cargo ship a few years ago, a crate fell on me. Almost broke my back in two. I was lucky to walk again, let alone fish and dive. Anyway, I got hooked on pain pills, and it's cost me several jobs. I thought I had the addiction licked when I signed up with Jimbo and Laurie. But during the hurricane, a shutter flew off a window like a missile, right into my back. Guess who offered me a bottle of his special pain pills so I could keep working?"

"The barfly on Davy Jones's locker?"

"You got it. A steady supply, free for a week, then cash up front. Just what the doctor never would have ordered." He quit fiddling with the bait, embarrassed, and turned away. "Pretty shameful, huh?"

At once, I understood the reason for the glued-on sunglasses, and why the one time I'd seen Fa-Fa's eyes, they appeared bleary. "You have nothing to be ashamed of. Terrible pain isn't a crime. So Jay was blackmailing you, really, counting on your addiction to keep you from going to the police about his coral business."

"That's about the size of it." He cast a line in the water. "Fortunately, I'm about out of pain relief. Never thought I'd say that. When I work up the nerve, I'll tell Jimbo everything. He has a right to know, no matter how bad I look in the end. He might agree to let me go into rehab in Miami, and maybe keep my job open. Not many people would."

I cast out again, brain clicking along with the reel. "You must have had a real love/hate relationship with Jay."

"Loved the pain relief the drugs brought, but no love lost where Jay was concerned. That man was the devil. The devil himself."

WHEN WE RETURNED to Camp Iguana, I volunteered to help unload the boat until I spied Constable Nettles marching in quickstep out of the main building, Jimbo and Curious George in tow.

"Wonder if they found Jay's body. I'll just be a minute." I sprinted off to hear the latest news bulletin. "Hello! Yoohoo, Constable! Any word?"

"Oh, good afternoon, Flip. No," he said in a hurry, barely slowing down. "No news."

"Sorry to hear that." I skipped in front of Jimbo and George. "How long will the search go on?"

"This is the third day of our effort. We'll search two more days, at least, but the weather, I fear, may be a factor. We're in for a bit of a brew tonight."

"Oh, too bad, it's been so perfect. Not another hurricane, I hope."

Jimbo grunted. "Bite your tongue."

"Let's hope we don't have to go through anything as bad as that." The constable backed away from us. "I'm sorry to have to run. See you later, Jimbo. George, thank you for your candor. Sorry, I do have to meet someone."

"Someone connected to the investigation?" I called, but he whipped around and jogged away.

"Well!" George shuffled his feet. "I guess I'll go see what Henrietta's up to."

He scurried off, fast as a sand crab. I watched him, puzzled. Not one to shun the company of others to seek out his sour wife, normally George would have lingered, extracting as much information as possible.

Jimbo combed a hand of fingers through his cropped hair. "Just when you think you know how the wind's blowin', the weather vane flips around. George just dropped a little bomb on us. Told me and the constable something I'd never have guessed."

"Really, what?" What in the world did Curious George know about Jay's disappearance?

"A member of Jay's family has been on the island for a couple of weeks."

"Jay's family? Did he mention it?"

"No. Jay didn't know she was here. She didn't want him to know."

"Interesting," I said slowly, imagination whirring. "His mother? A sister?"

"No." Jimbo bent down, looking me square in the eye. "His wife."

THE AFTERNOON PASSED at the same, mud-slow pace as most afternoons, with guests trudging toward hammocks or retreating to their cabins to snooze through the hottest part of the day. Tom and I, worn out from hours of fishing in the sun, eased into the two hammocks beside our cabin and pulled wide straw hats over our faces. Through a tear in the brim, I could see flashes of boats on the water, a reminder of the serious, even dangerous business being conducted below the surface.

Sometime later, in the middle of a glorious wedding dream, I awoke with a start. Voices in the thicket behind our hut filtered through the heavy afternoon air. I listened, half awake, gradually connecting the British accents to the faces of George and Henrietta.

"Yes, George, we *will* discuss this again! We'll discuss it until you can give me some straight answers! Why didn't you tell me Jay was married and you know his wife? You never said a word."

"I told you, I promised Liza Carruthers absolute silence on the subject. I only met her this past spring, a month after our trip to Barbados. When she realized I'd met Jay there, she begged me not to tell him where she lived, or even acknowledge that I knew her. They had an awful row and she left him months ago, barely escaping with her life. She feared for her safety enough to rent a flat in Knightsbridge under an assumed name. She had a fake passport made up so she could travel here."

"But why not tell *me* you'd met her? Oh, don't answer that. You don't have to. I can read the reason all over your pasty little face. Is that why she's here now, Georgie? So the two of you can have a holiday of your own, laughing behind my back all the while?"

"It's not like that, not at all."

A boat sped by and I prayed it wouldn't drown out the argument. My eyes bugged out beneath the straw hat. Jay's wife was George's Lady of the Lake! Fortunately, the couple's acid encounter required moments of silence and when the boat passed, the fight took up right where I'd left it.

"Well, what is it like? Why don't you explain every disgusting detail to your lawfully wedded wife?"

"I told Liza that Jay had asked us to come to Little Cayman, to give our opinion of this new eco-resort he'd invested in. I knew he'd try to persuade us to kick in more than a few dollars, too, and would be frightfully attentive. Liza asked me to help her, to spy on Jay and gather information so I could act as a witness in her divorce suit. She's swimming in money, the reason Jay could make this sort of investment. He led quite the high life in Barbados, if you recall, but Liza's sure he spent what he had. She said he would never agree to a divorce without demanding a huge settlement, based on her abandoning the marriage, which could drag the thing out for years. As I said, she asked me to collect evidence against him, but we didn't know how hard it might be. Fortunately, Jay had an eye for the ladies, telling everyone he was single."

"Yes, he had a real talent for chronic lying. Like my husband."

"I am not lying, Henrietta! This is the truth! I was the one who told Liza he'd gone missing and she'd best come clean with the constable. I was afraid . . . I was afraid if she didn't, she would look . . . I would look . . ."

"Guilty? Guilty of murder? Or . . . conspiracy to murder?"

"Good God, what are you saying? You don't really think I had anything to do with Jay's disappearance!"

"I don't know! Oh, what's happened to us, George? What's happened to *us?*"

A painful silence drained the heat from the air.

"The question is, Henrietta, what has happened to you? You're not at all the woman I married. Liza . . . Mrs. Carruthers . . ."

"Don't bother trying to hide the obvious. I can see how besotted you are with this woman. But for all you know, she's using you, George, and I don't just mean to gather information! How do you know she's telling the truth? What if she planned all along to rid herself of that horrid, money-grubbing man, and use you to bolster her story?"

"You can't be serious. The man had an accident. He was drunk. He shouldn't have been in the water."

"Well! You're certainly in over *your* head, aren't you, Georgie? Or is it head over heels? Or both?"

Curious George didn't answer. But what he didn't say rang loud and clear.

# Chapter 13

THE SKY SHOWED little sign of approaching turbulence. Bare hints of steel slowly edged toward us over the horizon, the gorgeous red sunset, a near perfect duplicate of the past few evenings, primed for another knockout performance. Only the wind delivered a hint. What had been up until then a pleasant breeze stiffened and grew chilly as we made our way to the dining room for dinner.

Advised of the latest dirt, Tom preferred to sweep idle gossip under the rug and concentrate on more serious matters. "Darling, that indescribably green golf skirt is sure to turn heads."

"It is not a golf skirt. I do not play golf. It is a skort—shorts made to look like a skirt. See?"

"Whatever it is, it's certainly a bold fashion statement that will have all tongues wagging. Murder and mayhem and mysterious wives have nothing on you." He tugged at the collar of his Terps T-shirt. "Should I wear a tie? I bet Sam is wearing a tie. I hate it when he shows me up."

Sam, of course, didn't even bother to change the ratty

shirt he had worn fishing that morning or his lucky baggy shorts with the frayed back pockets. Lee dressed for dinner, however, wearing a pink flowered muumuu she'd borrowed from Miss Fizzi. They sat on the terrace, sharing a drink. The words sprang out when she spotted me. "Did you know Jay was married?! And she's here! The Wife is here!"

"Word travels fast. Just like home. What does she look like? Where is she? Boy, do I have something to tell you!"

"Honestly," Tom scoffed. "It's as if we never left Solace Glen. All this gossip. Yak, yak, yak."

"I tell you what," Sam made a hand motion like a flapping mouth, "we might as well be sitting at Garland's Bistro. You women are evil creatures." He toasted us with his beer, and leaned forward to listen.

"Constable Nettles met with the Wife," Lee barely drew breath, convinced I knew nothing, "and she's been here for two whole weeks! Jay didn't even know she was here!"

I slid into a chair and sat straight as a royal palm. "I know all about it. It's raw-ther suspicious, don't you think? Nobody knew he was married, and now we learn he's not only hitched, but the Wife is camped out nearby, spying on him. Not only that . . ."

Before I could connect the dots for Lee about Liza and George, Buddy and Dempsie strolled up. As usual, Buddy had the inside scoop. "Jimbo invited Liza Carruthers to stay in Jay's bungalow while the search goes on, said it's the least he could do. Laurie pitched a fit. Went on a regular warpath."

Lee's face lit up at the prospect of more drama. She popped out of her chair like a jack-in-the-box, and suggested we head for the dining room, no more lollygagging. "I saw the other couples go in already."

As we hurried inside, Frank called Jimbo to his table. "I hear Jay's wife is on the island, and she's gonna stay here."

"You heard right."

"That's a surprise, huh? That he's got a wife?"

Jimbo's bleached brows twisted at Frank. "Are you interested for a reason, or just making conversation?"

Frank's chummy, disarming side came through. "Ho-ho, nothing slips by you, does it? Interested for a reason, you bet. You and I both know they're never gonna find Jay. He's history. Probably as much of a relief to you as to me. What I do hope to find, however, is my money. He took my money, OK? And I'm sure his wife can help. I mean, she's got a right to his stuff now that he's dead."

"He's missing." Jimbo bristled. "Not dead. At least, not declared dead."

"Oh, he's dead," Frank replied firmly. "He's dead. And I *will* get my money back."

We breezed past Frank and filled our plates at the buffet, returning to our usual table for six, the one painted with buzzing hummingbirds. No sooner had we picked up our forks than Dempsie's round face broke into a grin, chipmunk eyes darting to the lobby doorway.

Her back to us, the Wife engaged in a somber discussion with Jimbo and Fa-Fa. A tall woman with beautiful, sleek, honey-colored hair tied neatly with a black satin ribbon, she spoke quietly. When Frank loudly cleared his throat, she turned and glanced his way a moment, giving us a view of her breathtaking profile. A strong, chiseled jaw, full lips, pixie nose, cheekbones any aspiring model would kill for, and eyes dark as magnolia leaves. How Jay could exact cruelty on this angel come to earth, or why he would ever give her up, I could not imagine.

Frank twisted in his chair, impatient to speak to her, ignoring Renata's plea to sit still and bide his time. Renata's lovely new hairstyle, I noticed, appeared tangled and unkempt. She wore the same lifeless, beige cotton dress she wore to dinner every evening. Across from Renata, Henrietta sipped a chilled martini, silent and sulky, as if every swallow added to her misery. Equally miserable, Curious George sat nailed to his chair. He dared not sneak a peek at the honey-haired vision behind him, his Lady of the Lake, and dared not lock eyes with the embittered woman by his side. He stared at the floor, contemplating a dive.

From the kitchen, Laurie swung through the door, mouth curled into a frown, in her arms another platter of shrimp for the buffet table. When she caught sight of Liza, her soft brown eyes hardened into lumps of coal.

Buddy followed my line of vision. "Laurie's none too happy, is she?"

"No," I said flatly, "she's not."

"You know, I saw them," he said close to my ear. "Jay and Laurie. The first night we were here."

"You saw them . . . together?"

"In the boathouse. I went down to store some fishing rods, and heard them. You better believe I sent Jay a message he'll never forget. May he rot in hell."

The blood in my veins stopped running. "Oh, no. Buddy . . ."

No sooner had I spoken than Dempsie threw an arm around Buddy's linebacker shoulders and giggled. "I finished that drink already! I tell ya, I'd be a dead woman if I lived down here year round! Would you get me another one, honey?"

"Sure. Sure, baby." He forced a smile the size of North Carolina, and offered to buy everyone a round.

"Hey, what's wrong?" Tom placed a hand on my knee. "You look like you've just been told gossip is illegal in the Caymans."

"I'll tell you later."

The dark, hawk eyes read every line on my forehead. "Whatever is bothering you, don't worry." He patted my knee. "I'll help." Two little words that went straight to my heart. I planted an appreciative kiss on his lips.

"Oh, *puh-leeze*. Take it outside, you two!" Before she could take the joke any further, Lee's eyes popped. "What in the world is that girl wearing?"

Tipped off to Liza's arrival and drop-dead looks, Tootie decided to show up and show off. If she were going to check out the Wife, she'd give the Wife something to check out, too. She entered the room swishing her hips, affecting Richter scales all over the world. Her favorite bloodred string bikini top left nothing to the imagination, and a matching sarong fluttered around her long legs. Crimson lip gloss drenched her pouty mouth, and a glitzy ruby barrette held her sweep of sun-kissed hair to one side. A very pretty package that hid every insecurity.

"She's acting out," I said to Lee. "It's kind of sad, isn't it?"

Lee rolled her eyes. "Oh, spare me."

Fa-Fa drew back as Tootie approached and Laurie closed in from behind. "I promised Dirk I'd ferry the *Tyrol* over to Brac for repairs. Laurie," he gently took her elbow, and ferried her away from the flash point, "he took Jimbo's boat, right? Any idea when he'll be back?"

Laurie raised her shoulders, one eye on Liza, but allowed Fa-Fa to lead her into the kitchen. Jimbo performed the introductions. "Tootie, this is Liza Carruthers, Jay's wife."

Tootie lifted her chin and flipped her hair back. "Yes, I know. Jay told me all about you."

Cool as an English cucumber, Liza said bluntly, "I doubt that very much, young lady."

Tootie rose on her painted toes. "Are you calling me a liar?"

"No, I'm calling my husband a liar. After I left him, he apparently decided to start a collection of women, neglecting to mention to them his marriage to me. You just happen to be one of the many dolls in the collection."

Tootie paled. "I don't know how you . . . I mean, we never . . ."

"Oh, I know. Believe me, I know. You started to fall for him, though, didn't you? I can see it in your eyes. I don't blame you, dear. Jay was handsome and charming and— most of the time—knew how to treat a lady. But it was play acting."

Jimbo shifted his feet. "Tootie, we have a kind of delicate situation here."

She stared at him, thrown out of her flip-flops by Liza's cool, steady gaze. "What kind of situation?"

"I need to get my husband's things," Liza answered. "*All* of his things. You have a couple of his boxes in your bungalow."

"Yes, but . . ." Tootie stammered, "that doesn't mean we . . . it doesn't mean anything."

"I told you, I know you weren't having an affair. Working in such close proximity, he couldn't hide his true colors from you for long, poor boy. Consider yourself lucky. He left some things in your care, though, didn't he? It was his clever way of using you, and making you feel important at the same time. What did he tell you? That he felt paranoid about leaving documents in his own bungalow?"

"Yes, yes!" Frank cheered from the sidelines. "The lady has a right to have her husband's things! Bank accounts and what have you."

"Frank!" Renata timidly placed a hand on his arm as if to restrain him. "This is none of our business."

"What are you talking, 'none of our business'? You heard what the lady said. Jay hid things in Tootie's bungalow. She could have my money and not even know it!"

"Wait one minute!" Unfortunately, Tootie found her voice again. "Who do you think you are, sweetie? I'm not gonna hand over Jay's stuff to some stranger who pops up from nowhere! And, anyway, he could still be alive! You're mighty quick to declare him dead, swooping in like . . . like a vulture!"

Liza sighed and turned plaintively to Jimbo. "Now, Tootie, calm down," he said. "I don't want to have to call the constable. He had a long talk with Liza here and said she has every right to collect Jay's things. That's our bungalow. You're not exactly paying rent, ya know."

Tootie stomped her flip-flop. "That bungalow has been my home for weeks, and I work around here, in case you forgot! I've *earned* my rent! And I say *she cannot come in!*"

"Tootie." Frank butted in again. "You're not on solid

ground with this one. Better let the lady have her conjugal rights."

"Oh, put a sock in it! All you care about is pinching my rear end and finding that money you gave Jay! You *gave* it to him, remember? It's his."

The friendly dining room would have turned into a free-for-all, but Tom took matters in hand. He introduced himself to Liza as a stateside attorney, and offered to accompany her, along with Jimbo and Tootie, to the bungalow. "Frank, I'm sure if Liza finds your money, or evidence of where it is, she'll inform you, and the two of you can work it out once we know something more definite about Jay."

Liza responded with gratitude. "Thank you, Tom, for your voice of reason." She spoke directly to Frank as they left the dining room. "I'm sure the gentleman who wants his money back will have satisfaction at some point. I'll do my best."

Pleased, Frank's sallow complexion blossomed into pink. He had laid his one issue on the table, and Liza picked it up. Laurie swung through the kitchen door with an offering of bread that she didn't offer anyone. Instead, she rushed to the window, eyes glued to Liza as she entered Tootie's bungalow.

"Hey, Dempsie," Lee launched the inquest, "what's your take on the Mrs. showing up and wanting to go through Jay's things? Think she's looking for anything in particular?"

"Probably his bank book, but whatever she finds, she's welcome to it, in my opinion. Can you imagine? The widow having to go through another woman in order to gather her own husband's belongings?"

Buddy grunted and slathered jam on a biscuit. "I think the lady's gonna be disappointed, that's what I think."

"What do you mean, honey? Oh, listen to that wind outside."

"Yeah, it's blowing pretty stiff. What I mean is, Jay's

been missing two and a half days. Don't you think Tootie tore through his pockets already? The constable went through his stuff, too, looking for signs he'd faked his disappearance. Didn't come up with anything."

"It wouldn't surprise me if Tootie did go through his things," I said, "but somebody else could have, too. I wonder if Liza will say something's missing." I stared out the window, tossing questions around. Was Liza searching for something in particular? Something incriminating? Something that could tie her to Jay's disappearance?

A clap of thunder boomed across the sea and found its resting place in the center of the dining room. Half the women in the room screamed. Even the men jumped out of their skin. Laurie scurried to close the doors and windows as Fa-Fa yelled, "I'd better get the *Tyrol* over to Brac! This is going to be a monster!" He raced out the door to the dock.

"Does he really have to go now?" I flinched as a bolt of lightning tore through the thickening clouds.

"Looks like it's blowing in from the southwest." Buddy peered out the window. A crash of thunder shook the building, so ferocious it left us speechless. Fa-Fa pulled away from the dock, the first drops of rain pelting his hatless head, flashes of light igniting the sky. "If he's going, he's got to go now. The mechanic who works on Dirk's boat has to have her in dock by tonight, so he can start repairs early tomorrow. He's the only one Dirk trusts to do the job right. Don't worry, Fa-Fa will get her there safe and sound, and be back by tomorrow afternoon."

The storm spurred us to finish early and run to our cabins, my juicy tidbit about George and the Lady of the Lake put on hold until morning. When Tom finally scrambled out of the rain from Tootie's bungalow, I grilled him about Liza for as long as he could stand it. He didn't have much to offer, though. He and Jimbo stood to one side talking fish talk for fifteen or twenty minutes, while Liza rifled through stacks of papers in a couple of boxes.

Tootie sat on her bed, puffing a cigarette, teary-eyed.

"Was Liza teary-eyed, too? I know I'd be, if I had to go through your mountains of paper."

"A very poignant sentiment, my love. Frankly, I didn't notice."

"For a lawyer, you're not very visual."

"They say that's the first thing to go. My hearing's still pretty good, though."

"Oh? Did she say anything interesting? Like, 'I'm so glad I did away with my cheating, wife-beating husband'? Or 'Hallelujah! Thank God, somebody did him in for me!' "

"Eh? What's that you say?"

I kicked myself. I should have volunteered to go to the bungalow with them. At least then we'd have something to go on. Surely, I could have dusted up some sort of evidence against the Lady of the Lake!

# CHAPTER 14

※

ALL NIGHT LONG the howl of the wind scraped across Little Cayman. The stinging rain poured. Thunder punctuated the ceaseless moan of the wind; bolts of lightning struck with fury. Waves pounded the beach that normally welcomed gentle slaps of water, while out on the sea, white caps rose and fell like flocks of drowning swans.

In the morning, proof of the terrible storm littered the landscape. Palm fronds and branches lay scattered around Camp Iguana. The white plastic chairs dotted the lawn, up-ended. A few slats dangled loose from shutters on the main house, and flowerpots rolled on their sides in the heavy breeze, lush blossoms of pink hibiscus reduced to shriveled fragments of slime.

"At least the sun is out." I hugged a sweater to my chest as we made our way to breakfast.

"It's still early. I bet it warms up later on. Maybe we could do a little 'snorkeling' at our secret love nest this afternoon." Tom slapped my backside and wiggled his eyebrows.

"Are all Methodists such sex fiends?"

"Only the best looking ones."

"Tom, isn't that Jimbo's boat next to Laurie's?"

"Yikes. Didn't do too well in the storm. At least they've got it secured now. Guess Dirk made it back in one piece." The boat listed to one side, a long, jagged gash stem to stern. Even Laurie's boat took a few dents during the storm, but Fa-Fa's smaller bass boat, tethered to the dock, had sunk. We picked our way past minor debris on the terrace and stepped inside to the buffet. To our surprise, PC Nettles and Arnaud sat at a table, engaged in an earnest conversation with Dirk, Laurie, and Jimbo.

At our approach, the constable rose. "A beautiful morning, but more bad news, I'm afraid. We received a report that a boat went down last night. I'm asking around the island, and stopped by to see if anyone from Camp Iguana was out on the water. The storm knocked the phone service down. We haven't been able to reach the mechanic at Brac to find out if Fa-Fa made it to the marina last night."

"Oh, no!" I gasped.

Tom, the practical one, simply suggested, "What about the boat radio?"

Dirk drummed his fingers on the table, pale as a bleached shell. "Unfortunately, that's one of the things the mechanic needed to repair. He's not answering the shop radio. There's been no word from Fa-Fa. Nothing."

"How do you even know a boat went down?" I slowly sank into a chair.

Arnaud relished the chance to convey important information, jumping into this new crisis with both sneakers. He stood, hand upon his heart. "A brave band of U.S. Merchant Marines happened into the vicinity and observed a boat go under. They could not tell the style or make of the boat. The conditions were so horrible, we can but imagine. They pushed their way to the scene of the tragedy, but alas, no sign of survivors could be found." His hand slid dejectedly from his heart, and he sat with a thud, as if the lost boat contained every last French/Irishman on the planet.

The Constable winced at Arnaud, trying to remember how good the junior officer looked on paper. "Now that we know the *Tyrol* may be missing, we'll drive back to the station and radio the police boat units. One of them can head to the marina at Brac. We'll know something soon enough."

I hated the thought of another drawn-out search. Thirty-five people, I heard, had scoured the waters for Jay the past three days. Tomorrow, the search would end. Would today be Day One of the search for Fa-Fa?

At that moment, the side door blew open. "You stole it! That's what you did! It was on the dresser last night and now it's gone! You stole it and I want it back!" Tootie's blonde head reared up when she saw Arnaud and PC Nettles. "Good! The police are already here! You there—Arnold, Harpo, Aardvark—whatever your name is! Arrest this . . . this . . ."

"Watch your language, dear," Liza purred. "I know how much you'd hate to say anything off color."

Tootie proudly fired off an impressive arsenal of obscenities.

I tapped a finger on Tom's arm. "Lee should be here."

"Oh, yes. Right up her alley."

Speak of the devil, entering stage left, Lee picked up speed at the sound of raised voices. Sam traipsed close behind, in his usual disheveled state. He made a beeline for the coffeepot, keeping one amused eye on Lee. She sidled next to me. "What's the commotion? Liza steal a bikini?"

"No, but she may have stolen something else."

"Ladies, ladies!" The constable patted the air for quiet. "What's this about?"

Arnaud wrapped his knuckles around the baton at his belt, prepared to beat either woman to a pulp. His free hand searched a pocket for his little notebook.

"She stole a sapphire ring Jay gave me!" Tootie anchored her bare feet to the floor and crossed her arms. "Go on, admit it. It's right there on your finger."

And, indeed, it sparkled.

"Honestly," Laurie spat the words, "do we have to waste time listening to this maniac rave about a stupid ring when a man's life . . ." She broke into tears.

"If you mean my husband," Liza said briskly, "there's little hope of finding him alive. As for the 'stupid' ring, it's my engagement ring. It's the only thing of value Jay ever gave me. I'm afraid I threw it at him the last time I saw him." She admired the deep blue stone.

Jimbo draped an arm around Laurie and drew her close. "Laurie didn't mean Jay. She's talking about Fa-Fa. We're waiting for word on whether the *Tyrol*'s missing."

Tootie clutched the neckline of her nightshirt. "Not Fa-Fa, too!"

"Oh, I'm sorry," Liza said perfunctorily. "I didn't know."

"Now, Tootie," Constable Nettles's chest heaved, "what about the ring? Let's clear this up before I go."

"Jay gave it to me," she whined, not very convincingly. "It's important to me."

"So important," Liza argued, "it wasn't on the dresser, as you said, but in a box of Jay's papers. Why weren't you wearing it?"

"I gave myself a shea butter treatment," she snapped. "Is that OK with you?"

"Watch it," Arnaud warned. He wiggled his baton at Tootie.

"Put that flute away," she squeaked. "Where the hell's your gun? I want this woman arrested!"

"The truth of the matter is," Liza said, ignoring the threat, "the ring belongs to me. It wasn't Jay's to give away, and I don't believe he did. He's the type who would have sold it. What do you think, Constable? What is your ruling?"

Impatient to fly away and attend to more important duties, Constable Nettles delivered his opinion. "You may keep your ring."

"Damnit!" Tootie stomped a little war dance. She glared at Liza. "You really are a vulture. Now I know why Jay . . . oh, hell!" She spun around and stormed out.

"Poor Tootie." Lee pouted sarcastically. "One less thing to wear."

"You're so compassionate," I chided, distracted by what Tootie had started to say about Jay.

A heinous crime exposed and justice quickly delivered, Arnaud warbled, "I'm very impressed, Constable! It will be a pleasure to work with you. A pleasure!" He scraped and bowed. If Arnaud expected a compliment in return, he shouldn't have. With a pained expression, his new boss herded him out the door.

"What's this about Fa-Fa?" Lee wandered toward the buffet as other guests dribbled in. Soon everyone was caught up with the latest bad news.

"Oh, heavens, not Fa-Fa!" Dempsie cried. "He's one of my favorite people! You know, he has seemed a little off kilter lately. Have you noticed, Buddy? Maybe he got sick, and lost control of the boat. Oh, this is terrible!"

Buddy nodded glumly, his attention on Jimbo and Laurie. She blew her nose on her husband's handkerchief and slouched into the kitchen, as wrung out and tired as anyone I'd ever seen.

Curious George, minus his spouse and no longer so curious, sipped his tea and openly worshipped Liza from a discreet distance. To my surprise, she walked right over to his table and sat down, his golden treasure. Sure that *his* pot of gold lay at the end of Liza's rainbow, too, Frank fell over himself with good morning wishes before drilling her about what turned up in Jay's bungalow. "We missed you after dinner last night, Liza." He hovered over her, plate in hand, hoping she'd invite him to sit down for a chat. "You didn't come back from the bungalow, but that's understandable. Must have been an emotional experience. My condolences."

My condolences went out to Renata. She trembled behind

Frank, anxious to know if the money she'd worked her fingers to the bone for turned up in one of Jay's pockets, or at least on an account number from a Cayman bank. "Yes. We're so sorry."

Frank's forehead popped beads of sweat. "Yeah, yeah. Jay was a great guy, really great. Top diver. I enjoyed knowing the guy. So, did you happen to find anything about my money? I'm sure we can get this matter cleared up pronto, right?"

Liza turned bewildered, dark green eyes on Frank. "I am so sorry to report that I saw absolutely nothing about your money. I spent half the night crying and the other half going through the papers I took out of Tootie's room. Believe me when I say I'm simply crestfallen that I didn't come across anything. You see, I hate to admit this, but Jay married me for money more than anything. He came from a good family, but hadn't a dime. The only reference to any banking activity I came across was a pitifully small checking account on Grand Cayman that he opened right after he arrived here. He had a good amount at first, drawn from our account on Barbados, but most of the funds went into this place. The history of the account shows he drained it fairly quickly."

"The way he drained his booze." Frank's rudeness knew no bounds.

"What?" Liza set her teacup in the saucer. "Jay didn't drink. The slightest taste of alcohol made him violently ill. He called it a saving grace, given all his other filthy habits."

"Add that one to his other lies!"

But Liza persisted. "No, really. I knew him for several years. Never, never did I see him drink anything stronger than grape juice. Once, someone even played a practical joke on him in Rio, and slipped vodka into his orange juice. It almost killed him. He had to be rushed to the emergency room at the height of Carnival!"

Everyone sat back to absorb Liza's revelation. How

many times had we seen Jay with a drink in his hand? Beer, Bloody Marys, wine, and rum. If Liza told the truth, and we had no reason to doubt her, then Jay's drinking added up to nothing more than a well-acted, calculated performance. I tried to think of a time he'd taken a drink from someone else, but every recollection featured Jay walking into a room, drink in hand, or Jay mixing his own cocktail from "his own stock," as Laurie assumed. And if the drinking amounted to an act—his "disappearance" could, too.

Suddenly, I thought of Tootie, and the words she started to say about Jay before she stopped herself. *"Now I know why Jay . . ."*

Could Jay be hiding close by, waiting for the coast to clear with Tootie's help? Or did he have more devious intentions? Did he, in fact, know that Liza arrived on the island under an assumed name?

I found myself staring at the Lady of the Lake, the source of Jay's dwindling bankroll. But also the source of great gain.

AFTER BREAKFAST (WHEN I filled Lee and Dempsie in on the George/Liza connection), most of us wandered outside to enjoy the sunshine and await word on Fa-Fa, although Sam and Lee, operating on the usual high level of ants-in-the-pants, opted for a bike ride. Five minutes into a lounge chair, Frank felt the same sting. He convinced Renata to take a walk with him. When I glimpsed their way twenty minutes later, the body language of the small figures in the distance beside the docks of rental villas betrayed a heated argument.

Meanwhile, Curious George and the lovely Liza enjoyed each other's company as if one didn't have a wife, hurt and fuming in a nearby hut, and the other didn't have a missing husband. The two watched the police boats plow back and forth, and waved at the people on board as if they were out diving for pearls instead of bodies. Both wore the carefree look of two people in love, out on holiday.

"Don't you find it bizarre?" I asked Tom, on the verge of a snooze.

"Wh-what?"

"Look over there. Don't stare. See what I mean?"

"Oh, yeah, that is bizarre. Two people having a conversation."

"Come on, you know what I mean. Don't you think it's strange that they both act like nothing's happened? Like Henrietta doesn't exist, and Jay is nothing to worry about?"

He yawned. "So?"

"So it's bizarre! Even if Liza doesn't love Jay anymore, the least she can do is act as if she's *slightly* caught up in the search. And look at George. He's completely mesmerized by her. Bet he'd do anything for her."

Just then, Buddy and Jimbo drew up chairs on the terrace. They waved at Dempsie, who sat near the water's edge reading a romance novel.

"There's another 'I'd-do-any-thing-for-you-dear' person."

"What are you percolating about, now?"

"Buddy." I lowered my voice. "Remember when he said he'd do anything for Jimbo?"

"Meaning?"

"Meaning he and Jay had a confrontation. Maybe it amounted to more than that, I don't know."

"So now Jay was murdered by George, or Liza, or Buddy, or all three. Why have you left me off your list?"

"You're on the B-list with Sam and Lee."

"As long as I'm not neglected."

I squirmed around. "Where did Dirk go?"

"He's probably out doing something to get himself on your A-list. Is Fa-Fa on the A-list, too?"

"Yes, although I'm praying he's OK. Dirk had it in for Jay, we know that, and we also know the power Jay had over Fa-Fa. When drugs enter the picture, anything can happen. Fa-Fa could have had a big fight with Jay and decided to add something to the oxygen mix, then grab the stash."

"My, what a street-smart vocabulary you've picked up. But I don't buy it. Fa-Fa doesn't seem the type."

"Doesn't seem the type to be a drug addict, either. And somehow, Tootie knows a lot more than she's letting on. If Jay faked his death, she knows it, and she knows where he is."

"How do you know Tootie wasn't the one to mix something into his tank? They'd had their share of public squabbles lately. Not to mention, Tootie had access and came out of the boathouse last."

"True. Maybe they'd had a bigger fracas than usual, and she decided to kill him and steal Frank's money, along with Liza's sapphire engagement ring. Anyone could tell she was lying about that ring."

"Think she's smart enough to plot a murder, and actress enough to pull it off?"

"I don't know. I just don't know."

Laurie stepped out on the terrace, nerve-racked and frayed. Jimbo offered her a chair, but she shook her head and stared mournfully at a passing police boat, hugging a sweater around her shoulders.

"She's taking Fa-Fa's disappearance really hard." I tried to concentrate on my beach book, but the words swam across the pages like a school of darting minnows. Too many questions filled my head, and too many things led to distraction. Police boats, yachts, fishing boats, live-aboard diving craft. The rustle of the breeze through palm trees and the sound of rakes, scraping up seaweed and fallen leaves. The perpetual drone of conversation, delivered on the wind and amplified by water.

Frank and Renata returned from their walk and set a straight course to Liza. Renata hung in the shadow of her determined husband. A little arm-twisting to warm things up, Frank loomed over Liza, blocking her sun. "Excuse me, Mrs. Carruthers, but we need to get a few things straight."

"Oh, please. Liza."

"No, I think for now I'll call you by your husband's name. You're cut out of the same cloth."

One side of her pretty mouth tilted, mildly amused. George shielded his eyes and wormed lower in his lounge chair.

"I'm gonna lay the cards on the table. I don't know what you think you're trying to pull, but your husband, and thereby you, took money from me under false pretenses. I gave him fifty thousand dollars on deposit to buy out his partnership interest in this resort. Now you can either give me my money back . . ."

"Or?"

"Or we'll sue the pants off you. It's the money or the partnership, or maybe even jail for you, lady, for theft and fraud."

Liza slid her sunglasses an inch down her nose. "Heavens." George opened his mouth to speak, but she tapped him to keep quiet. She could handle a gnat like Frank. "As I told you earlier, I found nothing. That is the truth. If I had found your money, or if I do find it, I assure you, I have no need of more wealth and would promptly return it. That being said, your business arrangement involved my husband, not me, in his capacity as a partner in this mosquito pit. I don't care if you invest in this place or not. That is between you and Jimbo and Laurie. If you still wish to sue me, sue away, but you'll end up holding the short end of the stick."

She batted her eyes, perhaps hoping he would blink away, but Frank stood firm, stuck in the sand, jaundiced skin reddening. Before he could say anything to worsen their chances, Renata hooked an arm through his elbow and dragged him away. "I told you this was a bad idea. If you could only keep calm and listen to me for once instead of flying off the handle."

Frank jerked his arm away, muttering expletives, glaring over his shoulder.

"Well! I do say! I say, I must say!" Curious George sputtered. "Well done, Liza! Brava!" He grabbed her hand and kissed it, just in time for a second assault. Henrietta veered into view. George gulped and slunk low in his chair, a decent imitation of a rabbit, head shaved down the middle by a whizzing bullet. Henrietta slowed, and tried to assume the superior posture she'd adopted for so many years. She clamped on the chilliest smirk she could muster under emotional stress, and faced the enemy head on. "Hello, Liza. Not out bobbing for dead husbands?"

"Henrietta!" George sat up so fast, his sunglasses toppled into the sand.

"Why so shocked, Georgie? Try looking at her without the rose-colored glasses. Take a good hard look at the woman. Enjoying the view, aren't you, Liza?" She placed a hand over her sunglasses, further shading her eyes from the sun dancing across blue water. "As far as the eye can see—no Jay Carruthers. Very tidy for you, isn't it? No messy divorce ruining one's reputation with nasty accusations on both sides. No more drain on the family fortune. Not even an expensive coffin to buy. So very, very tidy."

Liza remained unflappable, as amused with Henrietta's insinuations as with Frank's ham-handed threats.

"Henrietta, really. This is too much, even for you!" George almost grew a spine. "You used to be . . . you used to be so different, so much fun. That's what I loved about you. You were fresh and exciting and spontaneous, but over the years you've turned into exactly the kind of woman I've always found repulsive—proud, complaining, negative. I can't do anything right. Nothing pleases you."

"Re—repulsive?" Henrietta's proud posture drooped.

"Don't let her get to you, darling." Liza caressed George's hand before the astonished wife. "You don't have to play lapdog ever again."

If Henrietta didn't have sunglasses to hold them in, her eyeballs would have popped right out. "George! How could you? Oh, how could you?"

"How could he not?" Liza primly crossed her legs and pointed her nose at the sun.

George watched as his stoic wife shriveled in size like a piece of plastic wrap tossed into fire. She gripped her hands as if the tears might escape from that outlet, backed away, and fled.

"Oh, dear. Liza, I must go to her. I never expected this reaction. We've been on the outs for so long. I never expected."

"Forget it, darling." She wiggled down in her chair and glanced at her gold watch. "Good lord, I'm famished, and there's still an hour to go before luncheon. Stop whimpering, George. She'll be fine. Women like Henrietta always muddle through. Stiff upper lip, and all that. She's got a thick crust, that one."

I didn't think so at all. In my book, the one with the thick crust sat next to George. He eventually simmered down, and their shallow chatter recommenced where it had left off, before Frank, Renata, and Henrietta spoiled the sun from shining solely on them.

My friend Sally, a long time in the beauty business, often made the comment that people aren't always what they appear, and she ought to know. Rarely had I seen a woman more lovely than Liza, with a beauty as warm as the golden rays of the sun, but with a temperament as cold as the deepest depths of the Atlantic.

# CHAPTER 15

❋

"WHAT'S THE WORD?" Lee popped open a can of soda and collapsed in a terrace chair to hear what she'd missed all day. "Sam and I must have biked over this entire island twice, and back again." She looked down her nose at Dempsie and me, her sedentary friends. "Dempsie, honey, you need to throw away that romance novel and create some of your own. And you—I've never known honeymooners who needed so many naps. What will Solace Glen say when I blab about it when we call tonight? Any word on Fa-Fa?"

"No." Dempsie slapped the paperback down. "The phone service is still spotty, but Jimbo and Buddy left about twenty minutes ago to see if word had come in to the police station over the radio. I wish there were something I could do. I feel so useless." One hand fell to her waistline. She absently pinched at the roll of flesh.

Going about her business in a daze, Laurie wandered out on the terrace from the lobby and paused, waiting to remember why she'd left the kitchen in the first place.

"Laurie!" I waved her to our table. She inched forward, lips parted, quizzical, as though trying to recall our names and why we dropped by for a visit. I kept the subject up-beat. "Did you do any diving today?"

"Diving?" She went blank, voice strange and hallow. "I don't remember."

"Isn't this one of the days you normally go out with Picky?"

She jerked back, skittish, doe eyes large and luminous. "What do you know about Picky? He won't dive with any-one else. He doesn't want anyone else. You stay away from him. Just stay away." She backed into the lobby and disap-peared into the kitchen.

"My heavens! Poor thing!" Dempsie put her hand on her heart. "She's losing her mind. First Jay, now Fa-Fa. The stress is too much for her."

"Yeah, but there's something else going on here." I searched, but gave up. "She's so weird when it comes to Picky Jiffers."

"Laurie *is* weird." Lee rested her chin on a fist, brain clicking. "What if she's faking this la-la-land breakdown to throw us off?"

"Throw us off of what?"

"Maybe she killed Jay. Or maybe Picky did. Maybe they both did."

Before we could have a real roundtable discussion, Hen-rietta and Renata trudged up from the beach. The moment they saw the three of us, they hesitated, reconsidering plans to lounge on the terrace.

"Come on!" I called. "Pull up a chair."

"We're havin' a hen party!" Dempsie smiled broadly.

The hesitation melted; the ice broke. Within minutes, the five of us shared a pitcher of punch and each other's life stories. Henrietta gradually shed her well-performed reserve, vulnerable and needy in the face of a crumbling marriage. "There's never been anyone else but George. He's always been a dear, and treated me like a queen. Too bad I started acting like one. Now, I'm afraid I've lost him forever to that . . . that . . ."

"Block of ice," Dempsie offered, filling in the blank. "That's what I call her. It wouldn't surprise me one bit if she was the one who sneaked into the boathouse and fiddled with Jay's tank."

"But if she did," Henrietta blanched, "George might be implicated. Guilt by association. He may have fallen under the spell of another woman, but he certainly doesn't have what it takes to kill a man." We all cooed soothingly. "He moved his things out of our cabin this afternoon. Into hers. We had an awful row. I said terrible things. Ugly things."

I couldn't believe I didn't hear them, and *why* would George do something so stupid and suspicious?

"What will you do now?" Lee refilled Henrietta's glass. "Hold or fold?"

"Pardon?"

"Fight to hold onto your husband, or fold your tent and run back to England with your tail between your legs."

"Does he know how much you love him?" Dempsie placed a hand on the romance novel as if preparing to take an oath. "Would it make a difference if you told him you want him back, and forgive him?"

"But," Renata said sternly, "if Liza has blinded and brainwashed him so he can no longer see the open, caring heart in you, then he's not worth it! Cut him loose and take him for all he's worth!"

We stared at Renata as if the wind had swept in a winged unicorn.

"Would you do that to Frank?" Henrietta asked softly.

Renata didn't draw breath. "In a heartbeat! I told you at the spa, when you were so very kind to me, my marriage has become intolerable. I can't let that man destroy what has taken me a lifetime to build. Somehow," she clenched her eyes tight, "some way, I will find the courage to break out of this hell and live again, while I still have time. I've lost all hope, all trust. It's unbearable!"

"Wow." Lee sat back hard. "You've really thought about this, haven't you?"

Renata nodded bitterly and gulped her drink. "I haven't thought about anything else. To outsiders, Frank turns on the charm, but behind closed doors . . . well, let's just say I have my battle scars."

I shuddered. Like Garland, who secretly endured years of abuse from Roland, Renata would find the strength to walk away, I had no doubt.

"That's so brave," said Dempsie, mystified. "I wish I had your attitude, and wasn't afraid to try new things. Just the thought of leaving the house to work at a real job scares me."

"Why leave?" I looked her square in the eye. "Plenty of women work out of their homes, running businesses. Or out of their cars, like me. You're a whiz with a needle; I've seen your handiwork. Start an online shop."

"Start a Mom's Helper service," Lee suggested.

"Or sell your needlework to a local store on consignment," Renata added.

Dempsie stirred her drink with one finger, a faraway, wistful smile turning bright. "You know, I could do those things. I could do all those things."

An unmistakable voice screeched Jimbo's name. Tootie rounded a corner. She ground to a halt, confused, as if she'd stumbled upon the papal conclave. "What are you guys doing . . . together?"

"Big shock, huh, Tootie?" Dempsie poked her pink drink umbrella behind one ear. "Come yak with us!"

Tootie started forward with a huge smile until Lee sniggered, halfway mimicking, "Let's not go overboard. Got any shea butter?"

"Lee!" I could not believe her rudeness. "What's got into you?"

"Me? Why don't you ask Miss Tootie what got into Jay's tank!"

The faces around me flushed as pink as the rum punch.

Hurt and rejection filled Tootie's eyes. "Thanks, Dempsie. Maybe some other time. I was looking for Jimbo, but forget it. Just forget it."

As she started to leave, we heard the distinct chug of the camp truck, and Jimbo and Buddy jumped out, light on their feet.

"It must be good news!" Dempsie cried. "Oh, please let it be good news!"

"He's OK!" Jimbo shouted, galloping straight to Laurie, who flew out of the house. "He's OK!"

"Thank God! Thank God!" She collapsed in his arms, weeping. "Where did they find him? Did you talk to him?"

"I sure did. He had quite a night of it, quite a night. But when I told him what happened to my boat when Dirk brought it over the reef, he was relieved he got the *Tyrol* to Brac. He tried to steer around the storm and headed south. Ended up at the marina twelve hours late, but safe and sound!"

Laurie shook her head, confused. "What?"

"You can quit worrying!" Jimbo hugged her to his chest. "Fa-Fa's fine. He'll be back in time for dinner."

She stared at him and pulled away. The light dawned on us. She wasn't thinking of Fa-Fa. All this time, she wasn't thinking of Fa-Fa.

I knew it. Buddy knew it. And her husband knew it.


WHEN LAURIE WANDERED back into the safe confines of the kitchen, Buddy and Jimbo exchanged dark glances, although the rest of us erupted, prompting other guests to wake from hammocks or leave the beach, and congregate on the terrace.

"If Fa-Fa and the *Tyrol* are OK," Dempsie took Buddy's hand in hers, "then what about that other boat that went down?"

Sam yawned beside Tom, both waking up. "Who knows? Could have been somebody fishing, or a family crossing over to Grand Cayman or Brac. Or it could have been a boat like Laurie's, somebody's pride and joy, yanked away from its moorings and swept out to sea, pounded to a pulp by the vicious waves."

"Don't make me send you back to Solace Glen early, sweetie," warned Lee. "No sad thoughts."

"Speaking of Solace Glen." Tom drew a chair next to mine. "When are you two lovebirds winging your way back home? Soon?"

"Nice try," said Lee. "We're on the plane with y-o-u."

"Mmm. Miss Fizzi left no stone unturned."

The dull roar of an engine caught our attention and we cast our eyes on the sea. Fa-Fa made a wide turn and headed for the dock, behind the wheel of the *Tyrol*. Everyone cheered and waved. Dirk cantered toward the dock, the first to greet him.

"Thank goodness!" Dempsie hugged her husband before he and Jimbo lumbered toward the incoming boat. With eager hands to help, the *Tyrol* eased into her familiar place of repose, tied down and secured in no time. Fa-Fa accepted Dirk's clap on the back for returning the boat to port shipshape, despite the challenge of the storm. He placed an arm around Fa-Fa's shoulder for more serious words, a touching gesture, I thought, before Jimbo and Buddy joined in the welcome.

"Looks like another round of drinks is in order," Tom drawled. "This is getting monotonous."

We all agreed we could use a little more monotony and joined him. When the group reached the terrace, more claps on the back and hugs ensued. Dirk excused himself and hurried back to the *Tyrol* for a closer inspection. The rest of us gathered round to listen to Fa-Fa's tale of survival. Curious George and Liza blended into the herd, as did Tootie, who constantly skirmished with Frank's roving hands. I noticed him glaring at Renata at one point, seated safely among us.

Jimbo set a cold beer in front of Fa-Fa. "Tell us what

happened, from the beginning. You look pretty beat up, bro."

"Yeah, rough ride." Though shaken and ill at ease under the spotlight, Fa-Fa delivered his story straight from the hip. "When I left here, I could see the main thrust of the storm had swung closer than I'd expected. So right off the bat, I knew I'd miscalculated my timing, and there could be trouble. Sure enough, when the *Tyrol* cleared the reef, she started to struggle, and I almost brought her back in, but I figured she'd have a better shot at Brac than staying here, tied to the dock and getting pounded. In hindsight," he reddened, "it was probably a really stupid decision."

"No, no, don't say that," Jimbo chided. "You came through with flying colors."

Fa-Fa continued, humble, almost apologetic. "I set course for Brac at the fastest clip she could muster, but the storm caught up with me. Waves a good ten feet or higher. She was taking on water, the radio was out, so I figured my best bet was to swing south, try to skirt the edge of the storm, avoid the brunt of it. I went miles and miles, I don't even know how far, but the farther I rode, the better the weather. So I ended up well south of here, and it took all morning to make my way back to Brac. A police unit pulled up about the same time I did, and sent word to the constable. End of story. Not too exciting in the telling, is it? But believe you me, it was a night I'll never forget."

"You're damn lucky." Frank blew a ring of cigar smoke in the air that settled ominously on Renata's shoulders. She coughed into her hands. "A boat went down last night, you know."

"Yeah." Fa-Fa stared at the floor. "I know. The police told me. There but for the grace of God . . ."

The weight of the moment didn't escape us. He'd survived a very close call.

"Dinner's ready," a small voice announced.

I didn't recognize the speaker and turned around, surprised to see Laurie. She did not sound like herself; she didn't even look like herself—silky, black hair flat, features washed out and pale.

"My lord," whispered Dempsie, "she's gone right over the edge."

Jimbo crossed the terrace in a split second and wrapped an arm around her frail shoulders. "Thank you, darlin'. Listen, you look tired. Why don't you let me take over? You go on to our room and get a little rest. It'd do you good."

She nodded, pliant as clay, then suddenly trilled, "Jimbo! Why didn't you tell me he was back!" She swept into Fa-Fa's startled embrace and threw her arms around his neck. "They found you! You're safe! Oh, Jay, thank God, you're safe!"

Every jaw dropped to the floor, including Fa-Fa's. "No, Laurie," he said softly, tiptoeing through a minefield. "It's me. Fa-Fa. Remember? I took the *Tyrol* out last night, and got mixed up in that big storm?"

Jimbo gently eased her out of Fa-Fa's arms and into the main house. No one knew what to say until Liza sniffed, "Someone ought to tell her the man wasn't worth a breakdown."

Buddy knocked a fist on the table. "Do you mind! The woman's out of her head, thanks to that bastard you called a husband."

"I assure you," she replied drolly, "I had no hand in making him a bastard. I'm sorry for Jimbo and Laurie, but they never should have trusted Jay. There isn't a person here who's not better off without him. He did us a favor, stepping over the edge into oblivion. Isn't that true, Georgie?"

George nodded obediently, and they departed for the dining room, leaving cares, and the sore subject of Jay, behind, already debating the crucial issue of the menu. Renata rose and shuffled after Frank, followed by the others. But the Solace Glen crew lingered outside a few moments with Dempsie and Buddy.

"What is wrong with this picture?" Lee slapped a hand on her hip. "Have you ever?"

"That Liza truly is the coldest block of ice," Dempsie fumed. "Buddy, honey, I'm glad you gave her what-for."

Buddy stewed in silence. Finally, he said, "I'm going to have a little talk with the constable about her tomorrow. She had something to do with Jay's disappearance. I'm sure of it. She's too cool a cucumber."

"She's certainly that, and more," said Tom, "but I wouldn't jump to any conclusions."

*Good advice,* I thought. Buddy seemed overly anxious to point a finger at Liza. Did he sincerely believe she killed Jay? Was he protecting himself? Or someone else?

The evening meal proved a somber affair, despite the steady flow of good wine and perfectly prepared food. Laurie's pathetic display served as a reminder that the loss of life—even one as seemingly worthless as Jay's—always carried repercussions. Stepping in for his wife, Jimbo did his best to show a brave face, but Fa-Fa, rattled by the scene and exhausted from his battle with Mother Nature, retired early. We never saw Tootie or Dirk; the high spirits of the staff at Camp Iguana had sadly deflated.

To compensate, Lee and I dialed Garland's Bistro at peak Friday evening hours, as promised. Tom and Sam lounged on the deck of our cabin, pretending to tell fish stories, but tuned in to Solace Glen all the while.

The hubbub background noise of the Bistro gradually subsided as Hilda and Garland screamed at everyone to hush up for the latest tropical advisory. They clicked on the speaker phone.

"Hey, Flip"—an Egghead—"did they find the body yet?"

"Is anybody under arrest?" Another Egghead.

"Do they think you did it?" Suggs.

"Is Tom gonna be your lawyer?" Both Eggheads and Pal. Gales of laughter.

Lee told them to can it. "I'd bet anything the bimbo did it."

"How much you want to bet?" Pal shouted. "Right now, it's even money on the bimbo."

"Stop calling her that." I placed full blame on Lee. "Her name is Tootie. She didn't kill anybody. Nobody killed Jay. Nobody's killed anybody. It was a diving accident."

"Says you." I couldn't even convince an Egghead.

"Doesn't anybody want to know how we are, and how the honeymoon's going?"

Dead silence.

"I think that carpetbagger from New York did it," Miss Fizzi clucked. "What do you think, Margaret?"

"I put two dollars on his wife."

"Renata? Why in the world?"

"It's always the one you least expect. Ivory! What do you think?"

"I think . . ."

"Nobody cares!" boomed Screamin' Larry. He belched to emphasize the point. "The guy's brain exploded."

"The island is beautiful," I said, taking a whack at decent conversation. "The water's so clear, you can see all the way to the bottom when you're fishing. Tom caught a huge bonefish the other day."

"The wife did it!" Melody yelled, joined in chorus by Sally and Tina.

"How do you even know about her?"

"Lee called Sally two hours ago," Tina piped. "Is Fa-Fa single?"

Lee's mouth spread sheepishly. "I dipped into the ladies' room with my cell before dinner."

"Then what's the point of this call?"

"So you could tell about the water."

"George did it! He's the killer!" Ivory trumpeted. "Get away from me, you drunk fool." I heard a slap and a thud, and a call for Egghead assistance.

"We'll call again tomorrow," I said wearily, "but trust me, all bets are off. There will be nothing to report."

# CHAPTER 16

✳

SATURDAY DAWNED BRIGHT and beautiful, full of promise. "I think my appetite has increased tenfold since we stepped off the plane. No Halloween candy for me tomorrow." I plopped a mound of scrambled eggs onto my plate.

"That's right." Tom helped himself to pancakes and a slice of bacon. "Thankfully, I'd forgotten about Halloween. I hope they don't force us to wear anything out of the ordinary."

"Don't be difficult. You're not the only person on earth who hates costume parties. If push comes to shove, you can borrow that thing you call my golf skirt and go as me."

"There's an idea. You could borrow my hangover and go as me."

Jimbo poked his head out of the kitchen to ask if we needed anything, my opportunity to ask about Laurie. He swallowed hard. "She's OK. She's been under a lot of stress, ya know. We'll see how it goes today."

"We're very worried about her." I had hoped for more detail.

"Thank you. I appreciate that. I'll pass on your good wishes." He retreated into the kitchen.

I waited a moment and hissed to Tom, "I don't think she's OK. I think she's anything but OK."

He nodded without comment, and we sat down to eat our breakfast. Dirk drifted in with Fa-Fa. They loaded up plates and sat at their regular table, silent and morose. Fa-Fa's sunglasses covered his eyes, as usual. He ate his meal in slow motion, either from pain or heavy medication.

Sam and Lee traipsed in, rolling straight from bed to the breakfast table. "Yo, Fa-Fa, my man." Sam slapped him on the back. "How about a little reef fishing this morning?"

Fa-Fa bent forward, white as a sheet. "Sure. Sure. I was wondering what we'd do today to keep Lee out of trouble."

"As long as you keep me out of a bar." Lee pinged two fingers against her temple. "I feel like one big boo-boo. Too much punch in the rum punch."

"Speaking of boos," I called out to Fa-Fa, "anything special happening around here for Halloween?"

"Yeah, Jimbo wants to do something for the guests. We figure you deserve it. Thought we'd throw a costume party and dinner out on the dock."

Tom scowled and examined my hips. "What size do you wear again?"

A few other guests trickled in, minus Henrietta, and the various spats and alliances played out. Buddy and Dempsie took their seats at our table, and Buddy revealed what I feared, that Laurie had slipped deeper into a black abyss, speechless, staring out to sea as if she expected Jay to appear over the horizon, walking on water.

From across the room, Renata had a point to make with Liza, her friendship with Henrietta spawning courage. "Perhaps you'll be so good as to leave Henrietta alone until she can make arrangements to go back to London."

Frank grunted, but stayed out of it. If the subject didn't involve his money, why bother?

Liza sawed primly into a breakfast sausage. "Why would I bother her?"

"Apparently, you did last night. You threatened her."

Buddy's eyebrows shot up, at attention. He stopped eating and listened closely.

"I did no such thing."

"Yes, you did. She told me so herself, after you left. You tried to interfere with her separation arrangement with George. You threatened her and said you could make things very messy and expensive if she didn't cooperate. Now, why would you do that, a woman of such wealth? Why would it matter to you if George loses the shirt off his back? Could it be you're running a little low on funds? Did Jay drain more than you care to admit? It could take a very long time, I imagine, for Jay's life insurance to kick in, especially since no one knows if he's really dead. But, somehow, I think you know."

Liza dropped her fork with a clang. I expected her fury to focus on Renata, but strangely enough, she fixed her blue-hot gaze on George, as if he bore the fault, and had led her down a rosy path of doom and gloom. He, in turn, gave full attention to a poached egg, which he edged around his plate like a photographer positioning a subject for the best shot.

Liza reclaimed her sure footing. "I'm sorry if Henrietta misconstrued anything I said. I only meant to reason with her, and avoid future heartache for the three of us."

George quit shoveling and beamed up at her, his angel atop the Christmas tree once more. "Good show, old girl! That was good of you."

A no-show for some time, Tootie suddenly made a grand entrance, perky and bouncy as a toddler. She sashayed up to Fa-Fa and threw her arms around his neck, half sisterly, half flirtatious. "King Neptune! Back from your most excellent adventure." She plucked a bacon bit off his plate and popped it in her mouth. "God! I feel like I haven't eaten in a week!"

Lee grumbled, "What's got her motor running all of a sudden?"

Thrilled to see his favorite pair of legs in action again, Frank egged her on. "Whoa, look who's out of the gate running! How are you, missy? Care to join us?" He scraped his chair back, hoping she'd take a running leap for his lap. Renata's shoulders hunched.

Tootie shook her blonde mane and swished to the buffet, stacked her plate, swished back to the table, and squeezed into a chair between Fa-Fa and Dirk. She'd at least raised the energy level in the room, and we turned to a discussion of plans for the day. While Sam and Lee settled on reef fishing, Dempsie pressed Buddy to take her to the one museum on the island, or for a walk through the Salt Rock Nature Trail, but he insisted on paying a visit to the constable. With no desire to disturb the peace, Tom and I opted for a trek to our private beach following a couple of hours of books and magazines.

Around eleven o'clock, we approached the kitchen for a picnic basket. While the staff prepared sandwiches and fruit, Tom ambled to the bar to find a bottle of wine and a corkscrew, which I cleverly reminded him about. Nothing's more frustrating than finding yourself at a nice picnic with no way of entering the wine bottle short of gnashing your teeth.

Picnic and accoutrements packed into our backpacks, we set out on bicycles for Preston Bay. The temperature climbed into the low eighties, and the sky wore its brightest blue dress. Clumps of purple and red blossoms practically sizzled as we passed, the sun stroking all colors with an extra coat of high gloss. We slowly pedaled past the one house of worship, the one museum. As we passed the Booby Pond (about which, thankfully, the man I married would never make tasteless jokes), frigates flew overhead.

"How many red-footed boobies does it take to change a light bulb?" asked the man I thought I married.

"I don't know. How many?"

"Boobies don't have hands, silly."

"You made that up on the spot, didn't you?" I accused him. "Don't deny it. I thought I married a mature adult. This is what comes from having Sam around."

"What about Lee? Emotionally, she can't be more than seventeen."

Through the thickets, an occasional flash of water gleamed as we continued our pedaling. Cattle egrets and show-stopping snowy egrets stood in their favorite spots, stilt legs rising from the edges of little ponds.

"I have a confession to make," I said, lazily zigzagging the handlebars of my bike.

"Is it a true confession? Or a pretend confession, designed to cut me to the heart?"

"It is a true confession." I clapped the back of my hand across my forehead. "I don't like birds. You know that line in the old movie, *The Producers*? Zero Mostel sees some pigeons and says, 'Boids. Doity, disgusting boids.' That's how I feel in a nutshell."

"You don't even like toucans, or parrots?"

"Nope."

"You don't like the brilliant, colored markings of the mallard duck floating atop the Chesapeake Bay? You don't like peacocks?"

"Certainly not. Their finery means nothing to me. They are all 'doity, disgusting boids.' "

"I suppose this means boobies are out, too."

"Most assuredly. I am not enticed by their hideous red feet."

Tom ruminated on this startling confession, and finally remarked with some bitterness, "I wish I'd known this about you before."

"Before what?"

"Before I found myself shackled to you for all eternity."

We left it at that, having exhausted the topic of boids. As we approached the grass airfield, a plane made its slow, even turn and filtered down from the sky like a drop of distilled metal.

"More happy campers," I said. "Too bad Camp Iguana is full up. We could do with some new faces."

"You mean more backs to stab. Mealtime has become quite stressful. It's not good for my diverticulitis."

"I didn't know you had that."

"I've decided to develop it. Then we'd have something else to talk about besides boobies."

I threw him one of my disdainful Presbyterian sneers. We pedaled past the tiny building known as the airport and soon arrived at the turnoff for Preston Bay, parking our bikes in a clearing at the foot of the path. We trudged up the incline with the backpacks and snorkeling gear. The empty beach looked none the worse for wear from the battering of the big storm. We spread a beach towel in the sandiest area we could find, so much of our special place rocky, and decided to eat half our picnic before a swim. We munched in silence, admiring the incredible scenery. So peaceful. So tranquil. If you had asked me to paint the ideal honeymoon scene, this lovely spot would fill the frame. After a few minutes, Tom yawned and leaned back on his elbows.

"Oh, no, you don't." I wiped the last crumb off my lips and stood up, pulling him with me. "We're going to get some exercise if it kills us."

"It might kill *me,* but I suppose I can work up the energy. You know, except for fishing and a stroll or two on the beach, I had high hopes for a sedentary honeymoon." We donned rubber masks and plastic feet once more, laughing at our absurd appearance. "It would be a crime to take our picture. How fortunate we left the camera in the cabin. Open up." He stuck the breathing tube in my mouth. "This device could come in quite handy when I've had all of you I can take."

We plugged toward the water and eased beneath the surface. The sea, calm and resplendent, allowed us to splash easily around the rocks and coral, sighting more fish than ever. My head swung like a pendulum. I didn't want to miss even a minnow in this stunning, undersea world, my eyes zipping as fast as the fish, enjoying every second. I swam in this happy state for a good twenty minutes when something caught my eye. A bright orange net bag caught between two waving plants. I took a deep breath and dipped close enough to grab the bag and pull it loose. Fairly large, the size of a cotton mop head, and surprisingly heavy, I dragged it to the surface and swam to a shallow area where I could stand and take a peek.

Tom surfaced. "What have you got there?"

"I don't know. I saw it caught between a couple of plants." I pulled open the enclosure. "Looks like different kinds of coral."

"Mmm. Maybe the bag belonged to Jay."

"That's a creepy thought. Guess I better hand it over to the constable."

"Good plan. Are you hungry?"

"I'm always hungry."

We dragged the orange bag of coral up to our towel and resumed our picnic, adding the delight of a good red wine. Before the sun, the wine, and the food could lead to the inevitable nap and sunburn, I tapped Tom on the shoulder. "Come on, hup, hup, hup! We're going for a walk. I want to soak up as much of the island as I can."

"You are merciless." But he stuck water shoes on his feet. We began our hike on the edge of the sea, weaving between rocky spots and venturing up to the sand now and again. Relaxed and carefree, Tom sang catch phrases of old songs and challenged me to name the tune, or quizzed me on trivia, usually in a category he knew I could handle, like state capitols or the sixties. Not fifteen minutes into our trek, I glanced up to see something washing in and out at the brim of the tide.

"What's that? Driftwood?" I bent down and picked up the object, about the size of an express mail envelope.

"It looks like a waterproof pouch. Maybe Margaret and Lindbergh mailed us their ugly Chihuahua."

I unzipped it and gasped. "Tom! Look at this!"

He drew close and immediately removed his sunglasses. "Don't touch anything in that bag."

I handed it to him gingerly, and watched, open-mouthed, as he rolled the contents back and forth for a better view. "Looks like a pharmacy in here, there are so many bottles of pills."

"What about the money?"

"Oh, yes. There's a *lot* of money. Several thousand dollars, at least. Maybe tens of thousands."

I stumbled backward, mouth dropping wider. In that instant, a large form further down the beach grabbed my attention. Something floating in the water. "Tom . . . is that . . . ?"

"Yes."

We ran the twenty yards or so over the rocky beach to the dark, undulating lump. Tom handed me the pouch and waded into the water. He pulled the bloated form to the edge as I stood by, breathing hard, horrified.

"You better run for the constable right away." He turned his face from the body. For a moment, I thought he would be sick. "Tell him . . . we found Jay."

"Jay?" I froze, confused, expecting diving gear and a wet suit. "But he's wearing clothes."

"Not only that." Tom stared at me. "He was stabbed to death."

# PART THREE

✳

# Bold Swimmers

# CHAPTER 17

✳

THE PEACEFUL, TRANQUIL scene of the perfect honeymoon in paradise dissolved. The neatly framed landscape of azure seas, blue sky, and pebble beach crumpled
into chaos. A blitz of crime-scene photographers, consta-
bles, and technicians with latex hands trampled the quiet as
Tom and I sat slumped against each other on the picnic
towel, stunned.

Hovering on the fringe of the towel, notebook in hand,
PC Arnaud Fitzgerald glowed at the impressive responsibility handed him—interviewing Tom and me. Not that PC
Nettles hadn't talked to us at length, but when pulled to the
center of the crime scene, he couldn't hide his irritation at
the leech by his side.

"PC Fitzgerald?" He spoke Arnaud's name as if world
peace depended on the young man's response.

"Yes, sir, PC Nettles!" Arnaud snapped to attention.

"I would appreciate your further investigation of the
Scotts' experience here. Would you be so kind?"

Arnaud hiked up his pants. For close to thirty minutes,

an eternity, he circled us like a shark. He considered us dangerous suspects, subject to fleeing. I wondered where Arnaud thought we'd go, how we'd make our great escape. I could see the wheels spinning under his tufts of yellow hair. How we'd race to our bicycles, lugging snorkeling gear, picnic trash, and a sandy towel. How he'd trip us up. How, as we cowered against each other in the dirt, he'd brandish his baton like Dirty Harry and growl, "Do you feel lucky, punks? Well . . . *do* ya?"

Sadly for Arnaud, he got nothing much out of us. Instead of deadly, insane criminals, he had in custody two middle-aged honeymooners out on a snorkeling picnic. There wasn't even any food left, and we refused to share the last drop of wine.

Something in the salt air inspired him and he barked, "Why did you choose *this* beach to have your picnic?"

Tired to the bone and missing his power nap, Tom replied, "It's a good place to make love."

Arnaud reacted as if Tom had confessed to murder instead of marital bliss. He puffed his chest out. "So. It wasn't merely a picnic you had in mind."

I murmured in Tom's ear, "He may not look like an Egghead, but he could be their lost triplet brother."

"You are so judgmental."

"Yes, but you're smiling." I ran my tongue over a piece of ham, permanently stuck between my teeth. "Jeepers, Arnaud. We *are* on our honeymoon."

He didn't see that as an excuse. "This end of the island is very deserted. No one comes here."

"Except," Tom offered, "the tourists who are specifically directed here by their genial hosts."

Arnaud contemplated this, unable to imagine why the local innkeepers would do such a bizarre thing.

"Arnaud," I lay back on my elbows, "surely, you're not so new to this island that you haven't brought a lady friend down here for a little spooning. Attractive guy like you."

The compliment pleased him—I doubt he'd heard it

before—and his dull, gray eyes, small balls of lead, rolled up and down the length of the beach, picturing himself with such a friendly lady.

Constable Nettles completed his business and plodded toward us. Jay's body—like a dolphin inexplicably driven from the ocean to the shore—was hoisted into a body bag and carried off the beach, erased from the poetic scenery. A landscape that would never again be the same for me.

No one connected to Jay or Camp Iguana had permission to leave the island. We sat in the dining area with other guests and staff, gathered together once more by PC Nettles for an "exchange of information." Arnaud shadowed his boss like an extra appendage, writing furiously in the little notebook, barely able to keep up. The Constable called for calm, his principle occupation at times, and explained yet again that this time we had a murder investigation on our hands, not a diving accident. He focused a great deal of attention on Liza, to her annoyance and Buddy's delight. Elbows on knees, he leaned forward, looking for all the world like a defensive end, ready to spring forward and sack the guy with the ball.

"Why am I the only one questioned in this accusing manner?" Liza asked indignantly, eyeballs burning into Buddy. "Why not him? Or her? Or *her?*" She aimed a long fingernail at Tootie, who flicked a cigarette lighter, and squeaked, "Vulture."

Frank wasted no time. "Hey, Constable, you know that money in the pouch is mine. You know that, right?"

PC Nettles denied knowing any such thing, and tightened his focus on Frank's relationship with Jay, and his whereabouts on the night of the storm, sending Frank into spasms and Renata into a deep depression. The strain of the past few days had taken its toll on her. She wrung her hands, occasionally biting a nail. "How do you know Jay was killed the night of the storm?"

"It stands to reason. We know he didn't have a diving accident on Tuesday. We know he faked his disappearance and swam ashore. Obviously, someone stabbed him to death between Tuesday and today. The storm hit the island Thursday night, and the best estimate of death, given the state of the body, is within the past forty-eight hours."

"Oh, gross," said Tootie. "Do we have to talk about his body?"

Liza's green eyes hit the ceiling. "The fact that there *is* a body is the sole reason we're here!"

"It's the *only* reason I'd be in the same room with *you*. Vulture."

"Tension between the women," Arnaud jotted excitedly, unable to contain his zeal. "You there, the foreign couple, when was the last time you saw Jay Carruthers?"

"Arnaud," PC Nettles ground his teeth, "everyone here is a foreigner. This is a vacation resort." He bobbed his head at George and Henrietta. "I apologize to our visitors from England."

Henrietta leaped away from George as if he had small-pox. "We are no longer a couple, and I have nothing to add to this discussion. I barely associated with Jay except for two very brief conversations about investing in this awful property, which is why he suggested we come. We were not interested, and Jay dropped it. The day he disappeared, I was with Renata at the spa. Thursday night, I went straight to our cabin after dinner, and never left because of the storm."

"Constable," George's voice cracked like a schoolboy's, "can't you allow my wife to leave for London?"

"Soon to be *ex*-wife," Henrietta said quietly.

Liza rolled her eyes. "Why do you still call that woman your 'wife'? It grants her a respect she doesn't deserve."

As Henrietta burst into tears, Laurie wandered into the room wearing a white sundress with yellow daisies splashed across the fabric, seemingly right as rain. Jimbo flew to her side. "Laurie! You should be in bed, sweetheart. You need to rest."

"Oh, I'm fine! What a fuss you make over me!" The plastic smile and the glazed expression announced to anyone with a grain of sense that this woman had lost hers. "I need to see about dinner before Picky calls. He wants to schedule a night dive. Look, everyone is waiting on me. I feel terrible. I simply feel terrible."

No one said a word until Arnaud patted his stomach. "I could do with a bit of something. Haven't had time to eat a bloody olive all day."

The constable suggested he leave at once, and stuff a very large olive down his throat, but Arnaud, caught up in his first homicide, vowed to stay until the murderous cows came home. He turned to Laurie. "May I ask you . . ."

"No!" Jimbo cut him off. "Can't you see she's not well?"

We remained soundless as Jimbo led Laurie out. PC Nettles displayed no emotion, no annoyed tick of the eye or grim frown, no expression of sympathy or doubt. Nothing to give himself away. "Everyone went straight to bed after dinner? No one braved the storm?" Several bodies twisted uncomfortably. He picked one. "George? Were you safe and sound in your cabin Thursday night or not?"

"I can tell you for a fact he was not!" Mascara dripped down Henrietta's lineless face. "That was the first night Liza stayed here, and George sneaked out of our cabin. You thought I was asleep, didn't you, George? But I saw, I saw where . . ." She broke into tears again and collapsed on Renata's shoulder.

Liza powdered her pixie nose. "Of course he came to me. Who wouldn't, given the choice?"

Poor George. He couldn't decide which looked worse for him—the fact that he'd tried to hide his whereabouts on the night of the murder, or the fact that he cheated on his wife and had lied about it from the beginning. Under the scrutiny of a police constable, even a white lie scorched into black.

PC Nettles received this new information from Henrietta

as if she'd merely divulged her shoe size. "Yes, thank you. George, will you and Liza vouch for each other on the night in question?" When he meekly nodded, Liza arched a triumphant brow at Henrietta and smirked. "You'll both verify you stayed in the bungalow all night?"

"Yes, well, except for . . ."

"Except for a brief time," Liza interrupted. "I'd forgotten a piece of luggage and we drove back to my apartment to fetch it."

The constable paused and focused on an empty chair, deep in thought. "Who else braved the storm that night?"

"I did." Dirk raised his hand. "I took Jimbo's boat out for a scientific dive. As you know, the *Tyrol* had a few problems to iron out, so Fa-Fa took her to Brac for me. We both got caught in the storm."

"Where were you exactly?"

"I started out at Marilyn's Cut, and had to struggle back to camp. The reef, it was very dangerous. I barely made it through the pass. The boat took a bad gash on the side."

"Did you see other boats before or during the storm? And Fa-Fa, did you?"

"No," they replied in unison. Dirk hurriedly added, "From what I've been told, neither one of us made it near the area of the Merchant Marine and the boat that went down. We saw nothing."

"Nothing," Fa-Fa repeated faintly. He'd probably downed more than a few pain pills after his ordeal.

"Constable," I itched to join in, "if Jay faked his disappearance, then he could have been killed by someone who discovered his ruse and wanted him dead. Someone who thought the body would never be found, and we'd all think he drowned in a diving accident."

"That is certainly one possibility. Or he was killed by someone involved in his scheme, whatever that amounted to, out of passion."

Passion. Heads swiveled toward the women in Jay's life, and the men he'd angered. Liza had rejoiced at his death.

Did he come to her demanding more money, and find himself at the wrong end of a knife? Did he plan to run off with Tootie or Laurie, but instead betrayed one or the other and suffered the consequences? More than one head rotated toward Frank, George, Dirk, Fa-Fa, Buddy, and Jimbo, who had just stepped back into the room.

"There's something I don't understand."

The constable sighed. "Yes, Flip?"

"How did Jay end up in Preston Bay in the first place, with the bags of coral and money and drugs. Was he on a boat? Was he killed in the bay, or dumped there? Was he meeting someone, or trying to escape from someone?"

"All good questions." PC Nettles granted me the tiniest smile as a reward for my sleuthing. "Arnaud, you should take note. These are logical questions, questions that do have answers. And someone in this room, I daresay, knows every single answer to every single question."

# CHAPTER 18

✳

I SAT ON an outstretched towel on a beach chaise, watching my legs turn pink, and poring over the notes I'd written on one of Tom's legal pads.

"You're as bad as Arnaud." Tom swiped a fly away from the straw hat that covered his face and rolled over on his stomach. "I hope the backs of my legs eventually match the color of my knees."

"Too bad we can't hook you up to a barbecue spit."

"Very ingenious, Arrrr-no. Must come from the French side of you."

"We're *Scott*ish, remember?" I flipped a page and started a new heading: TOOTIE. "At least the police gave us the rest of the afternoon off. I only wish we could hear the results of the autopsy before tomorrow morning so we'd have something significant to add to our Bistro report tonight. And I thought we'd have nothing to tell!"

He turned his head toward me, handsome features hidden by the hat. "I know you're dying to try out your theories of the case on me. Go ahead, pull!" He raised an index finger, preparing to shoot my first theory out of the sky before it had a chance to fly.

"Try to keep an open mind."

"Yes, ma'am." He aimed the trigger finger at me.

A couple of police boats still plowed the water, searching for any debris from the mysterious boat lost in the storm. "I wonder if Jay was on the boat that went down."

"Could have been. Stands to reason."

"Do you think he stole it, and was trying to get away? But the owner discovered him in the act. Stabs him—ugh! Ugh! Ugh! And then, looking down at this pool of blood messing up his boat, realizing what a horrible thing he's done, he sets the boat adrift. Jay's body tumbles out. Voilà! The honeymooners stumble across the carcass and all the loot."

"We didn't exactly stumble across it. We're clumsy, but not that clumsy." His finger shot one across the bow. "Pull."

"OK, second theory. He was stabbed to death someplace on land, placed on a boat, and set adrift or motored out to sea. The boat capsizes, he washes up after the storm."

"Theory number two probably requires a conspiracy."

"Yes, but maybe not a preplanned conspiracy."

"For example?"

"For example." I swished back a couple of pages. "Jay sneaks into Liza's cabin during the storm. They fight, she stabs him, Curious George waltzes in, and Liza convinces him to help dispose of the body. Aiding and abetting, as you legal eagles like to jabber. They vouch for each other. No one's the wiser."

"Mmm. Not bad. Pull."

"Third theory. Jay promises Laurie he'll run away with her, absconding with Frank's money and whatever else they can make a buck on—the coral, the drugs. But he double-crosses his paramour. She discovers the ruse, and discovers him—hiding out at Preston Bay. He is killed on the spot."

"What about the lost boat?"

"Pure coincidence. It broke away from its mooring or dock, and went down with no one on board. Nothing to do with Jay."

"Uh huh."

I popped his bare leg with the back of my hand. "Are you falling asleep again?"

"No, you violent wench. Can't you tell the difference between sleep and mulling?"

"Oh, you're mulling."

"Yes, I am. You throw theories at me left and right, I deserve to mull."

"Then I'll leave you alone and work on theory number four."

"You do that." He switched his head to the opposite side. "Let me know when you decide to take me off the B-list, too, and add me to the A-list. I think I deserve a promotion." With that, he mulled himself into a nice, long snooze. Just as well. He never would have approved of theory number four.

Time to ring the Belles.

LEE COULD STILL ride a bike without using her hands. "Whoo-whoo-whoo! Look!" She pulled ahead of the pool of women in her wake. "I'll be doing this when I'm ninety-five, you watch!"

"I won't care," I intoned flatly. "I'll be dead."

"Don't you wanna live to be a hundred, Flip?" Dempsie huffed and puffed, almost weaving into Renata, who squealed and laughed like a nine-year-old.

"Not if it means sitting around all day watching Lee totter off a bike, acting like a big showoff. We'll spend our weekends shuttled around by the Eggheads in their ambulance. Isn't that a happy thought, Lee?"

"Let's see, when you're one hundred, I'll be ninety-three, and the Eggheads will be . . . about Miss Fizzi's age. Think what they will have learned by then."

"Who *are* these Egghead persons?" Henrietta clutched her chic sun hat to her head and tried to steer. "Your little town sounds so enchanting. And too, too comical."

"Oh, honey," Lee doubled over, "you don't know the half!"

A familiar voice rang out from the bushes ahead of us. "Slow down! You are breaking the speed limit!" Arnaud leaped into the road and planted himself directly in front of Lee, radar gun in hand. "You are traveling at a rate of speed of . . . *umph!*"

Lee sailed into him, arms above her head, and landed with a thud on his sprawling body. She stared into the wide, astonished gray eyes. "Arnaud, you scared the bejesus out of me."

He was splayed across the asphalt, a pinned frog in biology class. "Would you *please* get off?"

"Why? Aren't you comfortable?" Shameless, stooping so low as to flirt with Arnaud. Anything to avoid a ticket. She moaned to cover the giggles and waggled up.

Arnaud checked both arms for scratches and bite marks. "I don't know what kind of place this Solace Glen is, but in my country, we show respect for each other and the law."

I put my lawyer's-wife status to good use. "Exactly what law did we break, Arnaud? In case you hadn't noticed, there are no speed limit signs. Plus, we are on bicycles, in case you didn't notice that, either."

Dempsie straddled her bike and popped her gum, reminding me of Sally and the minty smell of her breath as she cut hair. "What's that gadget you got there, Arnaud? You find a weapon of mass destruction?"

He wobbled to a standing position and wiped his paws across the rear of his khaki shorts. "It's a brand new radar gun." He wielded the device with surprising agility.

"You don't say." Lee took a step forward, wearing her sauciest mantrap smile. "It's so . . . powerful."

"Stand back!" Arnaud ordered. He raised the radar gun, prompting Renata and Henrietta to duck.

"You better do what he says," I warned Lee. "The Force is strong in this one."

But to her, Arnaud posed little challenge. Quickly reduced to a driveling slice of pulp, he promised to show up at the Halloween party the next evening as Lee's spare date.

Time served, we commenced our rip-roaring tear through the countryside, stopping for ice cream before putting theory number four to the test. On the curb outside the general store, Dempsie licked the drip off a strawberry cone. "What was Arnaud doin' out in public, anyway?"

"Guess he irritated the constable's nerves for the fiftieth time today and got set loose."

Henrietta grinned. "Poor boy would have terrorized every soul who passed by, but now he's run home to fret about what to wear to the costume party tomorrow night."

"As your date," I reminded Lee. "So you know he'll wear something . . . powerful."

"I deserve to be impressed."

A man pulled up in a jeep, nodded hello, and stepped inside the store. Renata followed him with her eyes, attacking a fudgesicle as if it were the last thing she'd eat on earth. "I bet the store clerk here knows everything about everybody on this island. Reminds me of our first laundromat. I knew everything you didn't want to know about the neighbors."

"Yeah, bet so." I idly swirled my tongue around a cone of pistachio almond for a long moment. "You know, that gives me an idea that will save us a *lot* of time." I sprang up and whisked into the store.

A couple of customers milled around the shelves, but the store clerk had time on her hands. A pretty redhead with a band of freckles across her nose and a heavy Irish brogue, she rose from a stool when I approached the counter. "May I help you?"

"Yes. Mind if I ask you a couple of questions?"

"You need to know directions? You go this way, you go that way, you're in deep water."

I grinned. "No, no directions, thanks. I was wondering," I parked my elbows on the counter as if I might stake a claim, "you know about what's going on at Camp Iguana?"

The bright eyes glowed. "Hell, yes! A murder! That's all anybody's talking about."

I figured as much. I might as well have been talking to Melody in Connolly's Jewelry Store on Center Street in Solace Glen. "Has the constable talked to you?"

"Only briefly."

"Do you know a man named Picky Jiffers?"

"Aye," her eyes fluttered, "that millionaire nutcase. He walked into the store the first day he arrived in September, took one look around and said real haughtylike, 'I've seen cleaner horses' arses!' Then he left in a huff, never to return. When he discovered our Miss Laurie, what a grand diver she is and how kind, he made her his personal secretary. Paying her extra to do things like grocery shop, he's so antisocial. She was happy to do it, and would have, anyway, out of the goodness of her own heart."

"What does Picky Jiffers look like?"

"A little on the tall side, good physique, repulsive black goatee and slick black hair, like he'd got his head stuck in a barrel of oil. Wore big sunglasses and a silk scarf tied around his neck. Ridiculous in this heat."

"Know where he lives?"

"He rented the new villa near the east end of the island, sort of isolated, way past the Southern Cross Club. Got a red roof, last house down the road before you reach Sandy Point. He's supposed to be there until the end of November."

I thanked the sales clerk and joined my new tribe of Circle Ladies. Dempsie's chipmunk eyes lit up. "Did you find out anything? I know that's what you were doin,' you snoop."

"I gave her the idea," Renata bragged.

"Mount up, ladies." We pushed off simultaneously. "I found out just what we need to know to put theory number four into action. Follow me."

We picked up speed, sneakers pushing bike pedals at a moderate clip down Guy Banks Road, turning east along the edge of the island, past South Hole Sound. Several lovely homes drew our attention, a few smack on the edge of the gorgeous, aqua water. We sped past the Tarpon Pond with its prehistoric loveliness. All the while, only a couple of vehicles passed by, traveling in the opposite direction. At last, the pavement ended, and the wheels of our bikes ground into a packed sand road that stopped only when land met water at the very tip of the island. After a quarter of a mile, we jumped off and walked until spotting the turnoff. A red tin roof showed through the brush, cactus, and trees. A narrow dirt path made up the driveway, almost as rough as the passage leading to Camp Iguana. It ran through thickets as high as fifteen feet. We walked slowly, concocting different versions of introducing ourselves to Picky Jiffers while Dempsie fretted over trespassing charges. Renata suggested the old Hansel and Gretel story—boo-hoo, we are so stupid and lost, but Henrietta thought of a better excuse—the wrong address for a beach party.

The drive gradually widened, and soon we stood staring at a lovely pastel yellow home, two stories tall, with impeccable landscaping. The structure almost sparkled, brand new and freshly painted. I glanced around for signs of a car or jeep, but the carport beneath the house stood vacant, no vehicle parked on the side. Through the carport, the white beach gleamed. A long dock extended over still water.

"Hello?" I waited. No sound.

"Hello?" Lee echoed. Nothing.

We knocked down our bike kickstands and crept up the stairs to the front door, pausing on the landing to regain both breath and cool. Through a set of windows, we peered into a living room. Clean and neat, the room looked every bit the high-end rental property, with perfectly matched upholstered furniture and a large entertainment center against one wall. Artsy silk flower arrangements poked out of massive vases in two corners. Through open French doors, a dining room contained a Swedish-style distressed white set of table and chairs. Nothing appeared out of place.

"You'd never know a normal, sloppy man lives here," Lee whispered.

"That's because he's not normal," Dempsie whispered back. "This is creeping me out. Maybe we better go."

Lee shushed her and rang the doorbell. We listened for the tread of footsteps. I rang a second time, and Henrietta a third. Silence, but for the rustling of the breeze through the surrounding foliage and the distant lapping of waves.

None of us looked forward to the trek back to Camp Iguana, trudging down the quarter mile of dirt road, kicking up dust and dehydrating into skeletons. I wiped perspiration off my neck with a bandanna. "Too bad Little Cayman's Howard Hughes didn't open the door, suppress his revulsion, and invite his uninvited, sweaty guests to sit on the back porch under a ceiling fan."

"The least he could have done was leave a pitcher of icy lemonade outside the door for us," Henrietta puffed. "Renata, dear, you're kicking dirt in my face."

"I'm doing you a favor. When it mixes with your sweat, you'll have a mud pack, just like the spa."

We laughed and agreed to take a swim the moment our feet hit Camp Iguana. Theory number four would have to wait.

WITH THE AIRPORTS and ports advised of our temporary confinement, the Camp Iguana inmates felt like well-treated prisoners, limited to the lovely boundaries of Little Cayman. We could bike and swim, snorkel and fish, but we also had to put up with more questions. During the evening meal, PC Arnaud Fitzgerald paid us a special visit.

"What's he doin' here?" Buddy groused. "Did he bite through his leash and run away?"

As a matter of fact, he had. We soon realized that Arnaud relished a little investigation time all his own, hoping to score brownie points with his new boss. Jimbo dropped subtle warnings at each table to cooperate, at a minimum, but if Arnaud whipped out a flashlight to shine in our eyes, we could feel free to knock it to the floor. As we sat down to dinner, Arnaud's pink grapefruit cheeks swelled in anticipation. Who to grill first—the chickens at that table? The lamb kabobs over there? The slabs of steak sitting against the wall? He pigeon-stepped to the squabs, smacking his lips.

"You are the New Yorkers, and you are the woman from London," he announced, as if they did not know.

"And you are disturbing our dinner." Henrietta cracked a napkin like a whip and tossed it into her lap, employing her most regal air.

Arnaud clicked his ballpoint pen in return. "Police business cannot wait." He ran one finger down a page of his notebook. "Henrietta. Henrietta. You *hated* the deceased, did you not?"

"Oh, for God's sake. Go away."

In a slump ever since the constable decided to hold on to the pouch of money pending the outcome of the investigation, Frank growled, "Hit the road, buddy."

"Ah, yes," Arnaud's upper lip curled, "the ugly American."

"*Excuse* me?"

"I have a question to ask you, Ugly American. Since our last meeting, I have discovered some new evidence about you."

"Oh, really?" Frank shoveled a forkful of mashed potatoes into his droopy mouth. "What might that be?"

"On the night of the storm, you were not in your cabin the whole evening, were you?"

Renata lost all color, and Henrietta listed toward Frank, a question mark in her eyes. He knocked a fist against his chest, banging potatoes down his windpipe. "I'm sure I got up once or twice to go to the community john."

"Or to Jay Carruthers's bungalow, perhaps?" Arnaud rocked back on his heels, stubby nose in the air, lead eyes gleaming.

"What? I . . . I don't know. I may have passed that way. It was dark. There was a storm."

"Someone saw you go into the bungalow at a very late hour, when all good little Camp Iguana guests should have been fast asleep." Arnaud paced around the table, hands behind his back, boring into Frank like a stage Sherlock Holmes, building to a crescendo. "What were you looking for? What did you find? Who did you see? Was it Jay Carruthers, the deceased? Did you stab him with your American pocketknife?"

"Arnaud," Jimbo tried to cut in, "remember what I said about bothering my guests? I told you to wait until tomorrow."

"Is there some reason you don't want the investigation to make headway?" Arnaud pointed his sharp blue ballpoint pen at our host. "Where were *you* the night of the storm, Jimbo? You never said. You and your wife left the room this morning before that vital information could be extracted."

"I know where he was!" Tootie waved her arms in the air and rose high on her toes as if she might do a gymnastics routine across the center of the dining room. "I know where *everyone* was that night, and what *everyone* was doing! I'm dumb like a fox! I know about *you,* Jimbo. I know you and Laurie had a huge fight about *her* that night." She jabbed a finger in Liza's direction, the squeak in her voice rising rapidly. "Then you left camp at about two in the morning with *him.*" She jabbed another finger at Buddy, causing Dempsie to gasp. "And I know George and Liza left together, but it wasn't for a 'brief time' like she told the constable this morning. And I saw *you,* Frank. You snuck into Jay's bungalow after George and Liza left. You stayed in there at least twenty minutes. When I checked, you were gone, out the back way, I guess. Back to your cabin like the big rat you are."

I thought Arnaud would burst into applause over his star witness. "And where were *you* all this time, Miss Tootie, that you happened to observe this startling amount of activity?"

"I was in the bathroom, giving my hair a hot oil treatment!" She grabbed a blonde strand of material evidence and held it out for us to witness. "It takes at least two hours!"

At last, Arnaud had found the right lady friend to take on a picnic to Preston Bay. He practically levitated, a giant soap bubble rising above us. "Jimbo, I must ask for details. What did you and Miss Laurie argue about on the night of the murder?"

Jimbo, completely disgusted, but utterly defeated, heaved a sigh. If he didn't answer now, he would only have to answer tomorrow, or the next day, or the next. "Like Tootie said, we argued about Jay's wife, Liza, staying here at the resort."

"Yeess?"

"And we argued about Laurie's relationship with Jay."

Tom groaned, incredulous that Jimbo would admit such a damning fact. Laurie's affair put both of them under the spotlight.

Arnaud whirled around, making sure everyone in the room heard. "Your wife was having an affair?"

"Yes. Yes, she was. I think it's best to come clean, and tell the truth now that we know what happened to Jay."

Arnaud pursed his lips and closed his eyes. He had struck a chord in himself he enjoyed playing. "An affair. An affair. So, Mr. Jimbo, you had every reason in the world to want the deceased to become the deceased."

"Look, I didn't kill him."

Tootie went for broke. "But Laurie did!"

Every spine in the room snapped ramrod straight as Jimbo exploded. "What the hell are you talkin' about, Tootie! Laurie couldn't hurt a sand flea!"

"Ha! Gimme a break! I don't buy her tropical depression.

The whole nervous breakdown routine is nothing but a cover. I think Jay faked his disappearance to get away from her, to have his freedom, but she found him and stabbed him. If she couldn't have him, she didn't want anybody else to have him, either. That's what I think!"

Arnaud clapped his hands together in self-applause. He'd done it! He'd solved the case! Then he heard the muffled snickering from the Solace Glen crowd. "What do you people find so amusing? A man was killed!"

"Yes, Arnaud," I tried to let him down easy, "but you haven't got any evidence that Laurie committed murder. Didn't you hear what Tootie said? This is what she 'thinks.' It's a theory. A theory based on jealousy, nothing more."

You could almost hear the hiss of Arnaud's inflated ego as it shriveled. No picnic for Miss Tootie.

Jimbo, worn out and ragged, pulled Arnaud toward the exit. "We've had about enough for one night, Arnaud. Jay was probably alive at some point on the night of the storm, but I didn't see him. I didn't kill him. And neither did my wife. Now, good night. Time to go."

But Arnaud didn't budge. He glimpsed over Jimbo's shoulder at a figure in the opposite doorway.

"Hello, everyone! I hope you had a lovely day!" Barefoot and wearing a swimsuit, Laurie started making her rounds with a pitcher of iced tea, chatting as she moved around the room. "The weather was perfect today, don't you think? I really should call Picky tonight for a dive under the stars. Oh, I see the kitchen forgot to put the plantains beside the conch chowder. We'll have that taken care of right away."

"Laurie, honey," Jimbo practically tottered toward her, "please come back to our room with me. The best thing for you right now is rest. I told you—no diving." He attempted to take the pitcher of tea.

"No, no, I need that. What are you thinking?"

"Isn't it a little heavy?" Fa-Fa rose to the occasion. "Why not let me pass it around?" She stared at him, smiling sweetly, as he gently pried her fingers loose and took the pitcher. "There, now. Isn't that better?"

"Oh, Jay, you're always there when I need you."

I could see the quiver on Jimbo's lips. Arnaud did a double take. "Jay? But that's . . ."

"And guess what, darling?" Laurie reached up and touched Fa-Fa's smooth cheek with her hand, and held it there. "Picky Jiffers asked me to dive again tomorrow for a whole day! No husband to fret about. No slave labor. No nasty mosquitoes and complaining guests." She wrapped her arms around Fa-Fa's neck and held on tight. "Oh, Jay, I can't wait until we're free. Free. Free. Free."

AS THE MEN in our lives engaged in group therapy, the kind that involved fish talk and an ocean of beer, Lee, Dempsie, and I sat on the terrace under the stars and called upon a different technique to lift the blues.

"Are you gonna eat that whole piece of pie?"

"Yes, I am. Are you gonna finish that chocolate cake?"

"You betcha. Where'd the ice cream go?"

"Was that yours? Didn't have a name on it."

With the last crumb gobbled, we slumped in our chairs and patted bulging stomachs. "Bet I'm hungry again in an hour." Dempsie yawned. "I am worn out. Worn out! Honestly, I get mad whenever I think of that stupid Arnaud insinuating Jimbo and Buddy killed Jay. Buddy says they were just driving around in the truck gettin' drunk while Jimbo poured his heart out. I tell you what, between Buddy worrying about Jimbo, and both of us worried about Laurie, it's a wonder I don't have a stroke."

"I've never seen anybody literally lose her mind before," I said. "It's so pitiful, and I don't believe she's faking it like Tootie believes."

Dempsie agreed. "I wouldn't wish it on anybody, even if she did cheat on my husband's best friend."

"Ditto." Lee unbuttoned the top button of her pants and

exhaled. "I don't know who killed Jay, but I do know one thing. Miss Tootie hasn't got the brains to stab a meat loaf."

"Lee, stop it. Talking ugly about people doesn't help."

"Well, was she such a big help tonight—blaming Jay's murder on a woman clearly out of her mind?"

Dempsie sucked the night air into her lungs. "I wonder if Laurie's gone crazy because . . . she did kill him. What if Tootie's right, and she found out he was sailing away without her, and had swindled her the way he did Frank?"

"That's my third theory," I bragged. "It would really help if we could hear the results of the autopsy. Lee, did you steal my thunder and call the Bistro already?"

She popped loose the second button on her pants. "You know I did. I couldn't wait. Everybody was tickled pink to hear about the stabbing. The bets have doubled, and the money's on Liza. Did you know Ivory knocked Screamin' Larry out cold last night?"

"He had it coming. Hope he doesn't retaliate and blow her house up, but at least he's not a stabber."

"Shoot," Dempsie pouted. "I'm gonna dream about stabbings and sunken boats all night long."

"Me, too." I gazed mournfully out to sea.

"Not me." Lee popped open the final button. "I'm gonna dream about fudge."

# CHAPTER 19

❋

"HAPPY HALLOWEEN." I snuggled against Tom, his dark eyes blinking away sleep in the early morning light. "I did plan on going to the party tonight as a murder suspect, but there are so many to go around at Camp Iguana, I wouldn't stand out."

"You do so love the limelight."

"That's why I'm the town maid. Every day is a Hollywood production with me as the star."

"You're my star, anyway."

I kissed his cheek. "Well, sweet poet, what shall we do today? We only have today and tomorrow left."

"I know. Too bad we can't spend these last two days absolutely alone."

"Are you bemoaning the fact that Sam and Lee are here, or the fact that we're tied up in a murder investigation?"

"Both. Still," he threw off the covers and stretched, "no use crying over spilled rum. I'm starved. How about you?"

"Say no more."

Even though Tom and I skidded into the dining room a

few minutes after seven, a few other guests milled around, bleary-eyed and on the prowl for coffee or a strong cup of tea. Henrietta and Renata picked up mugs and a single helping of fruit each. As they stepped out on the terrace, Henrietta crooked her finger my way. I excused myself from Tom. "What is it?"

"Renata left Frank. She stayed in my cabin last night."

Renata's firm jaw told me she had no other choice. "I did it. I really left him, and I will not go back. Last night . . ." She almost couldn't finish. "Last night was the last straw."

I gave her a hug. "Don't worry. We'll keep you safe. You're not alone."

"One other thing," said Henrietta. "Constable Nettles is here. Shhh, we're escaping."

"Really?" Maybe I could slip in a little interrogation of my own. "Where is he?"

"In the kitchen with Jimbo."

"Flip!" Tom called from the breakfast table, and I stepped back inside. "No gossip on an empty stomach. Come on and eat. We need to fatten you up before we go home to Solace Glen, otherwise, people will say I abuse you. I can hear the old ladies tut-tutting about it now. 'Flip doesn't look the same since she married that cruel lawyer. She's so thin and weak, she can hardly fly on her broomstick.' "

"Very funny. Listen, the moment Constable Nettles walks through that door, he's mine."

"What a disturbing thing for a bride to say on her honeymoon."

As we ate, the door of the kitchen swung open and Fa-Fa appeared with a fresh pitcher of orange juice. "Hey, Fa-Fa," I said brightly. "How are you today?"

He paused over the simple question, eyes shadowed by the sunglasses, no spark of life. "OK, I guess. Not quite right as rain, but I've felt worse."

How much worse, I could only imagine. "Are you in

any pain? You took such a beating during the storm. How are you recovering?"

"I honestly don't think I'll ever recover from that night. Well, better get back in the kitchen." He started forward, but hesitated. He did not want to deal with the constable, no doubt, but threw out another excuse. "Right. Just thought of something I have to do in the boathouse." Shaking, he set the pitcher on our table, and crept out of the dining room.

"What do you make of that?" I asked Tom.

"Good orange juice."

"You don't have any curiosity at all, do you?"

"You, my dear, have enough for both of us. My nose stays clean. You can poke yours in all the mud piles you want."

Before I had a chance to break the conversation into an argument, Constable Nettles entered the room. He drew up when he spotted me waving frantically, like a motorist stranded on the side of the road. I gulped the food in my mouth. "Mmm! Constable! What's the latest, if you don't mind me asking?"

His two muscular shoulders rose and fell as if he did, indeed, mind, but responded courteously, "I'm sorry to have nothing to report, but I should hear the results of the autopsy sometime later this morning."

"And the missing boat?"

"That is still a mystery. We've contacted almost everyone on the island. There are very few leads left."

"Is there a reason you're here so early?"

He smiled indulgently. "Yes, I hear my young associate paid the camp an unexpected visit last night, and managed to ruin everyone's digestion. I apologize for that. I will say, however, the evening produced more than one interesting link in the chain."

I sat back and let Tom ask the questions, having reacquired his curiosity. "Such as?"

"Such as the absence of Jimbo and Buddy during the

storm, Frank's entry into Jay's bungalow, and of course, Laurie's affair with Jay. These things I did not know before. To think, Arnaud may have possibilities, after all."

"Do you really believe any one of those people is capable of murder? A stabbing, at that? So brutal."

"And personal. You saw the body yourself, Tom. Obviously, there was a struggle. More than one cut marked the upper torso."

"But not many, and only one looked deep enough to kill a man. Again, do you think any of the people you've named is capable of stabbing a man to death?"

"That's not for me to judge. I can only compile a list of suspects and make as thorough an investigation as possible, which is why I needed to speak directly with Jimbo. He's been most cooperative. Laurie, unfortunately, is another story." He mopped his bald head with a handkerchief. "I must leave you now, and find Buddy and Frank. First their dinner is disturbed, now their breakfast."

Before he could dash away, I blurted, "Will you let us know the results of the autopsy? And another question, are the guests free to leave yet?"

He hesitated. "That will depend upon the guest. Have a nice day."

TOM SOUGHT THE closest hammock after polishing off two plates of food. He even drank decaffeinated coffee so as not to interfere with the pleasant prospect of the sun on his face, feet dangling over the sides of a swinging bed. His last words before oblivion were, "Please, please, please. Buy me one of these for Christmas."

I tried to leaf through a fashion magazine, but the bruised orbs and white lips of skinny models in flimsy clothes only reminded me of ghosts. I threw down the magazine and shoved off for a walk on the beach. Throughout my leisurely hike, the different "links in the chain" the constable had referred to rattled around in my head, and I pondered my A-list.

Frank, still on probation for assault and battery over a deal gone sour, could have discovered the missing diver before anyone else the night of the storm. He could have argued with Jay over the money, stabbed him, and yet Jay managed to escape. I breathed a sigh of relief that Renata made the brave decision to walk out on this abusive man.

George and Liza might have acted in concert. Using an assumed name, Liza had the time and the brains to discover Jay's disappearing act. She certainly never relished the role of grieving widow. If he'd suddenly reappeared, the blood in her veins ran cold enough to take a stab at fate. On the night of the storm, did she and George really return to her apartment to pick up luggage, or did they drop something off—into the sea?

George and Liza weren't the only two running around in the storm. Jimbo and Buddy, the closest of friends, willing to do anything to help each other, also hit the road that night. Jimbo had reason enough to rid himself of Jay, and Buddy could have gone along for the ride. No psychologist, I couldn't discern if Laurie's breakdown bore the markings of the real thing. Was she Jay's victim, or was he hers? Did Picky Jiffers fit into this ugly picture?

Regardless of Lee's low opinion of Tootie's intelligence, I recalled her behavior before and after Jay vanished. Clearly attracted to him, she had not borne his humiliating treatment well—the hurt in her eyes at the pool, followed by anger. The high mood after the storm. Had she seen Jay that night? I couldn't imagine she'd stab a man, unless in self-defense.

Fa-Fa and Dirk both had issues with Jay. With drugs involved, anything could happen, and Jay's illegal harvest of marine life on Dirk's own boat struck him like a viral infection.

By the time I returned to our cabin at Camp Iguana, my short walk had stretched out to a good hour and a half. No guests lounged around the pool or on the beach. The dock harbored no boats. The hammock rocked in the breeze, empty. On the bed, I found a note from Tom. "Gone fishin' with the boys. Dragged me kicking and screaming. Be back for lunch."

I addressed the piece of paper in my hand. "I guarantee you one thing, Mr. Scott. After lunch, the hammock be damned. We are going on a bike ride to find another secluded spot in paradise."

I touched a finger to one red shoulder and pulled down the bathing suit strap. Proof of the burn, a white stripe ran down the skin from neck to breast. I scrounged around for the suntan lotion and massaged it in, too little, too late.

"Hey, Flip, you in there?"

"Come out, come out, wherever you are!"

I stuck my head out the door. "Yes, ladies?"

Dempsie carried a paper fan, just the type Miss Fizzi sported to church. "We decided Renata could use a stiff drink."

"Don't forget me." Henrietta had replaced her tight chignon with a cascade of reddish curls.

Dempsie waved her little fan in the air. "I wish all of y'all lived in Raleigh. There are too many Baptists in Raleigh. You have to be so good all the time."

"Gross." Lee stuck her tongue out. "I would hate to live in a place where everybody knows what side of the bed you sleep on, and what time your mail arrives, and what seeds you plant in your garden. Wouldn't you, Flip?"

"Oh, definitely. We're so lucky to live in a big metropolis where we just blend into the sidewalk and nobody notices a thing we do. And no one in Solace Glen would ever dream of injecting themselves in someone else's honeymoon." I joined the crowd.

"Wait, hold it." Dempsie reached into a pocket and pulled out some lip gloss. "The sun burns my mouth to a crisp if I don't do this every ten minutes. Tootie told me about this stuff."

"Where is Tootie?" I glanced around the empty grounds

of Camp Iguana. "She's kept a low profile since Arnaud's heroic effort to solve the case last night."

"Too bad he didn't," moaned Dempsie. "Buddy's been jumpy as a flea since then."

We reached the patio and the bar area. "Ghost town. Guess we better sign the honor roll." Lee picked up the clipboard. "Good thing we don't have to write down what time it is."

"You'd lie, anyway."

"Got that right. Even if I wrote down Sam's name instead of my own, he'd see the bill at the end of our stay and say, 'Man, I must have had a really good time.'"

We settled down on the terrace with cans of soda and a bottle of dark rum. "It's so quiet around here today." I made a slow circle in my chair. "Where is everybody?"

Lee unscrewed the cap off the rum. "The boys are fishing with Fa-Fa, that's all I know. I swear, if Sam says fishing is better than sex one more time, I'm gonna whup him upside the head."

"Tom doesn't actually say it, but I know he believes it."

Renata blushed, hands fluttering to her cheeks. "I've never really had any close girlfriends before. I didn't realize women talked about . . . you know."

"It's a whole new world, honey," Dempsie patted her hand. "You wouldn't believe the things I hear my boys say. I've washed their mouths out with soap so many times, they blow bubbles when they talk."

Henrietta threw her head back, and for a joyful instant, she owned laugh lines. The laughter distilled into a sigh. "I suppose any chance I had to have a family is shot to blazes now."

"Don't give up the ship." Lee poured an extra jigger in her glass. "From what I've seen of Liza, she's going to stab herself in the foot sooner rather than later."

"Interesting choice of words." I sat up straight as a flagpole, as much from the industrial strength cocktail Lee mixed as from the sight of Constable Nettles and Arnaud approaching.

"Must be looking for Jimbo." Dempsie raised her fan and waved, motioning them to join us. "I guess he's with Laurie. Hope she's feeling better."

Constable Nettles and Arnaud slammed the doors to the police jeep and made their way around the main building to the terrace. The constable greeted us in his relaxed, gentlemanly style, but Arnaud screwed up his nose at the bottle of rum.

"Arnaud's shocked. Shocked," Lee whispered. "Maybe he'll have a stroke."

"I'll drink to that," Dempsie said, smiling between clenched teeth, still mad at him on Buddy's behalf. "Hey! Lookin' for Jimbo?"

"Jimbo, Laurie, and a few of the guests, besides."

"Anyone at this table?"

Arnaud referred to his notebook. "You are Buddy's wife, are you not?"

"Yes, is something wrong?"

Constable Nettles took over. "I simply wanted to ask if you knew what time your husband left the cabin the night of the storm, and what time he returned."

"I couldn't tell you. I didn't want the thunder to keep me awake, so I took a sleeping pill. Knocked me right out."

"What time was this?"

"About nine-thirty. When I woke up the next morning, around seven, Buddy was right there next to me, fast asleep."

"Did he tell you what he did when he left the cabin?"

"Exactly what Jimbo told you. They left in the truck and drove around drinking a six-pack and talking about Laurie and Jay. You know, something two best buddies would do under the circumstances. Jimbo needed to unload."

"What else did he unload that fateful night?" Arnaud couldn't help himself.

Dempsie glared a hole through his anvil forehead. "Knowing my husband and Jimbo as I do, I believe they are telling the truth. That's all I have to say."

"Thank you," said the constable. "Now, can you ladies tell me where Jimbo is?"

We didn't have to. Jimbo raced around the corner and drew up short. He bent over, caught his breath, took two paces back, two paces forward, whirled around and finally saw us staring. "Constable! Thank God, you're here!" He crossed the yard in a single bound, and clasped two hands on the constable's shoulders. "Laurie's gone." He gasped for breath. "Her boat's gone, too. I just tried to reach her on the radio, but she's not answering."

Constable Nettles blinked, as if the words "Laurie's gone," read like pure fiction, and had no place in his ordered, investigative world. "How do you know she's gone?"

"I *know!* She's nowhere in the house or on the property. Look for yourself! And see, her boat's gone! She doesn't let anyone use it, not even me. It was here this morning."

I jumped out of my seat and offered Jimbo a chair, but he refused to sit still. He paced, one hand clutched to his chest as if his heart might fall to the floor. "We woke up early, and she promised me, she *promised* me she'd stay in bed and rest. She even called Picky and cancelled their dive today. You've seen how things are. She's sick! I thought I'd convinced her she needed rest and quiet more than anything."

"When did you notice she'd gone?"

"About fifteen minutes ago. I've been tearing around searching, then I remembered her boat and saw it's missing. She's gone."

The constable turned to us. "Have any of you seen Laurie today?"

I'd been on a long walk, so engrossed in my thoughts, I didn't notice any boats speeding by. Lee and Dempsie had shoved our husbands off on a fishing trip with Fa-Fa at nine o'clock.

"Was Laurie's boat there then?"

Lee bit her lip, thinking hard. "Yes. Yes, it was. The boys took Jimbo's boat since Fa-Fa's boat is there by the boathouse, getting patched. And a half hour earlier, Dirk left in the *Tyrol*."

"So as of nine this morning, the only boat at the dock was Laurie's?"

"Yes."

"None of you saw Laurie leave in it? Alone, or with someone?" When we all shook our heads, he said, "Surely, someone must have seen her between nine and ten o'clock. Are any other guests about?

"I think Frank's in our . . . his cabin," said Renata.

"I'm not sure where George is," stammered Henrietta, "but I'm sure he's with that woman. Jay's wife."

"Arnaud, let's snap to it."

Jimbo fell in step with the constable and Arnaud. "She's not well. God knows what she may do. She could be diving all alone, searching for Jay, she's so mixed up in her head."

We watched anxiously as they knocked on Frank's cabin door, and strained to see the nod of a head, or a smile indicating, Aha! Yes! I know exactly where Laurie is! But Frank, groggy from sleep, only shook his head. Just then, the men motored in from fishing, and our three husbands sauntered up to the terrace, comparing the size and weight of their catches, while Fa-Fa tramped to the boathouse to store equipment.

"What's going on?" Tom kissed my cheek. "Looks like Camp Glum."

"I'm afraid it is. Laurie's missing, and so is her boat. She's not answering the radio, and she cancelled her dive with Picky Jiffers. Jimbo's out of his head with worry." The happy, red faces grew somber.

"Damn!" Buddy watched Jimbo run from cabin to cabin, checking each one, just in case. "Somebody must have seen something, for God's sake. Has everybody been questioned?"

Henrietta gazed toward the bungalow George and Liza shared. "No, not everyone has been questioned."

"What about Tootie?" Renata glanced around. "She keeps pretty close tabs on people. Maybe she saw Laurie leave."

The drone of a motor drew our attention to the water, and the *Tyrol* rolled into view. Lee shaded her eyes from the sun. "There's Tootie, now. With Dirk."

We moved toward the dock and waited for the *Tyrol* to pull in. Dirk hopped out and secured her lines while Tootie managed the steering. They gathered their belongings and approached our group, along with Fa-Fa, wearing the same baffled expression.

Constable Nettles moved into the center of our circle. "Good, you're all here. For those recent arrivals, I have some distressing news to report. Laurie has gone missing, and so has her boat. She's not answering her radio, and we have no idea if she's alone."

Dirk appeared dumbfounded, and Fa-Fa tilted backward as if pushed by unseen hands. Tootie dropped her beach bag on the dock and popped open a tube of lipstick, always at the ready to keep those lips shiny in any emergency. She polished her lips as she spoke, making her squeaky words even more incomprehensible. "I don't get it. I mean, Laurie's so off her head, it's understandable she'd wander away like some farm animal lost in the snow like you read about in Wyoming, but her boat's another story. I saw it, and it's not with her, wherever she is." She applied a second coating. "I saw it while Dirk was studying groupers—no thank you, I don't need to see *that*—and from where I was sitting, I'm pretty sure that awful Liza and dumbbell George were winging their way to Grand Cayman."

"Are you sure about this?" The constable moved toward his jeep radio, just as Arnaud swung down from Liza's bungalow.

"I think those two have skipped! There are only a few clothes in the cabin," he reported breathlessly, "but no sign of a purse or wallet or anything of value. There are two large suitcases in the cabin, but no small carry bags, like most travelers have."

"But what about Laurie?" Fa-Fa breathed almost as hard as Arnaud. "Does this have anything to do with Laurie?"

"I don't know, but we're going to find out." As the constable rushed to his jeep from the dock, we huddled around like sheep. He grabbed the microphone and pulled the cord as far as it would stretch, alerting a unit to the fleeing boat, "possibly stolen," and its passengers, "possible murder suspects."

Henrietta clutched her chest. "This isn't like George at all! He's a poodle. He could never kill a man. It's that woman! That iceberg! She's responsible, I'd bet my life on it. Not George." She appealed to us, wailing, "Not Georrrrge."

Renata offered a hand and a shoulder. "Come on, now, buck up! Don't worry. This has got to be a terrible misunderstanding."

Jimbo paced around the jeep. "Look, I can't sit around here twiddlin' my thumbs. I've got to go look for her."

"Of course, of course you do." Constable Nettles appealed to us. "Do *any* of you have the slightest idea where she might have gone?"

Two places popped into my head. "You could try Picky Jiffers's villa. Even though she cancelled the dive, she might have changed her mind, or have been confused." I didn't want to name the second place, the spoiled scene still fresh in my mind. "There's a chance . . ." My mouth went dry. "Try looking at Preston Bay."

# CHAPTER 20

❄

THE KITCHEN STAFF managed to provide lunch for Camp Iguana's guests, despite our growing reputation among the islanders as the lowest of criminal types. Adulterers, drunks, murderers, and conspirators. Arnaud, no doubt, had a hand in shaping local opinion. He'd gleefully bounced into the jeep with Constable Nettles, while Jimbo and Buddy piled into the truck. Dirk and Fa-Fa, whispering as they walked, hustled off to shower and shave before lunch, promising Jimbo they would take care of preparations for our Halloween party on the dock that evening.

"Party?" Tootie's eyes boinged around in their sockets. She knocked ash off her cigarette. "Are they serious? That is the dumbest thing I've ever heard."

"You ought to know," Lee sniped under her breath.

"I heard that." Tootie marched over to Lee and looked down, a good three inches taller. A jet of smoke streamed out the side of her mouth. "Look, I don't know what your problem is with me. I've never done anything to hurt you.

Yet every time I turn around, you're saying something mean and nasty about me. I may not be the smartest girl in class, or as pretty as you, but nothing's wrong with my hearing. Plus, I have good friends around here. They've told me some of the ugly things you've said. Don't you think I have feelings? Well, I do, and you've hurt them pretty badly!"

For once, Lee's sassy mouth clamped shut, speechless. She couldn't wisecrack her way out of this one and she knew it. I added nothing to her flustered moment but an "I told you so" nose in the air. Finally, she had to plead guilty and apologize like a grown-up. "Tootie, I'm really sorry. Flip says I have a tendency to resent beautiful women because I'm so used to being the main attraction in our town. I'm just jealous."

This brief, but true confession pleased Tootie to no end. She stretched her polished lips wide. "OK, then. No hard feelings. I think you're really beautiful, too. But you need to wear more makeup. You could use an oatmeal facial, too. I'll show you how." Completely satisfied, she sashayed off to her bungalow, puffing smoke like the little engine that did what it said it could, on her way to whatever beauty treatment the schedule called for that day.

"In a strange way, I feel better." Lee patted herself on the back as we made our way to lunch. "Sort of purged. Have I been so awful? Don't answer that. Anyway, I have to agree with our Miss Tootie. It's a bit macabre to laugh it up at a Halloween party when your hostess is missing, presumed crazy. Two of your fellow guests are missing, presumed guilty. And a man presumed missing is found stabbed to death, presumably by one of our happy little campers or counselors."

I listened to Lee's bizarre litany of events, and after a moment of reflection countered, "Maybe a Halloween party is just what we need. The masks always come off at the end of a masquerade."

\* \* \*

THE SUN BLAZED high in the sky, battering any inclination I might have felt to race around on a bicycle, searching high and low for a new, private beach. Instead, I lay like a stuffed oyster in one of the hammocks by the humble little hut we called home, fanning my sunburned skin with a *Bass Fisherman* from Tom's stack of must-reads. My stack of must-reads consisted of two *Newsweek* magazines from April 2003, and a tattered mystery. Buck naked, without its enticing glossy jacket, the book baked in the sun atop the two magazines. So energized he made me nauseated, Tom zoomed through a copy of *Ghost Soldiers.* "Listen to this." Out poured a paragraph of graphic, wrenching war.

"I almost prefer the booby jokes."

"Good. Got a new one."

"Oh, please."

"All-time best booby put-down. 'Hey, buddy, got a neck to match those feet?' "

"Who came up with that fifth grade ha-ha?"

"Sam. He's good. He rolled out about five in a span of three minutes. We were on the floor of the boat, laughing our heads off."

I sipped at a bottle of water and stared forlornly at the half-baked mystery. "How did Buddy and Fa-Fa seem to you on the fishing trip this morning?"

"Fine. Why?" The hawk eyes behind the sunglasses drilled into me.

"It's just that both those guys have been under a lot of stress." Always a sly preamble to talk about people. "I'm not sure the constable buys Buddy's story that he and Jimbo rode around in a truck all night in the middle of a huge storm, drinking beer. Would you? Fa-Fa's had an extra load on his shoulders, too, since Laurie went off the deep end."

"He seems capable enough of taking up the slack."

"Yeah, job-wise, but to be the target of someone's mental collapse? Suppose you kicked the bucket and I started throwing my arms around Sam, mooning and calling him Tom?"

"I'd say Sam's a lucky so-and-so, but Lee doesn't like to share. She's selfish that way."

The camp truck rattled into view, and Jimbo and Buddy oozed out, slope-shouldered and dejected. I rolled out of the hammock to the tune of Tom's groan, and hurried to the patio where they headed for something cold to drink. "Jimbo? Did you find her?"

He didn't pretend to smile or act as if everything would turn out fine in our community bed of roses. "No, nothing. We drove down to Preston Bay and searched the whole area, but nothing came of it. Stopped by Picky's villa, too, but the place is locked up tight. Thanks for the idea, anyway. It did make sense. The constable's checking with the realtor's office and the airport to see if any new arrivals might know something."

"No word about Liza and George, either?"

"No, but there's a good chance we'll hear something soon. The police airmen should spot them in no time. I never figured those two for killers."

"I knew all along she did it," Buddy said without conviction. He rocked his beer bottle back and forth with one hand.

"Could have been an accident," Jimbo reasoned. He snapped open a can of soda. "Or self-defense."

Buddy's mouth skewed to one side. "No, Liza's a cold-blooded, two-timing hussy. I don't care how much money she has, or how high up in society. What surprises me is that they made a run for it."

"Yeah, me, too." Jimbo scratched his chin. "And in Laurie's boat. I just pray they didn't hurt her. She may have slipped into her own weird fantasy world, but she wouldn't hurt anybody. She's not violent. You don't think they hurt her, do ya, Buddy?"

As evil as he considered Liza, Buddy said the right thing at the right time. "No way! There's a chance she's with them, and Tootie didn't see her, and the police will have her back safe and sound in no time. But I bet they wrangled the boat keys out of her and dropped her somewhere kind of remote. In Laurie's state, she probably wandered into the thickets around Tarpon Pond. She's lost. She's confused. That's all. We'll find her, Jimbo. It's a small island. Don't worry."

The rambling answer seemed to satisfy him, and Jimbo slurped his soft drink. A thought occurred to me. "Did the constable mention the results of Jay's autopsy? Or say any more about the boat that went down?"

"As far as we know," Jimbo said between gulps, "every boat from Little Cayman has been accounted for, and no one was reported missing. The police are checking into boats at Brac and Grand Cayman."

"And the autopsy?"

"That was a bit of a shocker," said Buddy. "Seems Jay got into a short scuffle and got stabbed pretty bad, but that's not what killed him. He drowned."

"Drowned?"

"Drowned. Ironic, isn't it? The hot shot, deep-sea diver who we thought toppled over the Wall and drowned last Tuesday, actually got stabbed, then drowned on Thursday."

"Whoever stabbed him didn't do a very clean job of it," Jimbo added, "because all indications are he would have survived the cuts."

"That's another reason I think Liza did it." Buddy almost glowed, cheerful in his opinion, vindicated. "A man would have finished the job."

My eyes wandered to the glassy calm of the sea. "Maybe a man did."


AT SIX O'CLOCK, I giggled with Lee over our costumes as I dried my hair. "I could wear this towel to the party and say I'm a Desperate Housewife. I keep waiting for that call from central casting."

"No, no. I like my idea better. Anyway, the staff sacrificed two old sheets to the cause, and I'd hate my exquisite hand-iwork to go to waste." She held up one sacrificed sheet. "Not bad, if I do say so myself."

"It almost looks real."

"Do you like my hair?" She twisted her head around so I could see all sides.

"An exact duplicate."

"You're lucky. You don't have to do a thing to yours."

"Will that stuff wash out?"

"Oh, it's not permanent. I checked on the side of the can."

I stepped out of the towel. "I'm gonna have to stuff the sheet in a couple of places."

"Don't you own a push-up bra?"

"No, sounds too much like exercise."

We donned the sheets and admired ourselves in the mirror. Lee started adjusting my waistline. "Tighter. You're too loose."

"Speak for yourself. Watch out, don't mess up my sparkles. The color won't rub off, will it?"

"No, it's good and dry. Dempsie helped me before she started working on her own costume. She's a hen and Buddy's a rooster."

"How original. How many hen-pecked husband jokes do you think the boys will come up with tonight?"

"Anything to steer them away from those stupid booby jokes. Sam is driving me insane. Every night before bed, instead of sweet nothings he whispers, 'A Red-Footed Booby and an Irishman go into a pub.'" She snatched up her long-neck beer. "You ought to have one of these, too. As a prop."

We stepped out, arm and arm. The perfect Caribbean sunset beckoned us toward the dock, the sky ablaze with the colors of autumn: deep crimson, pumpkin orange, maple yellow. The other inmates of our prison in paradise tripped down to the dock as well, clutching glasses and bottles of fortification, dreading the long, odd social event in store.

The kitchen staff, along with Dirk, Tootie, and Fa-Fa,

made the most of Camp Iguana's meager supply of decora-
tions, adding creative touches of their own. Multi-colored
Christmas lights stretched from the boathouse to the dock,
and flames waved in the wind from a dozen torches staked
into the ground. Posters, personally painted by the staff,
adorned the dull walls of the boathouse, lending it an air of
excitement, as if we attended a New York gallery opening.
I particularly liked Tootie's rendering of an eel, complete
with gold hoop earrings and red lipstick, popping out of a
pumpkin, and Dirk's carefully drawn cartoon of the *Tyrol*
with the staff on board in costume. He stood to the side of
a table set up as a bar, dour in his lederhosen and German
hat despite the ale in his fist. Fa-Fa, a single Blues Brother
(perfect choice with the cool shades), mixed a drink for
Henrietta. She wore a homemade crown of kaleidoscope
blossoms atop her loose, red curls, and a pure, white sheet
draped toga-style.

"Is she supposed to be somebody British?" Lee whispered. "Or Greek, or *Animal House*?"

"We'll have to ask. Nobody's going to figure out who
we're supposed to be, either."

Sam slid between us, one hand on each of our bare
shoulders. "Well, if it isn't the Bush twins!" He kissed the
top of my head. "Lookin' good, Bar. That a preview of
your Inaugural gown? And Jenna, you fox. Where'd you
get that flashy green dress?"

Lee beamed. "At least one person figured it out. And
who are you supposed to be—Tom?"

"Right on the money, honey." He peered at us with serious eyes through Tom's wire-rimmed reading glasses, and
flicked a thumb against the tuxedo tie from our wedding.
"Tie looks good with the Terps T-shirt, don't you think?"

"And the black socks." I tightened the tie around his
neck. "Mission accomplished. You achieved 'simple.' I
don't see the cell phone, though, or the appointment book
with the little doodles in it."

Tom made a grand entrance, adorned in Sam's worst pair of torn shorts, worst shirt, worst hat, and barefoot. "Hey, there, baby." He grasped my waist from behind, planting butterfly kisses up and down my exposed neck until I shivered with goose bumps. "New on campus? I teach history, at least that's what they tell me. Normally, I'm too henpecked to hear."

I slid eyes at Lee. "What did I tell you? And you," I pushed Tom away, "you better stop flirting with me or my army of secret service agents will whack you."

Buddy and Dempsie, the rooster and the hen, strutted onto the dock, followed by Renata, who'd cleverly adjusted her plain, cotton dinner dress into a "farmer's daughter" rendition, complete with starched, calico apron. Pink ribbons decorated her ash blonde pigtails, a spirited, young girl again. After much clucking and scratching, and a couple of hen-pecked jokes, we moved en masse toward Henrietta and Fa-Fa. The widest part of the dock held three large, round tables covered with orange cloths and pretty hurricane lamps, with chairs enough for all campers and counselors and their invited guests.

Dempsie fluffed the pillow tied to her waist beneath a shredded sheet meant to resemble feathers. She'd painted a cone paper cup red and placed it over her nose as a beak. "Hey, Henrietta, who are you tonight? A Greek goddess?"

Henrietta fluffed her crown of blossoms with one hand. "I am Queen Mab, the Celtic Fairy Queen. From *Romeo and Juliet*, remember?

> " ' . . . she comes
> *In shape no bigger than an agate stone*
> *On the forefinger of an alderman,*
> *. . . And in this state she gallops by night*
> *Through lovers' brains, and they dream of love;*
> *. . . O'er ladies' lips, who straight on kisses dream,*
> *Which oft the angry Mab with blisters plagues . . . ' "*

Dempsie smirked. "I, for one, wouldn't mind if you planted a few blisters on a certain block of ice. Who's missing besides her and George and Jimbo?"

"I don't see Frank." Relieved, Renata glanced in all directions, but no sooner had she spoken than he made his way past the boathouse and its ingenious art collection, unimpressed with the whimsical transformation. As soon as his feet touched the dock, I started to giggle. True to character, true to form, true to nature, Frank sported a Greek shirt and sunglasses a la Onassis. Bringing up the rear, Tootie pranced into view, an exact clone of Britney Spears from the jewels in her nose and belly button to her low-slung, tight grunge jeans. She waved at a rotund figure in the distance, and soon PC Arnaud Fitzgerald caught up with her, proud and majestic in the unmistakable costume he must have invested a month of paychecks to own or rent.

"Well, Jenna." I poked Lee in the ribs, gesturing at her "date." "How does it feel to date Tom Scott and Henry VIII at the same time? Two such powerful men."

"Yikes. You know, Henry looks awfully excited, and I don't think it's because of me or Britney Spears. Maybe he's heard something."

And, indeed, he had. Striding confidently onto the dock, pushing ahead of the peasant, Onassis, Henry VIII raised padded arms, an important announcement to make. "May I have everyone's attention, please? Gather round, gather round. Before arriving here, Constable Nettles personally informed me that your criminal element was apprehended this afternoon. They are on their way here, as we speak. A police unit is expected at any moment with both the stolen boat and the accused. Constable Nettles is also expected at any moment with the owner of this establishment." He flattened his feet and crossed his arms in kingly fashion. "I will now take questions."

Tom responded to his offer in a deep, dramatic whisper in my ear. "PC Arnaud Fitzgerald . . . *why* did the booby cross the road?"

I shushed him away, straining to hear Fa-Fa. "Was Laurie with Liza and George? Did they find her?"

"No," Arnaud said mournfully, mouth forming a trench. "She is unaccounted for. Next question."

Fingers wrapped tight around Renata's arm, Henrietta stuttered through the dreaded question. "D-did George con-confess to anything?"

Arnaud jutted his button chin high. "It is my understanding certain statements were made."

Dirk whispered something in Fa-Fa's ear and slipped away.

Ever single-minded, Frank rasped, "Did Liza have my money with her? Ya know," he tossed an idea around, "maybe she had it all along. Maybe that money they found in the pouch was something different."

Arnaud had no time to answer. From the direction of the setting sun, we heard the buzz of distant engines, just as Constable Nettles and Jimbo screeched to a halt in front of the main house.

# CHAPTER 21

※

WHILE RENATA ATTENDED to Henrietta, frantic with worry, Dempsie removed her beak and offered Jimbo a pep talk, his face haggard and drawn. "Don't you worry. I'm sure Liza and George can tell us where Laurie is."

"Like I told you," Buddy said firmly, "they probably dropped her off somewhere." He shoved a beer into Jimbo's hand, standard consolation from a fraternity brother. "I'll beat the answers out of that woman if I have to."

Jimbo focused bloodshot eyes on the two boats drawing close. "Hey, Fa-Fa? You and Dirk help tie those boats up when they get here."

Dirk had excused himself moments before, but Fa-Fa pointed out the berth for Laurie's boat, and the officer at the helm pulled in. The second boat, a police vessel (so familiar to us lately), motored smoothly to a halt at the side of the dock. Liza came into view. She sat in the stern, lovely features distorted and furious. Curious George poked his head up. "I say, are we having a party? Costumes, splendid, splendid."

"Oh, George," Henrietta groaned, "what have you done?"

"Look at Liza," scoffed Buddy. "Caught like a fly in a web. She's mad about it, too. Look at her face."

"Nobody's handcuffed," Dempsie complained, disappointed. "I thought they'd at least be handcuffed."

A host of sparkles floated off my fancy ball gown as I moved toward Jimbo. "Do you know what Liza and George told the police when they finally tracked them down?"

"No, the constable got a call saying they were in police custody, and on their way back here for questioning. Guess we'll hear the whole story now, unless they ask for a lawyer." He threw an annoyed glance at Tom, who merely replied, "That would be their right, but don't look at me."

Two officers escorted George and Liza off the boat, and Constable Nettles greeted them somberly. Arnaud rushed to his side, instinctively patting his padded chest and sides in search of the indispensable notebook. Panic-stricken, he grabbed a cocktail napkin and borrowed a pen from Frank.

Constable Nettles used his magnificent tonsils to great effect. "I have a few questions. However, I must inform you, because of your unexpected flight during a time you were told not to leave the island, you are both under suspicion for the murder of Jay Carruthers, and larceny, for stealing Laurie's vessel."

"Yes, we know," George spewed, "and it's utterly ridiculous! We told these gentlemen as much, and we can explain everything, if you care to listen."

All of us did.

The constable nodded and nailed his black pupils on Liza. She returned his stare with slitty green eyes and a rock-solid jaw. Unable to contain himself, Arnaud boomed, "Well? Are you willing to answer our questions, too, Liza Carruthers?"

The green slits flatlined into needles. "May I sit down, please? I've been smashed about in a boat all day. I'm on the verge of a blackout."

She bustled past Henrietta in her crown of blossoms as if someone had left out the trash, and gracefully slid into a chair. Arnaud hurried around to the other side, blocking her escape route. He aimed the ballpoint pen at his cocktail napkin, eager to begin. The constable motioned George to take a seat, also, as three police officers ringed the table. The rest of us gathered round, a grand jury of cartoon characters.

Gravely, slowly, his two hands folded together in a gesture of equality and patience, if not prayer, Constable Nettles commenced the examination. "Why don't you tell me how this day began?"

"Ladies first," said Curious George, entranced with Henrietta's voluminous red hair and soft, pastel blooms.

"Gladly." Liza clenched her teeth sarcastically. "My morning actually began last night when I received a call on my cell from my solicitor in Barbados."

"That's right," George affirmed. "I was there when she received the call. I heard everything."

"Do you mind?" Liza's needle eyes pricked George. "When Jay's body splashed up on the beach yesterday morning, I contacted my solicitor in Barbados to let him know of Jay's death. I hadn't spoken to the man in months, not since Jay and I separated. My husband and I owned several properties on the island. I felt I should get the ball rolling on the legalities."

"Vulture." Tootie flared the jewel in her nostril.

Liza bristled like a porcupine, but continued. "My solicitor wasn't in when I called, so I left a message. He returned the call late last night, naturally shocked to hear of Jay's death, and then he shocked me by disclosing some financial matters Jay had accomplished without my knowledge."

"Such as?"

"Jay mortgaged every single one of our Barbados properties to the hilt, forging my signature a number of times. He'd also employed a fraudulent power of attorney, granting him the power to rent, sell, mortgage, or dispose of our properties in any manner he saw fit."

"How much money we talkin'?" Frank grew into the role of Onassis. We all screwed our noses in disdain, as if such a crass question would never cross our minds, and leaned forward.

"I don't know. Several million pounds. Eight, ten, something like that."

Arnaud, spouting sweat in the hot, padded costume, poked a hole in his makeshift notepad. "More cocktail napkins!" But no servant scampered to fill his order.

"Quite a large sum," said the constable coolly. "This was the first you'd heard of Jay's treachery?"

Liza's shoulders drew back. "Yes. I had *absolutely* no knowledge before last night."

"Yeah, right," Buddy sneered. "And I've got some land in the Everglades I want to sell you."

"What did you do next?" Constable Nettles continued his line of questioning, calmly and methodically. Meanwhile, the grand jury huddled closer.

"What would anyone do?" Liza said disdainfully. "I knew I had to meet with him immediately, but he couldn't leave for the Caymans for another week. I offered to fly to Barbados, but the damnable airlines are not up to snuff because of the blasted hurricane, and I couldn't get a ticket, not to mention two."

"Two?"

"You didn't expect me to leave Georgie, did you?" She patted George's hand perfunctorily. "He's been such a rock."

I examined the rock beside her. His teak-colored hair stood on end from a day at sea, clothes rumpled and wet. He couldn't keep his eyes off Henrietta.

"Go on."

"I was a complete mess, absolutely frantic. Afraid I'd be stuck on this godforsaken sand spit for the rest of eternity while my holdings evaporated. That's when George suggested we go by boat to Grand Cayman, and catch a commercial flight or charter a plane to Barbados."

George nodded affirmatively. "Righto. By sea."

"So we borrowed Laurie's boat."

"With her permission?" The constable cocked his bald head.

Liza's cheekbones burned cranberry red. "Of course with her permission."

"The hell you say!" Jimbo exploded. "She never let anybody take her boat out, not even me!"

"Well . . ." Liza lifted one shoulder. "She wasn't exactly herself, was she?"

"What did you do to her? I swear to God, I'll wring your damn neck with my own hands if you laid a finger on my wife!"

Buddy and Fa-Fa swooped in to hold Jimbo back. Liza sat perfectly still, impervious. "Is that what you did to Jay after you stabbed him? You and your 'drinking buddy'? Jay laid more than a finger on your wife, didn't he? I was on this island for two weeks, remember, before his so-called diving accident. He played her like a fiddle. You had every reason to kill Jay." She added slyly, "So did Picky Jiffers."

"What are you talkin' about?" Jimbo snarled.

"Oh, come now. Don't tell me you didn't know about Laurie and Picky."

"You're lying," he rasped. "There isn't anything going on between Laurie and Picky. She's his guide. He's a customer."

A woman without a heart, Liza cackled, "Yes, he did pay for it."

If not for Buddy and Fa-Fa, followed by a couple of policemen, Jimbo would have mowed her down and strangled her on the spot. Instead, the constable rose slowly, and paced in a tight circle. "How do you know Laurie and Picky were involved?"

"I saw them." Liza relaxed in her chair and examined one row of fingernails. "What else did I have to do on this island but spy on people? The third day I arrived, I caught Jay and Laurie kissing like a couple of sneaky teenagers behind the bicycle shed. The next day, I decided to follow Laurie around. Imagine my surprise when she flew to Picky Jiffers's villa and into his arms."

"You actually witnessed them do that?"

"Of course. She rushed up the stairs, and I saw her throw her arms around the man. They were in the house a good thirty minutes before I heard a motor start and saw the two of them pull away in one of those cigar-shaped racing boats." She paused at the sound of Jimbo's whimpering. "I'm sorry if you didn't know about Picky. At any rate . . . my original point . . . you had every reason to kill Jay."

"Me and a lot of other people!" Jimbo bellowed.

The squawking, denials, and finger-pointing commenced. "Well, don't look at *me!*" Tootie's vocal chords shot over the moon. "Why is everybody looking at *me* all of a sudden? I didn't kill him! The last thing he told me was to wait, and he'd be in touch . . ." Her purple fingernails flew to her lips. "Oops."

"'Oops,' indeed." Constable Nettles twisted around, eyebrows connecting across the top of his bare head.

"I knew it!" I pinched Tom's side, delighted at my brilliance. "She did see him the night of the storm!"

The constable loomed over Tootie. "There appears to be something you've not told us, Miss Tootie."

"Out with it, Miss Tootie!" Arnaud burst at the seams to dictate a real confession.

The staff of Camp Iguana fixed quizzical, lemur eyes on Tootie. She snorted, causing the fake jewel glued on one nostril to pop off. "Oh, hell. I guess it doesn't matter now, anyway."

"When did you have this conversation with Jay?" the

constable pressed. "When did he tell you he'd be back?"

"Thursday night. The night of the storm." The audience gasped at Britney Spears. "After *she* finished going through my bungalow."

"As was my right," Liza snapped. "You're telling us you knew all along Jay was alive? You put everyone, including poor Constable Nettles, through such torture?"

Accustomed to brownnosers, he waved her silent with one hand. "Did you know Jay planned to fake the diving accident?"

"No! I thought he was dead!"

"What time did he come to the bungalow?"

"He was already in my bungalow, hiding in the bathroom closet. He jumped out right after everyone left. Scared the crap out of me." Tootie squinted, conjuring up the memory of a whole three days before. "He was in a big hurry, and kind of mad that he'd had to wait on account of Liza going through his stuff. He said, 'She'll get what's coming to her soon enough.' He said he had to get some things in order, money or documents or something, and then he could take off and start over. Like in Mexico or Belize."

"What else did he say?"

"I asked what he had in mind. He said not to worry, to wait, and he'd be in touch with me. Then he kissed me on the forehead, really sweet, like when I first met him, and said, please, don't tell anybody, no matter what. He'd be forever in my debt."

I piped up. "Did he have anything with him?"

Tootie's brows joined. "Now that I think of it, he had some papers. Yeah, papers folded in half."

Documents so important, or damning, the contents compelled Jay to risk returning to Tootie's bungalow. He never meant to run into her but, true to form, managed to manipulate silence, and time to get away. "Tootie, why didn't you tell us you saw Jay the night of the storm when Constable Nettles questioned us yesterday morning?"

"Because," she played with a ring on her finger, "I was afraid you'd think I killed him. The day after the storm, I'd almost made up my mind to tell Jimbo when I ran into all the women on the terrace, and Lee accused me of messing with Jay's tank. When his body washed up the next day, stabbed, I figured Laurie did it, and I'd better accuse her before she accused me. But now . . . I don't know. I guess it could have been anybody."

"Can you remember anything else about Jay that night?" asked the constable.

"That's it. I don't know where he came from or where he went, it happened so fast. Got me so rattled, I had to go through four hair treatments to calm my nerves. That's when I saw *him!*"

She pointed straight at Aristotle Onassis.

Frank blanched. "Whoa, wait a minute. I've explained, already."

"Maybe you better explain again, now that Tootie has shared this new information with us."

"Aw, come on." He touched his heart, drawing from a shallow well of personal charm. "I told you, I just wanted a closer look-see in Jay's bungalow, in case Liza missed something. When I didn't find my money, I left out the back door and returned straight to my hut. Honest to God."

"You didn't see Jay that evening? You did not run into him and argue about your money?"

"No! No! I swear I didn't. I ain't lying."

"It's not too hard to tell who is." Buddy directed his venom at Liza. "Make her finish her story! Where's Laurie?"

Constable Nettles placed his hands behind his back. "Yes, Liza . . . and George. Go on with your story."

"And remember," Arnaud pointed his pen at a new collection of cocktail napkins, "everything you say *will* be used against you."

Liza pursed her lips, reflecting upon the faces surrounding her as if she rather enjoyed the attention. She held us in the palm of her hand. "Early this morning, after Jimbo left to work in the kitchen, and the others were at breakfast or asleep, I paid a visit to Laurie. I presented her with a proposition. Georgie and I didn't think she'd simply hand over the keys of her boat to us, especially to motor all the way to Grand Cayman, so we decided to tell her something that would cajole her into the boat, and we'd explain the situation later."

"What did you tell her?"

"We'd witnessed her pitiful display last night in the dining room, tripping around in a swimsuit with a pitcher of tea, and she mentioned a call from Picky Jiffers. I told her that Picky and I were old friends. The whole time, she looked at me with a god-awful blank expression. She said she didn't realize Picky had any friends, and wasn't that nice. Then she said, 'I'm supposed to take him diving this morning. I couldn't get away last night.' And I said, 'Yes, I know. He wants me and George to tag along with you.'"

"And she believed you?"

"Absolutely. After that, it was easy. We waited until Dirk and Tootie buzzed away, then Fa-Fa and his fish people. Jimbo was busy, Henrietta . . . ," her eyes wandered to the lovely Queen Mab, who raised her chin defiantly, "was sequestered in her cabin with Renata. Frank had passed out, Flip had gone on a walk, and Lee socialized with Dempsie. The coast, as they say, was clear."

"What time was this?"

"Around nine-thirty. We convinced Laurie we'd already stowed the diving equipment on her boat. She stepped aboard like a lamb. We wore bathing suits and took along our clothes in a carry case so as not to arouse suspicion. I must say, she looked marvelous, so excited to meet Picky for a dive."

"Did you pass any other boats? Did anyone see you?"

"No, we didn't see anyone."

"So no one can corroborate your story, thus far, but the

two of you." The constable slipped that one in before asking, "When did you tell her you wanted to 'borrow' her boat?"

"Now wait a minute. We did not *steal* her boat, if that's what you're getting at. We *rented* the boat, and paid good money for it."

"Yes, yes, I did," George wagged his head. "I gave her a thousand dollars in Cayman currency. Oh, yes, we did everything by the book, Constable."

The tips of Constable Nettles' lips twitched. "I have yet to hear anything that's actually *in* the book. Do go on."

"When Laurie spotted Picky's villa, she pointed it out to us, and that's when we urged her to stop. We said we desperately needed to talk to her. She quit the engine almost immediately—really, such a sweet woman—and listened as I poured out my tale of woe. She wore the same blank expression. We offered her the money and said, 'If you don't want to drive us there yourself, and we doubt you do, we'll drop you off here at Picky Jiffers's villa. But come hell or high water, we're going!'"

"You threw her overboard, didn't you?" Tootie's neck stretched up like a stork's. "You made her walk the plank!"

Liza's green eyes rocketed skyward. "She opted for the money, you twit. We dropped her at Picky Jiffers's dock, as promised. The next thing we know, an army of police swoop down and arrest us, babbling about murder, theft, treason—every crime known to man!"

George heaved a sigh. "It's been a bloody grueling day."

"You're lying!" Jimbo balled his fists. "It's all a lie! Buddy and I were at Picky's villa not two hours ago. Laurie wasn't there."

Constable Nettles combed his fingers through nonexistent hair, suddenly aware of the strange faces hovering over his shoulder. "Does anyone have anything to add to this story before we check it out?"

"I do." The words popped out of my mouth.

Tom drew back as if I'd confessed to kidnapping. "You do?"

The constable took a good look at me, probably wondering why one of the President's daughters would involve herself in a seedy murder. "Yes?"

"We were getting ice cream down at the store, and I asked the store clerk what she knew about Picky Jiffers. The more I thought about it, the more it made sense that maybe he'd know something about Laurie, but he wasn't at the villa when we went by yesterday, and Jimbo and Buddy didn't find him there today. I was wondering . . . has anybody questioned him since the storm?"

The constable turned to Arnaud. "Did you?"

"Did I what?"

"Did you question Mr. Jiffers?"

"His name wasn't on the list."

"Picky Jiffers wasn't on the realtor's list of renters? The one drawn up after the storm?"

"No, I'm sure."

Jimbo offered an explanation. "It's possible his name didn't make the list because he gave strict instructions not to bother him for anything. I bet he even paid under the table, he made such a big deal about his privacy. Buddy and I stuck around awhile when no one answered the door. We looked the place over real good. It was empty, and his boat was gone. We figured he'd gone to Grand Cayman."

"I would imagine," the constable said slowly, "that his boat isn't registered or licensed in these waters."

"Nobody would have reported it missing," I said. "It could have been Picky Jiffers's boat that went down during the storm. It wasn't at the dock when we stopped by yesterday, either. Nobody was there. At least . . . we *thought* no one was."

# CHAPTER 22

❈

LEE AND I held on for dear life in the back of the camp truck along with Fa-Fa, Tom, Sam, and Renata. Dempsie and Buddy sat in front with Jimbo, only slightly more comfortable as the truck jostled and jolted over Camp Iguana's craggy driveway. Behind us, Tootie, looking none too happy, sat squeezed between Constable Nettles and Henry VIII in the police jeep. Arnaud's costume, so magnificent an hour earlier, slowly unraveled, panel by panel, stuffing by stuffing, like a Christmas turkey gradually carved to the bone.

Lee called out to me, "Think Curious George and Liza will try to escape from those policemen?"

"No. As stupid as their story is, I believe it! Liza's probably barking at the kitchen staff right now to produce dinner or die, and I saw George making puppy eyes at Henrietta."

"I hope it works out for her!" Renata shouted. "She really does love George!"

"I noticed Frank stayed behind, too!"

She nodded, pigtails flying. "I'm sure he'll offer Liza 'help' in recovering her millions!"

I turned to Fa-Fa and yelled, "What happened to Dirk?"

He did not answer or smile or even acknowledge me. Tom and I exchanged a worried glance, but didn't pry. Minus the Blues Brother coat and tie, Fa-Fa wore only shorts and a white T-shirt. Even his sunglasses lay on the ground back at camp, discarded in the haste to trample onto the truck. It occurred to me that Dirk's lederhosen—in this setting, under these circumstances—would have made our rushed trip to the villa all the more ridiculous, a Boy Scout along on a drug bust. Not that Lee and I in our chic Inaugural gowns, or Renata in her pink ribbons and apron, blended into the scenery.

"Don't worry!" I shouted to Fa-Fa. "Laurie's probably at the villa, safe and sound."

The worried shadow failed to lift, and he yelled back, "But how sound in mind?"

Lee hesitated before asking the awful question, "Do you think she'd try to hurt herself?"

Little Miss Sunshine, I answered, "Maybe Picky Jiffers is taking care of her. Maybe that wasn't his boat that went down, and the two of them were out diving this afternoon. Maybe . . ."

Their skeptical stares silenced me, and a chill settled over my shoulders and down my back. *Or maybe Laurie's there, in the house. Dead by her own hand. Or the hand that killed Jay.*

THE HIGH HOPES at the outset of our journey plummeted. Jimbo burned rubber as fast as the old rattletrap could go, tearing down the road, white knuckles wrapped around the steering wheel. As far as he knew, Laurie waited at the villa for him to show up, her knight in rattletrap armor. Her mind clear as a bell, she'd have realized the error of her ways, and had spent the day inside the villa, quietly recuperating. The two would put Jay, Picky Jiffers, and the ugly past behind them.

Seated between Jimbo and Buddy, Dempsie took turns tick-tocking her head from side to side. First, a frightened glimpse at Buddy, then one at Jimbo. Once, she corkscrewed around to see if any of us had fallen overboard. Renata, Lee, and I smiled encouragingly.

Buddy's focus on the pavement ahead bordered on the phenomenal. Only when we hit the sandy road leading to the end of the island did he rouse himself out of the trance to look at Jimbo. Their eyes locked. Whatever the outcome, they'd fight through this thing together.

The truck ripped through the packed sand the whole quarter of a mile to the turnoff to Picky Jiffers's villa. The dim headlights barely lit the way. Behind us, the jeep chugged along, lost in the dust storm we kicked up. Britney Spears coughed and hacked while Henry VIII fought to cover his royal mouth and nose with the remnants of a floppy beret. I could just make out the top of the constable's bobbing head.

The truck ground to a halt a few feet forward of the driveway, and Jimbo practically tore the gearbox out when he jerked the shift into reverse. He backed up, forcing the constable to slam on the brakes and throw the jeep into reverse on a dime. Every woman screamed, and every man said his favorite cuss word. Tootie did both. "I can't believe I came on this witch hunt! If I'd known you people were going to ruin twelve hours of beauty treatments, I would have stayed with the vulture back at camp! At least I'd have something in my stomach besides dust!"

The truck lurched forward and we made our way down the drive. "I sure hope we find her," Lee wheezed.

"If we don't," Tom shook the dust off Sam's ratty shirt, "it's going to be a hell of a long night."

The Halloween moon, not quite full, wore a jaundiced cast, as if deathly ill. The mournful face, partly shadowed, gave our trip down the driveway an aura of doom.

"I have a bad feeling about this," Fa-Fa murmured, clinging to the back bar of the truck.

"Think positively," Sam advised. "There's every reason to hope."

The truck's headlights could barely illuminate the view, and the sickly moon threw little light on the house. When the jeep pulled up beside us, though, with stronger bulbs, we captured a decent picture of the property.

"Nice place," said Sam. He hopped off the back of the truck and offered two arms to his well-heeled date for the evening. Lee flapped in the wind, deserving clothespins. In the light of the headlamp, my costume took on the attractive appearance of a lumpish, middle-aged Tinkerbell outfit, molting pixie dust at every step. The rest of the misfits piled out and we stood in the eerie, harsh light, visitors from another planet, come to take E.T. home.

"Doesn't look like anybody's here." Dempsie spoke with a voice so muted, I could hardly hear the words. Like most of us, she looked incongruous and Mardi Gras–garish in the hen costume. "I don't see any lights on in the house."

A porch swing, chained to wooden beams over the carport, creaked in the sway of the breeze, a fitting complement to the bewitching season. "Does anyone see a vehicle about?" Constable Nettles handed us an assignment.

"No." I started forward. "Should we go up and knock? Anybody got a flashlight?" Suddenly, three or four flashlights clicked on, wide-eyed fireflies, and we moved as one unit toward the house.

"This is spooky." Tootie tripped on a root and grabbed Arnaud's arm. "Don't you have a gun yet? Where's that flute?"

We inched our way toward the stairs leading up to the first floor of the villa. I daintily held the ball gown sheet over my sandals as if my name were Cinderella. Lee tripped along beside me in sneakers, equally ravishing. I peered beyond the carport to the sea, trying to adjust my eyes to the weird light, but couldn't see a thing. The constable led us up the stairs to the front door. Through the windows, a couple of flashlights shined into the living room, revealing nothing but the scene I'd studied the day before.

"Nothing's changed," I murmured. "Should we ring the bell?"

The constable rang the doorbell and knocked politely, but forcefully. We huddled in the background, a restless band of trick-or-treaters waiting for the door to fling wide so we could cry out. The only sound came from the creak of the carport swing and the repressed coughs and hacking of people who'd swallowed too much dust. He knocked again.

"Shall we force our way in?" Arnaud shuffled side to side, anxious for combat.

"We may not," the constable counseled. "This is private property. We are here on inquiry alone. We have no reason to believe anyone's life is in immediate peril."

Jimbo cleared his throat of grime. "Wait one minute there. You heard Liza and George. This is where they dropped Laurie off this morning, and no one's seen her since. She might be inside, all alone, in a daze."

"Or worse," Buddy wheezed helpfully, inspiring the rest of us.

"She might have fallen and cracked her head," advised Dempsie.

"Or swallowed a bottle of pills to calm her nerves and passed out," Lee offered. "We have to save her."

"She could have slit her wrists," Tootie cheerfully suggested, "and the bathtub's filling up with blood as we speak. She might even drown."

Arnaud felt the lack of a cocktail napkin and pen. "We must do something, Constable Nettles!" He levitated, straining to see inside the house. "Good heavens! I think I saw someone with a flashlight!"

"Maybe the door's unlocked," Sam reached out and shook the handle, but it held fast.

"Let's try all the windows and doors!" Buddy banged on the first window.

A riot ensued. Constable Nettles raised an arm in the air. If he'd had a gun, he'd have shot it. "Please! Please!" He gave up. "At least do this in an orderly fashion! Men cover the front and sides. Women cover the back. Check any sheds and the dock."

People scampered in all directions, rabbits racing around the property. Tootie attacked the job of shaking screens as though filming an MTV video; I'd never seen her so animated. Lee and Dempsie flew to an upstairs porch. Covered head to toe in chalky dust, Renata grabbed a screen beside Tootie and shook so hard she caused a sandstorm.

I started to shake a few window screens at the rear of the house, but something caught my eye on the sea. A pale reflection, ghostlike. I squinted, unsure of what I'd seen. An instant later, the small reflection flashed again.

Above and behind me, voices cried out, "Here! Here! It's open!" And feet stomped up and down.

But the reflection drew me out toward the water, away from the house and the noise, away from the mad search as bodies crashed through a dozen rooms. I quickly realized that the location of the reflection lay not on the water, but over it, at the end of the long dock. I slowly made my way toward the spectral shape that glimmered and dimmed like the filtered beam of a lighthouse. Golden mushroom clouds parted, revealing a host of stars. The moon, a pat of butter in the sky, suddenly flooded light.

"Laurie!" I gasped. "Are you all right? Everyone's been looking for you."

She sat at the end of the dock, feet dangling over the edge, a soft cashmere blanket, dark as the night, swaddled her body. She rocked back and forth as in self-lullaby, the beautiful, pale white of her skin rhythmically catching the night's natural light, the answer to my spectral vision.

"I'm fine." Two simple words, but something made my knees lock. Something cold and defiant. Somewhere, millions of light-years away, a star summoned all its strength and self-destructed, sending out, in that one instant, the spark of light that fell on the blade of a knife. "I'm fine."

"What are you doing?" I forced myself to remain calm. And kind.

"I'm waiting." The rocking body, in, out, in, out like a tide, changed to a sideways sway, the slow tick-tock of something designed to explode.

"Are you waiting for something . . . or someone?"

"Someone."

I unlocked my knees and stepped closer. "Mind if I wait with you?"

"Guess not." She looked up at me and smiled like an angel before her gaze returned to the sea.

I eased down to a sitting position a few feet to her right, the opposite side of the knife. Over my shoulder, lights clicked on in the villa as people poured through the rooms. It wouldn't be long before they stampeded outdoors, and we were discovered. "Laurie, who are you waiting for?" *And who is the knife for?*

"I'm waiting for the one responsible."

"Responsible for what?"

She looked directly at me with her lovely brown eyes, eyes that zipped through my head and out the other side. "Responsible for killing Jay, of course."

Some semblance of reality had reconnected the dots. "So you know he's dead."

"Yes." She turned her snowy face to the moon and stretched her neck, a trumpeter swan, straining toward her lover. "I know. And I know who stabbed him."

One eye on the knife, I heard footsteps on the dock, and breathed a sigh of relief to see Fa-Fa hurrying toward us. The closer he came, the slower his pace. I turned, widening the whites of my eyes in warning. He drew up, almost crept to the end of the dock, and stopped a couple of yards behind Laurie. We could hear the sound of his panting.

She didn't bother to turn around. "You came."

"Yes." He tried to catch his breath. "We've come to take you home."

"Who's 'we'?"

"Me. Jimbo. Buddy and Dempsie. Your husband. Your friends."

"Ha!" Her swan neck snapped back. Strands of silky dark hair waved in the wind. "Friends! Like *you're* my friend, Fa-Fa?"

My mind swirled. Laurie's dive with Picky Jiffers the day Jay disappeared. Jay's ill-timed return to the bungalow to retrieve papers the night of the storm. Fa-Fa in the *Tyrol*, Dirk also on the water. The boat that went down. Jay's body in Preston Bay. Picky Jiffers's boat gone.

"Of course, I'm your friend." He swallowed hard.

Fa-Fa was the one she was waiting for. He didn't know she waited with a knife.

Instinctively, I started to rise, but Fa-Fa stood, paralyzed at the sight of her. Her hand cupped the knife.

"Laurie!" I slipped between her and Fa-Fa, a sudden movement that caused her to switch focus. "Tell me about Picky Jiffers."

Her lips parted, tears welled. "He's gone. Gone for good."

"Yes, I know. You loved him, didn't you?"

"I loved him very much. Very much."

"And his boat went down in the storm?"

She stared out to sea. "His boat went down in the storm. But not before somebody—a good *friend*—killed him!" She leaped up, and lunged at Fa-Fa with the knife.

"No! Laurie! No!" Two voices yelled from the middle of the dock. Jimbo and Dirk swooped down on the woman I tried to grab, a deadly blade in her fist. Two bare arms jerked awkwardly up in defense as the five of us collided.

"He didn't do it!" Dirk fought to take the knife out of her hand. "Fa-Fa didn't kill Jay!"

"Yes, he did!" Laurie struggled with all her might. The cashmere blanket bundled into my hands as the knife slashed the air. "He was in the *Tyrol*! He was out on the water when Jay was in the racer! You found out he was going to take me away, didn't you, Fa-Fa, and you killed him! Killed him out of jealousy!"

I heard a groan of pain. The knife slashed through the air again, the tip dark and glistening.

"No!" Fa-Fa fell to his knees. "It was an accident! It was an accident, Laurie! His boat was in trouble, and I went to help! I thought it was Picky Jiffers! That's when I realized Jay *was* Picky Jiffers! He admitted it! He had to abandon his vessel and come aboard with me. I understood, then. I accused him and he admitted everything! The money he bilked out of Liza and Frank. The fake identity, the phony bank accounts, the coral, the drugs. All the schemes he had, all the people who fell for his con game! How could you do it, Laurie? Why him?"

Dirk shoved me out of the way. He and Jimbo pushed Laurie down. Fa-Fa tumbled over as the knife dropped from her hand, through the planks of wood, into the water. Stunned, I clutched the blanket in my lap, almost fainting at the number of slashes and tears crisscrossing the soft fabric.

Laurie's wild eyes flashed at Dirk. "What do you mean, Fa-Fa didn't kill Jay? What are you talking about? He stabbed Jay!"

"No." Dirk rolled to a kneeling position, speaking calmly as Jimbo cradled his wife. "Jay tried to kill Fa-Fa because he'd been discovered. He tried to hijack the *Tyrol* when the racer floundered. Fa-Fa fought back in self-defense and Jay was wounded. But the stabs didn't kill him. Fa-Fa did not kill him."

"The autopsy." I clutched the ripped blanket that might have saved my life. "Jay didn't die from the stab wounds. He drowned."

"Drowned?" The wintry, white skin caught the starlight. "But he didn't go down in the racer. You said he was on board the *Tyrol* with you."

When Fa-Fa didn't answer, Dirk answered for him. "I found them. The racer had drifted away. That's the boat the

Merchant Marine saw go under. We scraped the hull of
Jimbo's boat pretty badly getting Jay aboard. I told Fa-Fa
to get the hell out, get to Brac with the *Tyrol,* and to say
nothing. Nothing! I didn't trust the police, they'd only mix
up the facts to get the wrong result, and Fa-Fa didn't need
their endless questions. We didn't know if the stab wounds
were fatal, if Fa-Fa would be accused of murder. It would
have been vintage Jay to accuse Fa-Fa of the attack on a
hospital deathbed. But in spite of that, and in spite of the
storm, I did the right thing. I made a run back to Little Cayman instead of heading south to safer waters. To save Jay's
life."

Laurie wept, a gut-wrenching, grief-stricken wail. "You
could have saved him! But you killed him! You shoved him
overboard and he drowned!"

"No." Dirk crawled toward her, shaking. "I did try to
save him, Laurie. I made it through the passage, through
the reef, at the risk of my own life! I swear to you, one
minute Jay was there. The next, he was gone. He grabbed
his stuff and slipped overboard. Maybe he counted too
heavily on his abilities as a diver. Maybe he thought he had
a better chance to swim in and find you than to face Liza
and Frank and the police."

Fingers spread across her face, Laurie's body shook.
"Did you look for him? Did you even try?"

"I tried." The words came haltingly. "But the sea, the
terrible waves, the darkness, were too much. Jay took a
chance. I knew I couldn't. The next day, when Fa-Fa returned, I told him to let the dead rest. Let everyone believe
Jay drowned in a diving accident."

"But you knew I didn't believe it! You both knew I was
going to run away with 'Picky'!"

"Yes, and we agreed to protect you! When Jimbo and
Buddy didn't find you here today, Fa-Fa and I, we knew.
We knew you were here hiding, grieving, all alone. I left
the party tonight to find you before the police did, bring
you back to your husband, and destroy all evidence of

'Picky Jiffers,' as if every trace of him sank into the sea with his boat."

A strange calm fell over Laurie. "I wanted Jimbo to move on, but he never would have. So we made plans. Jay would fake his death, a final, noble gesture, and sooner or later, Liza would get the money from the life insurance in return for what Jay took from the properties. I did the same for Jimbo. The Friday after Jay's diving 'accident,' I was going to leave a suicide note and disappear. It was perfect. It would have been so perfect. But when I heard a boat had gone down, I knew. I just knew in my heart, I'd lost him." Her head bowed to her knees. "How can you help who you fall in love with? Is there a way? Fa-Fa . . . is there a way?"

But he did not answer.

# CHAPTER 23

✻

Fa-Fa could thank the Little Cayman Clinic for saving his life. They kept him going until he could be flown to Faith Hospital on Cayman Brac, seven miles across salt water. Tootie volunteered to go with him.

"She views the hospital as a species of spa," Lee confided, "and the nurses will polish her up while Fa-Fa's getting his 'stitch job.'"

Dempsie choked on her rum punch. "Does she think he's going in for a little voluntary cosmetic surgery?"

"That's about the gist of it. Don't you just love her?"

Our Halloween moon had risen, and shone down on the tattered charter members of Camp Iguana. No police boats rubbed against our dock. No investigative Henry VIII lurked behind our palm trees. Peace and quiet reigned supreme on our very own parcel of paradise. And it did feel very much our own.

Jimbo remained at the clinic with a sedated Laurie; Dirk offered to have a very long chat with Constable Nettles and Arnaud at the police station. The kitchen staff had long since departed, leaving us with a host of goodies on the dock, and an inexhaustible supply of booze. We arrived at the sober conclusion we should make the most of the evening, and give ourselves a real Halloween treat. No blues or jazz or reggae—oldies music blared from a hooked-up stereo system. Screamin' Larry would have committed hara-kiri.

Buddy poured something green from a pitcher. "I'm just thankful Fa-Fa's gonna be OK. That was a close call."

Tom caressed my hand and kissed it. "Yes. It was." The hawk eyes clasped onto mine as deeply as when we spoke our wedding vows.

"Buddy," I had to know, "did you really think Liza killed Jay?"

"No," he admitted sheepishly. "But I was scared to death Jimbo did. Liza made such an easy target, I guess I went overboard."

"I say." George, burned to a crisp from his all-day sea adventure, couldn't get enough of the story. With his name cleared, he'd bid adieu to the woman who almost ruined it, and begged Henrietta for forgiveness and a fresh start. Liza sulked in her hut, but not alone, consoled by the brilliant businessman from New York and the promise of a hefty fortune. She could now plan to collect the funds from Jay's life insurance, and the various Cayman bank accounts in the name of Picky Jiffers. Inside the villa, Dirk had discovered a box of bank statements and other financial documents, along with a can of temporary black hair dye and a fake goatee, which he handed over to Constable Nettles. We could only conclude that the papers in the bungalow, now lost at sea, were the damning evidence that compelled Jay out of hiding and connected him to his false identity, Picky Jiffers.

"I have a question." Sam, rumpled and dirty, still sported Tom's tuxedo tie. "Why didn't Jay just call Laurie and tell her to get the papers out of the bungalow?"

I thought about it. "Timing, I suppose. And ego. When

Jay realized he'd forgotten the hidden papers, he thought he was smart enough to sneak in and grab them while we were at dinner. It must have given him a real thrill to take such a chance. Laurie must have known, though, she was so nervous that night. I guess he thought he was protecting her. If she'd tried to sneak into the bungalow herself, someone might have seen her, and raised a red flag—why is Laurie in Tootie's bungalow? Tootie would sure want to know."

"Poor Miss Tootie." Lee beamed. "I'll sure miss her."

"Poor Miss Tootie?" Renata threw up her hands. "I'm out fifty thousand dollars and a husband! Although," she half-smiled, "I can do without that particular husband."

Pollyanna to the core, I said, "I'm sure Constable Nettles will do the right thing and turn the money in the pouch over to you and Frank. You can split it—if you get your hands on it first."

"I hope it's not soggy." Renata tugged at a pigtail. "I'm kind of sick of humidity."

"Not me." Henrietta twirled a finger around a red curl, and drew closer to her husband, eyes aglitter. "What do you say we stay a few extra days, George? There's a *little* something we need to work on."

George lit up like a neon sign. "I say! I do say!"

The party took off from there. We danced under the harvest moon to Motown and the Beatles. Lee danced with George, Tom danced with Sam, Jenna Bush danced with a rooster, and the farmer's daughter learned how to do the shag from a hen.

Camp Iguana rocked all night long, and the sunrise couldn't be beat.

# POSTSCRIPT

✳

THE MOSQUITOES COME back in the spring, fresh, rested, and zooming to go after their long tropical vacation. We had to leave the Caribbean much earlier than they did, but not as early, we discovered, as Sam and Lee.

Soon after we toasted the first sunrise of November, and tottered off to our huts for some shut-eye, we heard a piercing yelp from Lee's cabin. She'd casually glanced at the airline tickets lying by her bed, and realized she and Sam had barely half an hour to pack up their suntan lotion and hightail it to the airport. Unbeknownst to Miss Fizzi, Tom had extended our trip for a day.

A member of the kitchen staff drove us to the airport, and we waved our two honeymoon partners onto the small island hopper—such a big help with their baggage, such huge grins on our faces. Once the plane lifted safely into the air, I turned to Tom and asked what he wanted to do with our twenty-four hours of freedom. He rested his head on my shoulder and yawned.

Our precious, private time on the island did not pass

without discovering yet another beautiful, deserted beach, another poem by Walt Whitman, another memory to press into our hearts for safekeeping. When we departed the next day, we held in our hands the addresses of new friends, with promises to visit their homes and, in return, welcome new faces to an historic, old town just west of Baltimore and east of Frederick, Maryland, where dogs are talked about as much as people, and the women keep secrets for generations.

Back at home, the subject of our dangerous, tropical honeymoon of death and intrigue gradually gave way to more exciting topics, like the next wedding. Miss Fizzi, delirious over the success of her Honeymoon for Four, immediately launched plans for Margaret and Lindbergh's wedding trip. At last count, the number of participants stood at fourteen. The chosen December nuptial date would collide with a full, wintry moon, in between Christmas and New Year's Eve. The town would already be decorated just the way she likes, said Margaret, so that fact alone could save them a bundle of money. Wise, old birds, they knew how to squeeze a quarter out of a nickel. Not like those youngsters, Hilda and Sidney, whose expensive dating habits coated everyone's tongues.

With a real December wedding to look forward to, the Belles of Solace Glen had more than enough to cluck about, but the added attraction of Marlene's lawsuit against Roland plowed new ground. She claimed she'd contracted salmonella from an egg salad sandwich at his Café and Grill, with the medical data to prove it. The Eggheads thrilled at the thought of taking the witness stand, stars in a case as big as Michael Jackson's. They'd saved her life, they told everybody in town six times a day (three times each), performing such delicate procedures as tracheotomies and lung transplants.

Melody and Michael remodeled Connolly's Jewelry Store, and added a clothing accessories department. Tina complained the hats are never big enough, even the stretchy ones, and Sally complained they're too dull. She offered to design a few hats herself under the witty label "Headway," but she and Melody had a breakdown in style. Even Reverend G.G. couldn't negotiate a truce until Garland stepped in. She suggested Sally sell her hats at the Salon, and both Melody and Sally could decorate an advertising mannequin once a week that she'd prop up in a window of the Bistro. Everybody was happy, everybody won, and the whole town loved the mannequin. Lee dubbed her Mrs. Toady-Face, and called her Plain Jane's best friend—until Dear John asked her on a date and stayed out till dawn. Sam testified on Dear John's behalf, claiming he and Tom, hen-pecked husbands, sneaked out and drove the two of them around one night in the backseat of the car telling booby jokes. But I know this to be a falsehood. Tom would never do anything that immature.

Pal updated the Crown station, inspired by the gussy-up of Connolly's Jewelry Store. He and Suggs decided to step into the glamorous world of art. They enjoyed painting the outside of the building so much, going crazy with Key West kinds of colors, that they attacked the interior next, even coloring the hydraulic thing that hoists your car into the air. Now, when you drive by, it looks as if somebody's car is surfing the lava on top of an exploding volcano. Next, they attacked the tools, and recently accomplished the magnificent, inventing a new medium—tire art. At least one Baltimore TV station has called.

While we were away on our honeymoon, C.C. made one comment too many about Ivory's dusting strategies, and Ivory fired herself, steaming out of C.C.'s fancy country house like a freight train, never to look back. Whenever C.C. and Leonard are in the Bistro, rather than beg, they start to moan and whine to each other about how terrible it is to find good help. Ivory and I snicker into our sleeves and keep counting the money, business has been so good.

Everything is good. I wake up each morning and ponder the man lying next to me in the huge, antique four-poster bed he bought as a wedding gift. I fling an arm out and gently tickle his nose until he says, "Oh, hell. Not again."

The green of spring and summer is hibernating, sleeping, but I know the buds of our cherry and pear trees will burst into color like a full orchestra, trumpeting joy at just the right moment. Now, the moment calls for hot cocoa and mittens, my greatest worry what recipe to use for the Thanksgiving Day picnic. I walk into my lovely dining room each morning and imagine it filled with friends and family at Christmas, gathered around the long table, toasting each other and our good fortune. Long enough had my table been empty. Long enough had I 'dream'd contemptible dreams.'

The dreams I have now, I share with Tom, the man who regards me as 'the dazzle of the light.' Now, together, we are bold swimmers, jumping into the midst of life like kids holding hands as they sail off a rope swing into the river. They plunge in together. They rise to the surface together. They nod. They shout. They laugh.

The current whisks them, light as autumn leaves, downstream. You can hear their laughter ringing, pure and wonderful, long after they are gone.

# Don't miss the first book in this series

## THE BELLES OF ✳ SOLACE GLEN

"A moving, charm-filled novel of lost loves, mysterious old letters and small-town friendships."

—EARLENE FOWLER

by

# SUSAN S. JAMES

Flip Paxton is forty-two, single and the town maid in quaint Solace Glen. With no husband, children or relatives of her own, she's always taking care of everyone around her. But now she's involved in a mess that's going to be hard to clean up—a murder.

0-425-19713-1

Available wherever books are sold or at penguin.com

# The Siren of Solace Glen

by

## SUSAN S. JAMES

When an impossibly beautiful blonde arrives in town—fleeing a stalker—Flip must clean up after the dangerous flow of violence that follows her.

0-425-20200-3

**Praise for the series:**

"Flip's outlook on life is fresh and appealing... Both touching and revealing with sparkling moments of gentle hum or and honest emotion."
—Earlene Fowler

"Susan S. James brings to life a small town, especially the quirky characters that live there...there are many surprises."
—Midwest Book Review

Available wherever books are sold or at
penguin.com

# GET CLUED IN

berkleyprimecrime.com

**Ever wonder how to find out about all the
latest Berkley Prime Crime mysteries?**

# berkleyprimecrime.com

- See what's new
- Find author appearences
- Win fantastic prizes
- Get reading recommendations
- Sign up for the mystery newsletter
- Chat with authors and other fans
- Read interviews with authors you love

# Mystery Solved.

# berkleyprimecrime.com